Kentucky Green

By Terry Irene Blain

HER PROTECTOR

"How're you getting on? Any of the men bothered you?"

April surprised him by giving a small laugh that sounded like delight. "Mr. McKenzie, the only man on this wagon train who has made 'improper advances' is you."

For a moment Dan had no idea what she was talking about. Then the memory of his offer that night on the inn porch came rushing back. He hoped the gathering darkness hid the flush creeping up his neck.

"And if you remember, I'm able to take care of myself," she teased in the same light voice. She made a fist and gently placed it against his belly.

She was so close he caught the light scent of violets from her hair. Unable to resist, he slowly brought his hands up and gently grasped her shoulders. She didn't move, but her breathing deepened as if she were waiting to see what would happen next. His hand glided up over her shoulder, up the side of her neck, and under her chin. His heart thudded, but he moved carefully, allowing her the chance to stop him. This time, when he tilted her face up to his, she let him. He breathed her name and gently covered her lips with his.

Kentucky Green

By Terry Irene Blain

www.BOROUGHSPUBLISHINGGROUP.com

KENTUCKY GREEN
Copyright © 2015 Terry Irene Blain

ISBN 978-1-942886-09-9

For my ancestors who passed on the stories of who we were and where we came from, so that the next generations would know where to go in the future.

CONTENTS

Title Page

Copyright

Dedication

Chapter One

Chapter Two

Chapter Three

Chapter Four

Chapter Five

Chapter Six

Chapter Seven

Chapter Eight

Chapter Nine

Chapter Ten

Chapter Eleven

Chapter Twelve

Chapter Thirteen

Chapter Fourteen

Chapter Fifteen

Chapter Sixteen

Chapter Seventeen

Chapter Eighteen

Chapter Nineteen

Chapter Twenty

Chapter Twenty-One

Chapter Twenty-Two

Chapter Twenty-Three

Chapter Twenty-Four

Author's Note

Author Bio

Synopsis

A man needs three essentials:
a good horse, a good rifle, and a good wife.

—Daniel Boone

Chapter One

Philadelphia, Spring 1794

April Williamson slowed her pace as she approached the Twelve Tankards Inn. Cool morning sunlight bathed the wooden steps and wide front porch. To bolster her courage she wore her most flattering gown, completed before Richard's death had dressed her in mourning. Enough time had passed to make the dark-green watered silk acceptable. She shivered, more from apprehension than from the crisp morning.

Male voices drifted from the common room as she climbed the inn's steps. On the porch she paused. For inside, just through the inn's open double doors, was the man who could turn her dreams into reality. Please, don't let me mishandle this. Please make Daniel McKenzie agree to take me to Kentucky.

Swallowing her nervousness, she entered the inn. The dusky interior caused her to hesitate just inside the doorway while her eyes adjusted.

Light streamed in from the open door behind her, throwing an elongated patch on the wide planks of the pegged floor. A stone-flagged fireplace bearing a huge oak mantel dominated the north wall. Solid oak tables and ladder-back chairs dotted the room which held only two men and the lingering aroma of bacon and sausage. The men sat at one of the tables, steaming cups of coffee before them.

The innkeeper's message had given her just a name—Daniel McKenzie. But which one was he? Her gaze went first to the taller man. With his dark hair and tanned complexion, he didn't appear particularly Scottish. She looked to the second man. Slightly older, he had the fair skin and sandy-red hair which characterized so many Scotsmen.

While she hesitated, the dark-haired man rose, and with long booted strides started across the common room toward the fireplace.

Concluding the seated man must be Mr. McKenzie, she moved toward the table with a determination she hoped camouflaged the butterflies in her stomach.

April stopped before the table, heart beating in her throat. "Mr. McKenzie?" The smaller man stood to acknowledge her presence and she said in a rush, "I understand your company has a commission to carry supplies to General Wayne."

The man nodded.

She hurried on, not giving him a chance to speak. "I would like to accompany you on that trip."

"No." The flat reply came not from the man before her, but from the tall, dark man standing by the fireplace. Startled, she twisted to look at him.

Lean and hard-looking, he stood tall enough to rest his arm easily across the high mantel. His muscles bunched under his linen shirt as he brought his arm down. With easy grace he strode across the room toward her.

A sinking, fluttery feeling intensified with his approach. A new and different feeling, certainly not the apprehension she had felt up to now.

Tight buckskin riding breeches fit his slender hips and strong thighs without a wrinkle before disappearing into glossy top boots. Hair, dark as India ink, was brushed straight back from his brow and tied at the nape of his neck with a plain queue ribbon. And his beautiful eyes: a striking pale blue-gray with long lashes, framed by high cheekbones and thick, dark eyebrows. She'd seen that particular shade of blue-gray before. But this wasn't the time to try and remember when.

He stopped before her. Under the intensity of his gaze, she instinctively took a small step backward.

"No," he repeated. "The McKenzie and Murray Trading Company transports army supplies." His rough-textured baritone held the faint drawl of the frontier. "We don't take passengers."

Fear of failure made her words sharp. "I beg your pardon; I wasn't speaking to you, but to Mr. McKenzie." She gestured to the man standing across the table.

"I'm McKenzie," the dark-haired man replied. "This is my partner, James Murray."

A heated flush of embarrassment crept up her cheeks. To think this was the man whose help she so sorely needed. She didn't know whether to laugh or cry. Mr. Murray saved her from doing either.

"Pleased to meet ye," James Murray said, pulling out one of the ladder-back chairs and gesturing toward it. "Will ye no' sit doon?" A hint of laughter flickered in his voice, but she couldn't tell whether he directed his amusement toward her or Daniel McKenzie.

With as much grace as possible, she took the proffered seat. In open amusement, James Murray continued, "Dinna trouble yoursel', lass. 'Tis common for strangers to mistake us one for t'other. As ye ken, I am a Scotsman, ma'sel'. I answer to 'Scotty' as easily as James."

Since he'd tried so hard to put her at ease, she smiled her thanks. She watched Mr. McKenzie out of the corner of her eye. He, too, drew out a chair. To keep her hands occupied, she tugged a lace handkerchief from her reticule. The neutral look on McKenzie's face became a frown.

"Now," Mr. Murray continued, "tell us why a young lass would want to go to the Ohio Territory?"

"In any case," Mr. McKenzie interrupted, "we're taking supplies only as far as Cincinnati for transhipment to General Wayne. Then we're going home to Oak Point in Kentucky. I won't return to Ohio until late summer."

Oak Point! She smothered a gasp and let the sweet words in his faint frontier drawl wash over her. These traders lived in Oak Point. Her goal of home and independence. His wonderful words deepened her longing and intensified her determination.

Perhaps fate was on her side. She struggled to keep her composure. She must convince them to give her passage. Because looking at Dan McKenzie made it difficult to concentrate and because she sensed Mr. Murray was more sympathetic, she kept her eyes directed to his kind face.

"I seem to have started in the middle. Let me explain. My name is April Williamson and I need transportation to Oak Point."

Mr. Murray looked intrigued. April chanced a glance at Mr. McKenzie. If anything, his frown had deepened. With a prickle of annoyance, she turned to him and asked, "Is something wrong?"

"Where are your menfolk?" His voice held a tone of manufactured civility.

Meaning of course, where is the man who takes care of you? He would, of course, expect a young woman to be attached to some man. A measure of her self-confidence returned. She had the perfect, irrefutable answer. "I have no menfolk. My husband died last November."

With satisfaction she noted Mr. McKenzie's surprise and discomfort. "I've inherited property near Oak Point. I appreciate it's unusual for your company to take passengers, but there's no other means of getting to Kentucky."

"Aye," Mr. Murray agreed, "but the trip is verra difficult. 'Tis too much for a visit."

"It's not just a visit," she replied. "I plan to live there."

"Don't be silly," McKenzie looked pointedly at her bonnet and the lace handkerchief clutched in her hands. "You couldn't survive."

"Really?" she challenged. His peremptory dismissal stung. "I survived there for eight years. I was born in Kentucky."

McKenzie blinked and his gaze sharpened. A chill shivered up April's back.

"Why did you leave?"

She drew a deep breath. "My mother and I came to Philadelphia in '82," she said, smothering any emotion in her voice, "after Indians killed my father at Blue Licks."

A strange look flashed across Mr. McKenzie's face, the expression so fleeting she couldn't identify it.

She must convince McKenzie and Murray to help her. Going to Kentucky wasn't just a return to home. Kentucky was her hope of a new life, different from the one she'd been obliged to live in Philadelphia. The compelling desire for freedom and the frontier came from deep inside her. A desire that even her closest friends considered so extraordinary as to be incomprehensible.

Why should these two strangers understand? A material reason would be easier for them to accept. "The property I've inherited in Oak Point is my only asset. I'm determined to reach Kentucky," she said simply.

After a moment, McKenzie leaned forward in his chair, resting his forearms on the oak table. One look at the closed expression on his face and her heart sank. Instinct told her if she pushed for a definite answer now, it would be negative. The pale blue-gray eyes under their dark brows also warned her this man, once an answer was given, would never change a "no" to a "yes."

She tried to think of some way to get the response she needed. Unable to give up hope, she turned to the kindly face of the Scot. "Mr. Murray, is it me you object to, or do you refuse all passengers?"

"Well... ah... 'tis... ah..."

"You have taken passengers to Kentucky before, haven't you?"

"Aye." The Scotsman glanced at his partner. "But nae a woman traveling on her own."

With a small point scored in her favor, she decided to retreat for now. Using her best smile and most reasonable voice, she said, "I see my query was unexpected. Please take a few days to consider my request. I promise I won't be any trouble on the trip."

The look of patent disbelief on Mr. McKenzie's face brought her close to panic again. Desperate to keep the "no" in his eyes from coming to his lips, she impulsively leaned forward and placed her hand on his.

"All I ask is that you think it over. Please consider helping me."

His expression didn't change. After a heartbeat, he looked down and her gaze followed. The deep tan of his skin accentuated the soft ivory of hers. Touching him confused her. His warmth imparted a feeling of comfort while at the same time caused her heart to thump at a disconcerting pace. Unable to move, her hand rested on his large, work-roughened one.

She lifted her eyelashes and her gaze locked with his. The force of his blue-gray gaze made her throat dry. She gently withdrew her hand and rose to her feet.

Both men stood.

"I apologize for interrupting." She kept her voice calm. "All I ask is for you to consider my request."

Dan McKenzie sat back down in his chair. He stared for several long seconds at the open inn door through which the young woman had disappeared. He'd noticed her earlier as she paused just inside the doorway. Her dress, made of some material which changed color as the sunlight struck it, had flickered hundreds of shades of green, like a breeze ruffling the leaves on hillside trees back home.

He straightened in his chair, seeing her in his mind's eye. Her face resembled a square more than an oval because of that firm chin. But her mouth looked soft. Between the low light and her bonnet brim he hadn't got a good look at her eyes and he wondered what color they were. But even in the dim light, her hair gleamed like polished mahogany.

She put him in mind of a porcelain figurine on the mantel in a rich man's parlor. Nice to look at but of no practical value. On the frontier, practicality measured everyone and everything. He knew firsthand what the harsh life on the frontier could do to a woman.

A chuckle jerked Dan back to the present. He turned to the grinning face of his partner.

"Well?" Scotty questioned.

"Well, what?"

"We could take her. 'Tis nae beyond the realm of possibility."

Dan didn't bother to reply, but reached for his coffee. He stared into the cup, then with a resigned sigh looked up. "Yeah, reckon we could. But we won't. She and her lace handkerchief should stay here." He pushed the cup away. "Life's hard enough for women used to living out there. The frontier would chew her up and spit her out."

"I'm nae so sure," Scotty countered. "I admit she's a right wee lassie, but she's got courage enough to want to go. And she was no afraid of ye, rude as ye were."

Dan snorted. "She would be if she knew what I am." At Scotty's puzzled look, Dan explained, "Any girl whose pa was killed by Indians might not want to travel with a half-breed."

Scotty started to speak, but Dan motioned him silent. "Maybe in Scotland I'd only be a quarter Indian, but here the son of a half-breed is still a 'breed.'" Dan accepted what he was. Funny how Scotty never quite grasped the idea.

"Ach, nae wonder ye looked peculiar when the lassie mentioned Blue Licks."

Blue Licks! Dan controlled a shudder as the words again knifed across an old wound. He changed the subject. "Next you'll tell me she wouldn't be any problem on the trip."

"I couldna' say that," Scotty replied with a laugh. "Don't ye go a' telling my Mary I said so, but woman ha' been trouble for man since Adam met Eve."

~ * ~

"Now, April, you cannot go traipsing off to Kentucky. It's not suitable, my dear, not at all suitable." Mrs. Browne's voice brought April's head up from her embroidery.

She'd been wool-gathering, her mind still on the morning's interview with McKenzie and Murray. The eight ladies seated in the Browne parlor suspended their conversation and awaited April's reaction to their hostess's pronouncement.

"I'm not 'traipsing off to Kentucky.'" April paused a moment to ensure her voice remained respectful. "I intend to live on the property I've inherited. Since my parents were among the first settlers in Kentucky and I was born there, I'll be going home."

Mrs. Browne glared at her over the rim of her china teacup. "Utter nonsense! Your dear mother is turning over in her grave. That wilderness wasn't a proper place for a widow with an eight-year-old daughter. Nor is it a place for a twenty-year-old girl, widow or no." She put her cup and saucer on the table next to her Queen Anne chair.

Not surprised Mrs. Browne already knew of her plans, April bowed her head over her embroidery. She suspected it hadn't taken more than a few hours for word to get around she'd met army contractors this morning, asking for passage to Kentucky.

She smiled to herself, thinking how apoplectic Mrs. Browne would be if she only knew about the letter April had written weeks ago. A letter to her husband's old friend, Anthony Wayne, who as general of the army, now had authority over the western territories.

"You don't need to go running off to Kentucky." Elizabeth Jefferies's faded blue eyes twinkled in her wrinkled face. "There are plenty of men here in Philadelphia. Get married again."

"That's always your advice," April replied, biting back a smile at the older woman's suggestion. Why, she wondered, would she want to subjugate herself again? When a woman married, she lost her legal identity. All her property and her decisions given over to another's authority. Still, she couldn't help but smile at enthusiastic Widow Jefferies. "You've suggested marriage four times already."

"It's good advice," the widow countered. "I put my third husband in the ground last fall with the yellow fever, same as you did your Richard. If an old lady like me is ready for another husband, you should be, too." Under cover of the conversation, the spry old woman leaned over and patted April's hand. "Get a young man this time, one who'll treat you like a wife, instead of a daughter."

April glanced sideways, wondering if Elizabeth guessed the truth of her marriage. "Thank you for your advice," she said politely, "but I plan to remain a widow and keep my freedom to do as I please." For the first time she was the one making decisions affecting her life. She was free. She meant to keep her freedom and she meant to go home to Kentucky.

In Philadelphia her only choices were to marry again or live on the charity of friends. In either case she'd become dependent upon others, obliged to live her life as they directed. But in Kentucky she had land—her own land. The start of a new life beckoned. Ever since she'd written to General Wayne, the thought of going to Kentucky made her spirit come alive. No matter the difficulties involved in travel, in spite of her fear of Indians, she was going home.

She glanced around the parlor of Mrs. Browne's spacious two-story house. What a contrast with her memory of Kentucky. She recalled the single-room log cabin, the clearing in which it stood, the path to the spring, the barn and the hayloft. She vaguely remembered the cabin-raising, playing with other children while the men heaved the logs into place and the women quilted before setting out dinner. And later, the quiet as she snuggled under her quilt in the attic, contentedly drifting off to sleep to the murmur of her parents' conversation.

Beautiful and expensive furnishings filled the Browne parlor but laughter and love had filled the cabin in Kentucky.

The clatter of teacups drew her attention as tea and small cakes were served. Needlework aside, a lively discussion ensued. Since they lived in the capital city, politics were as much a topic of discussion for the group, as babies and home remedies.

One lady commented to the group in general. "My Robert said a lawyer from Kentucky went around to all the Representatives last week, saying how bad the situation is in the West. This lawyer claims with the British backing them, the Indians are unbeatable." With a condescending look, the lady turned toward April and said, "Maybe you ought to reconsider your trip."

"That's right," Martha Allen exclaimed. "What about Indians? Aren't you afraid? Remember?" she said, her face serious, "I was with you last summer when the Indian delegation from the Six Nations rode in for the Peace Conference. You went positively pale."

She remembered. Feathers, beads, and buckskin fringes dancing, the Indian delegation rode bold as can be down the Philadelphia street. While others stared in curiosity, terrible memories had frozen her to the spot. She'd been four the winter of '78 when during the war, the Indians, supplied with British arms and ammunition, besieged the three small forts in Kentucky. She'd hidden her face in her mother's lap trying to block out the yelling, the screams of pain, the bang of gunfire.

"The sight of Indians riding through Philadelphia scared lots of people," she countered.

What Martha didn't know was since making the decision to return to Kentucky, April's childhood nightmares had returned. Several times in the last six months she'd awakened sick and shaking, having been chased through her dreams by screaming, half-naked Indians. But everyone knew Indians no longer roamed freely over Kentucky since the army was pushing them out of the Ohio Territory. She might be afraid, but she wouldn't let old fears prevent her from pursuing her future.

"Whatever will you do in Kentucky?" Martha kept her voice low, glancing in Mrs. Browne's direction.

"I can make a decent living as a seamstress," April replied. "And I'll have my property."

Sheltered by the small talk that rose around her, April sat and stitched and planned. She put on a determined face and carried on as though she knew she would succeed.

Of course the reply to her letter to General Wayne would come, or she would convince McKenzie and Murray to take her. And if not, then she'd have to think of some other way. She was going home to Kentucky.

~ * ~

Dan McKenzie arrived at the inn late for supper. He hung his black broad-brimmed hat on the last empty peg by the door. Across the crowded room, he spied Scotty seated near the fireplace and maneuvered his way to his brother-in-law's table.

With minimum conversation the partners turned their attention to pot roast, potatoes, carrots, and turnips in a thick, dark gravy, followed by apple pie. Hunger satisfied, Dan pushed the empty plate away. "Everything will be ready by next week." He leaned forward to be heard over the hub-bub of voices enveloping them. "Payne had a good selection of horses, but he's upped the price this year. He knows we'll sell the horses to the army at Pittsburgh."

"'Tis expected. I'll nae fret as long as we can make a profit."

"We'll make a profit, but we'll earn every penny of it. I saw Colonel Barker and we're set with the army supplies. You satisfied with the merchandise for the store?"

"There'll be nae problem." Scotty related arrangements made for the wide variety of goods and supplies for the McKenzie and Murray store in Oak Point. He took a sip of coffee and then, glancing about the room, said, "I picked up information on our other problem."

"What problem?" Dan asked, instantly suspicious of the self-satisfied look on the Scotsman's face.

"The wee lassie."

Chapter Two

April Williamson, just who Dan didn't want to think about. He reached for his tankard, determined to ignore the matter.

"I had a wee chat with the innkeeper this afternoon."

Dan took a long swallow, then put the tankard back on the table. Scotty was going to tell him whether he wanted to listen or not. He leaned back in his chair and crossed his arms.

"Innkeeper's an old friend of the lass's family." Scotty related. "Folks like her but think she's daft to want to go to Kentucky."

"She is." Dan's interruption earned him a stern look.

"The lass is well thought of," the Scotsman continued. "She's got no family left. Her mother and stepfather died of the cholera in that grand epidemic five years back. She married Williamson then, though she was nae but fifteen."

Dan shifted in his chair but couldn't help asking, "What about her husband?"

"According to the innkeeper, he was her stepfather's older brother by fifteen years. With both the girl's mother and stepfather dead, Williamson was the only family she had left."

"Anything else?" He kept his voice neutral.

"Nay. Innkeeper's the one who told her we're army contractors. She helps out around the inn once in awhile as her husband was friends with the innkeeper. He just wanted us to know that the lass is serious about going to Kentucky. 'Tis not the wild idea of a young widow."

~ * ~

The dinner hour at the inn over, April decided to take a short rest before tackling the dishes. The special dinner party in the Congress Room, in addition to the regular supper served in the common room, made for a busy night. When Sam had asked her to help out, she jumped at the chance.

She stepped from the warm kitchen onto the back porch, letting the cool evening air caress her overheated body as she looked over the peaceful alleyway, the gravel path pale in the moonlight. A three-quarter moon hung low in the southern sky, its cool brilliance lighting the evening. Relaxed, she leaned against the porch railing.

How would she get to Oak Point? Her thoughts turned once again to her hand, pale against Dan McKenzie's brown one. In his warm, solid hand, she'd felt his strength. A man who was capable of taking her to the frontier. The memory of that warm strength under her fingers still made her feel peculiar. She'd never felt such sensations before. What ailed her anyway?

She shook the thoughts away. Time to get back to the kitchen. Before she could move, the crunch of gravel on the alley pathway announced someone's approach. A tall, lean man appeared, his strides rapidly carrying him from the shadows into the light that spilled from the kitchen windows. With a quick intake of breath, she recognized Dan McKenzie.

Dan walked back from the stables, satisfied with the re-shoeing job the farrier had completed that afternoon. Unlike most frontiersmen, he always kept his horse shod. On the frontier, a fast horse was just as important as a good rifle in escaping trouble. A mindful man took care of his equipment, no matter where he was.

The shadowed alley gave way to the muted light of the inn yard and Dan noticed the Williamson girl on the back porch. Did she have to turn up again so soon? This evening she wore a plain, dark dress with a square neck and elbow-length sleeves. To his surprise, her hair was uncovered like the women back home. He frowned. Why did she have to look so natural without the fancy dress and bonnet.

Dan slowed as he neared the steps. One of her hands grasped the porch rail, the other smoothed the apron as if she was nervous. He touched the brim of his hat. "Evenin', ma'am."

"Good evening, Mr. McKenzie. Was your day successful?"

He nodded.

After a moment, she smoothed the apron again, and glanced over her shoulder. "I help in the kitchen here," she explained.

Dan leaned his hip against the step railing and looked up at the girl. "So I understand."

She stood straight, her shoulders back, as if prepared to challenge him.

"You're serious about going to Kentucky, aren't you?" He climbed the first two steps, close enough to see her face in the muted light.

"Of course I'm serious." Her voice held a hint of exasperation, making him think she'd said the same thing over and over. Her gaze searched his face, now level with hers, as he stood one step below her. With a shake of her head, she continued, "Why can't you believe that a woman could want a life on the frontier?"

The answer was so obvious it took him a second to put his thoughts into words. He didn't want to take any woman west. Especially not this pretty little girl on her own. She wouldn't stand a chance. "Life is hard out there. Some folks don't survive. Women should stay where they belong."

"And where would that be, Mr. McKenzie?"

"At home, doing what women do."

"Oh, I see. Women should do women's work, such as cooking and sewing, and leave the men to do men's work?" He nodded, and after a moment, she spoke again. "So tell me, how long does the journey to Pittsburgh take with the wagons?"

He could see no connection between her questions, but answered, "About three weeks."

"And you stay at inns along the way?"

A prickle of suspicion made him hesitate before he answered, "Only once or twice. We camp along the route."

Her voice, which had been soft, now sharpened in accusation, "So tell me, if women do women's work and men are to do men's work, who does the cooking all the way to Pittsburgh?"

"The men do," he said, not bothering to hide his irritation. "That's what has to be done."

"Then why can't women travel or live on the frontier? We can do what has to be done, too." The look on her face could only be called a smirk. "There's no difference."

Dan's irritation became full annoyance. Just like a woman to twist a man up in his own words. He pushed his hat back a bit, then very pointedly he ran his gaze over her, ignoring her flinch when she realized what he was doing. "No difference?" he asked with a slow drawl. "Well, ma'am, appears to me that there is a difference."

He sensed, as much as saw, her flush under his scrutiny. If she was that delicate, maybe he'd shake her a little more, scare her out of the idea of going to the frontier.

But she stood firm, refusing to acknowledge his remark.

His irritation faded into shame. Now he was uncomfortable. The uppity little widow made him feel... he didn't know what. Just the fact she made him unsettled, caused his anger to return.

April gripped the porch rail while she drew a deep breath. No man had ever looked at her like that. She'd never even suspected a look could make her feel embarrassed and all shivery at the same time. With a struggle, she composed herself. She had to make him understand the seriousness of her request. She made sure her voice sounded calm when she spoke again, "I'm returning to Kentucky. Any way I can."

Breaking the silence, pots clanked together in the kitchen, reminding her of the dishes waiting. She suddenly wondered if he was worried about money. She'd forgotten to mention payment this morning, and now he saw her working in the kitchen. Perhaps he thought she couldn't afford the trip.

"I could pay you," she blurted.

She watched his eyes blink slowly, as if he were turning her statement over in his mind. A heartbeat later his gaze narrowed.

"Pay me how?" he questioned in a half-whisper as he took the last step up to the porch. He lightly gripped her waist, leaving only a scant few inches of cool night air between them. His hands were two warm spots on her waist.

"H-How?" She stammered. His warm breath against her forehead carried a distinct masculine scent with undertones of the smoky common room and a hint of ale. Her heartbeat doubled, and she had trouble breathing. "I'll pay you to take me to Kentucky," she managed to get out.

"That might be nice," he murmured, pulling her closer. He put his head down next to hers, his voice hot and soft against her temple.

Her senses swirled. She tried to get her thoughts in order, but he slid his hands up her sides, stopping just below the level of her breasts.

"Reckon I can console a widow."

His heated touch almost obliterated what he said. Then the words 'console' and 'widow' jumped out at her. Warmth turned to rage and disgust as she understood his meaning. The first offer to console her had come from Mrs. Browne's nephew, when he backed her into a corner in the Browne kitchen. It took her a while to realize what he wanted, and after she did, it had taken him a while to explain the red mark on his cheek to his aunt. She was a lot smarter than she had been six months ago, better able to fend off such offers. "Take your hands off me!" she demanded in a fierce whisper. She pushed against his chest.

A surprised "Wha...?" came from him, and his grip loosened, but he didn't let her go. In fury and embarrassment, she pulled back her hand and punched him as hard as she could. He clutched both hands to his midsection with a muffled "oomph," allowing her to escape. She turned and fled into the kitchen, slamming the door with finality behind her.

Suddenly alone, Dan stood on the porch, one hand lightly rubbing his belly. She hadn't hurt him, but she sure as hell surprised him. One instant he'd had a warm, soft woman and the next it was like trying to cuddle a wild red fox. He couldn't suppress a grin. He shrugged as he walked around toward the common room, not bothering to wonder why her refusal pleased him.

~ * ~

The slamming door echoing in her ears, April stalked across the kitchen. She'd never been so unnerved by anyone in her entire life. She refused to think about how Milton had made her uncomfortable and then a little frightened, while Dan McKenzie had made her breathless, made her head swim.

She grabbed the kettle from the stove and sloshed hot water into the basin. With great vigor, she attacked the stack of dirty dishes. How dare he think that she... the gall of the man! How dare he be like those others who had offered to console her.

Her fury had abated by the time the door from the common room opened. Sam the innkeeper poked his head into the kitchen. "When you're done, come on out front and I'll walk you home."

A few minutes later, April waved goodbye to Sam and let herself in the side door of the small, two-story brick house Richard had rented. She lit the lamp left ready on the kitchen table and carried it into the hall where she paused to hang her cloak on a peg. As she started toward the stairs, she passed the door to the bedroom that had belonged first to her mother and stepfather, and later to her husband.

Her own attic room was small, but she'd always felt the gently sloping ceiling gave the room character. She hung her dress and petticoats in the maple wardrobe and pulled on her white cotton nightdress, then washed her face and cleaned her teeth. Pale moonlight filtered into the room as she removed the pins from her hair and undid the braids. Taking up her brush, she hoped the familiar action of brushing one hundred strokes would soothe her, but images of Dan McKenzie dominated her mind.

Even with her eyes closed, she could see him stride across the common room. She saw every detail, from his pitch-black hair to his shiny black boots. Then, there was this evening's encounter. Her initial fury now past, she recalled the warmth of his body against hers. She shook her head at her thoughts, and pulling her hair over her shoulder, she braided it into one long braid. She blew out the lamp and snuggled down into the covers.

The moonlight played across the room, shifted again and became the moonlight slanting across the back porch of the inn.

"Pay me how?" his low, rough voice breathed against her ear. This time when he leaned down toward her, she turned her face up. His embrace tightened and brought her against the length of his warm, hard body. His mouth moved to cover hers and...

April's eyes fluttered open.

She lay quietly, half-awake in the faint morning light. Then she shot upright in bed, her hands covering her mouth's 'oh' of astonishment. Then she giggled. "No wonder you woke up when you did," she chided herself, "you don't really know what comes next."

Her wardship-marriage had precluded such things. The title of wife gave her entry into the adult world. Being a member of the Ladies' Wednesday Sewing Circle had taught her in theory what she lacked in practice. For the last five years she'd been privy to the intimate conversations of married women, the jokes and teasing remarks that provoked laughter and blushes. She knew the problems of conception, how to improve or reduce its chances, as well as the graphic details of childbirth. But such things had not been part of her marriage.

Widowhood, the legacy of marriage, proved to be the true key to a woman's emancipation. A widow was free to do whatever she would, be it live alone or go to the frontier. The thought brought a familiar uplifting to her soul. But wishing never made anything so, she thought with a sigh. If she wanted a life in Kentucky, she'd better get busy. Somehow she had to make McKenzie and Murray agree, or find another contractor. She climbed out of bed and prepared for the day ahead.

~ * ~

Two days later, the answer to her prayers arrived in the form of a letter from General Wayne with the promise of his help. That same afternoon she received a message from Colonel Barker, the Philadelphia officer Wayne told her to contact, asking her to come to his office Friday morning.

At the appointed time, April sat in Colonel Barker's office. She smoothed her hand over the green silk of her skirt while she absorbed the shock of the colonel telling her he had also requested Dan McKenzie to attend their meeting. Something in her fluttered at the thought of seeing him again.

The colonel, in a paternalistic drone, began telling her of the dangers of the frontier. Not again. She was so tired of hearing warnings. Instead she wondered why the colonel had asked Mr. McKenzie to come. General Wayne's letter had given her no details, but the direction of Barker's comments became clear as Colonel Barker informed her McKenzie and his brother-in-law, James Murray, carried supplies for the military, as well as goods for their own store in Kentucky. He also managed to suggest she put her trust in Mr. Murray as the more reliable of the partners.

She realized Colonel Barker had no idea she'd already approached them. As she debated whether or not to mention it, she heard someone enter the outer office. After a few moments, Barker wound up his lecture, rose from his seat, and marched to the door.

"Ah, McKenzie, you're here," Barker said as he opened the door. From her seat, April looked through the doorway in time to see Dan McKenzie straighten from where he leaned against the far wall. Barker gave him a cold look and a brusque nod. Without offering his hand, the colonel turned, leaving McKenzie to follow him into the office.

"You sent for me?" McKenzie strode into the office and came to an abrupt halt when he caught sight of her. She offered a polite smile while the colonel introduced them. If Dan McKenzie's frown as he studied her through narrowed eyes was any indication, he wasn't too happy to see her again.

"Sit." Barker waved at the empty chair as he continued around behind his desk. McKenzie sat with all the care of a man expecting an attack, but uncertain of the direction from which it would come. The colonel cleared his throat. "I've asked you here on direct orders from the general himself."

"Wayne?" McKenzie's tone held a hint of wariness.

"The general has requested I help Mrs. Williamson travel to Kentucky. In fact, he has directed me to contact you personally, to take care of this matter. It seems he has great faith in you." The last sentence carried an undertone of sarcasm.

The colonel held out a folded sheet of paper. "Here's a letter for you. The general enclosed it with my orders."

The expression on the trader's face said he'd be happier accepting a rattlesnake.

Turning to her, the colonel went on, "It seems the general has been quite impressed with McKenzie's abilities these last two years." He glanced toward McKenzie as if waiting for comment, then went on, "McKenzie and the 'white Indian,' William Wells, act as the general's personal scouts for the Legion. Very good with Indians, aren't you, McKenzie?"

"I'm good at what I do," the frontiersman replied in an even tone, his gaze locking with the colonel's.

After a moment, Colonel Barker looked down muttering "Well, yes," as he shuffled papers on his desk.

April wondered at the cause of the hostility evident between the two men. The long silence continued as Colonel Barker perused the papers on his desk. To her surprise, Mr. McKenzie stood and offered her his hand.

"Mrs. Williamson and I can discuss the arrangements elsewhere," he said. Urging her to her feet, he took her elbow and walked her toward the door. Tension radiated from him as he hustled her through the outer office and out the door. Once out on the bricked sidewalk he dropped her arm. His pale blue-gray eyes had a faraway look in them as he stared at nothing. The muscles in his jaw clenched, while at his sides, his hands worked themselves in and out of fists.

"Mr. McKenzie?" She spoke his name hesitantly.

His beautiful eyes blinked, then focused on her.

Chapter Three

Dan gazed at the questioning look on April Williamson's face. With conscious effort, he unclenched his jaw. "Mrs. Williamson, writing that letter to Wayne was a foolish thing to do."

The young widow looked away, but surprised him by muttering, "It worked, didn't it?"

His anger jumped back up a notch. Drawing himself to his full height, he gave a sarcastic half-bow as an acknowledgment of her success. "It appears McKenzie and Murray is now a passenger service. Where may I escort you, ma'am, so we can discuss travel arrangements?"

"Back to the Twelve Tankards, sir." She dropped a slight curtsy and gave him a tentative smile which he ignored. He gestured and they started back toward the inn.

At the busy corner, they waited while a heavy brewer's wagon loaded with hogsheads of beer pulled by four draft horses rumbled past.

"When did you hear from the general?" Dan asked.

"The letter came yesterday, but I wrote asking for his help earlier this year."

He raised an eyebrow.

After a moment she answered his unspoken question. "Anthony Wayne and my husband Richard were friends. I wasn't sure I would receive an answer in time, so I asked you. I had no way of knowing the general's letter would specifically name you."

Just my luck, Dan thought bitterly. Once across the street, he kept his steps slow, shortening his stride to accommodate her.

Abruptly, she asked, "Why doesn't Colonel Barker like you?"

Dan stopped and turned toward the woman at his side. "The colonel and I don't get along. It's me, personally, he doesn't trust, not my ability. I'll get you to Kentucky."

Damn, he'd almost blurted out Barker considered him a 'dirty half-breed.' But since Wayne had ordered him to escort her, his mixed blood wasn't any of her concern. Their business arrangement was just that—business. "Come on," he said, not wanting to answer any more questions.

Damn Wayne and Barker for giving him this job. Usually he shrugged off the colonel's hostile behavior. Never offering his hand, never putting a Mister in front of his name. Attitudes like that hadn't bothered him for a long time. He suspected part of his present irritation with the colonel was somehow connected with this small widow—and he didn't like that thought one bit. He'd been right from the beginning. She was nothing but trouble.

Just as Dan and April started up the inn steps, Scotty appeared in the doorway. Dan turned to her, and making sure his aggravation didn't show in his voice, said, "Mr. Murray can answer all your questions. We leave next Wednesday."

Turning to his partner, Dan told him in short, clipped sentences about the letter from Wayne and that Mrs. Williamson would be their passenger. "Don't wait for me for supper," he concluded, then strode back down the street. The Twelve Tankards Inn was too respectable a place to get as drunk as he planned.

~ * ~

Late that afternoon, in a tavern three ranks down from the Twelve Tankards Inn, a different sort of meeting took place. The Blue Pheasant was an unusual setting for the man buying the drinks. His aristocratic face, as well as his manner of dress marked him out. He sported a fine linen shirt, with coat, breeches, and waistcoat of wool broadcloth. His stockings were silk, silver buckles adorned his shoes. The customary patrons of the Blue Pheasant invariably wore homespun, and those none too clean. But they weren't particular about who paid for the drinks or for any other service that might be purchased.

The handsome blond gentleman knew his welcome would last only as long as his money held out. Throughout the afternoon he provided whiskey and ale with a lavish hand. By evening he found two rough-looking men who indicated they were looking for employment. They also indicated as long as it paid good money, they weren't overly particular about the type of duties involved.

Briefly bringing his handkerchief to his nose, the blond man surveyed his catch. The stench of the place and of its inhabitants were a trial. But he willingly made any sacrifice if it helped achieve his purpose.

Like the tools they were, he'd use these men for his own purpose. Direct them by his superior intellect. He was a gentleman, and a true gentleman never dirtied his hands. Instead, he used subtlety and shrewdness to accomplish his tasks. Doing the dirty work for their betters was all American scum like these two were good for.

His new companions were dressed in clothes which had apparently seen water only when the wearer had been caught in the rain. The first man, heavyset with bad teeth, had introduced himself as Moose and his companion as Jonesy. Jonesy had the skinny, pale look of a man who spent his money on drink before food.

"Do you think you can handle the job I've outlined?" the would-be employer questioned.

Moose scratched an unshaven cheek. "Ya want us to give the McKenzie wagon train a rough trip to Pittsburgh."

"Correct. But remember, it should look like accidents or bad luck." Always the indirect approach. There might be suspicions, but there would be no proof.

"Sure, sure. We've arranged bad luck afore, ain't we?" Moose grinned at Jonesy, who answered Moose's snicker with one of his own.

"What ya got against this McKenzie feller? If'n you don't mind me askin'."

Everything, the gentleman thought fiercely. But that was personal. As always for a gentleman, duty took precedence over personal pleasure. Keeping supplies from Wayne was the chief consideration at this point. And, should the wagon train make it as far as Pittsburgh, he had other plans for the half-breed and his supplies.

"Why?" The gentleman leaned back in his chair.

"We was wonderin', see," Moose shifted uncomfortably in his chair, "if'n these supplies is going to Wayne's army, waylayin' 'em seems almost like helpin' the Injuns somehows."

"Yeah," Jonesy chimed in. "We don't wanna be helpin' redskins."

"I assure you, my plan is not to hinder the Legion. As I said, this is a matter of business between McKenzie and myself." He paused as if a thought had just come to him. "As a matter of fact, slowing the wagon train will hurt at least one Indian. McKenzie's a half-breed." Even these roughs looked down on a half-breed. He leaned forward and pushed over a handful of bright coins, the first payment on taking care of McKenzie's wagon train.

After exchanging a glance and nod with Jonesy, Moose swept the coins into his hand. "We'll take the job, Mister. Don't you worry, we'll make sure it's a long, hard trip for that there wagon train."

~ * ~

Too restless to sleep, April found Wednesday's dawn overcast and cool. Her trunks packed and taken away to the supply depot the afternoon before, she'd spent her last night in Philadelphia as a guest of Sam Rogers at the inn.

This morning, anticipation easily overrode apprehension. She hummed under her breath while she dressed, remembering the first time her father had put her on the back of a horse. Scared, she'd begged to get down. But Papa stood next to her, his arm around her as they walked the short distance from the cabin to the barn. "It's natural to be afraid, April," he'd spoken soothingly. "But don't let the fear stop you. Go ahead and try. Never be afraid to try." Now she would find out if she possessed the determination to build her own life in Kentucky.

Mr. Murray smiled at her while they walked the nearly deserted early morning sidewalks. "Ye're truly happy to be setting out, are ye lass?"

Her cloak around her shoulders against the early morning chill, April all but danced as she walked. "I feel like a child at Christmas."

A few minutes later, they turned the corner. "Here we are then," Mr. Murray said with a wave of his hand. Men and horses swarmed around the large Conestoga freight wagons on the hard-packed earth of depot yard.

Clustered into two groups, she counted nine wagons. The first five set to go, while teams were being harnessed to the remaining four. Scotty led her toward the lead wagon.

"This is the provision wagon. 'Twill carry our supplies for the next three weeks. Your trunks are in here, lass."

April peeked through the dropped rear gate of the wagon at the provisions there for easy access, her trunks stored toward the front, her quilt and blankets made into a sleeping pallet.

Voices raised in anger from near the rear wagons drew her attention. Mr. Murray gave her a quick glance. "Stay here, lassie." She waited for a moment, then curiosity took over and she followed Mr. Murray at a prudent distance toward a growing group of men at the rear of the wagon train. By the time she reached the fringe of the gathering, voices had calmed.

She saw Dan McKenzie in the middle of the group, obviously having separated two men about to come to blows. Today wearing typical frontier garb he stood out from the other men in their shirts and knee breeches. His linsey-woolsey shirt, so long it brushed mid-thigh, was cinched at his waist by a wide leather belt. A sheathed knife rested at his right side.

"What started this?" she heard him ask as he folded his arms across his chest. When neither spoke, he turned to the older man, his graying hair partially concealed under an old-style tricorn hat. "Tucker?"

The older man shifted his feet. "I asked the hostler, here, if'n he greased the wagons. He allowed he did, but I started checkin', just makin' sure, mind you. Found the rear axle on this wagon pert' near dry. Hardly a lick o' grease."

McKenzie's glance toward the hostler caused him to step back a pace, but he spoke up willingly. "I checked all the wagons, I did, Mr. McKenzie. Greased 'em all up on Monday. 'Member, you were by that day. Saw me doing it." He gave a small nod of his head, as if to encourage agreement.

Nobody had noticed her, so she took couple of steps closer.

Lifting his broad-brimmed hat, McKenzie ran his hand through his hair. "I remember." Settling his hat back on his head, he told the hostler, "Throw some more grease on that axle. We're late as it is."

"But, Dan—," The older man started to protest, but a wave of McKenzie's hand cut him off.

"Leave it for now, Tucker." He clasped the older man's shoulder. "Good thing you were on the lookout. Thanks." Raising his voice, he addressed the group of men, "Everyone back to work. We roll out in half an hour."

The crowd began to disperse and April hurried back to the lead wagon. She stood where Mr. Murray had left her when Dan McKenzie, along with Tucker, approached. The frontiersman greeted her with a curt nod and a brief, "Morning, ma'am." Even in such a short phrase, the warm, rich timbre of his voice disclosed the soft drawl of the frontier.

"Tucker," he called the wiry-built man over, "this is Mrs. Williamson. She'll be traveling with us to Kentucky."

"Pleased to make your acquaintance, Mr. Tucker." April smiled at the gray-haired man as he yanked off his tricorn hat.

"Just 'Tucker,' ma'am," he replied in a gravelly voice. His deeply tanned face held a pair of friendly brown eyes, surrounded by an abundance of wrinkles. "I'm the head teamster and the cook."

"You ready?" McKenzie asked her.

"Yes," she replied, trying to read his closed expression. Why did she feel he constantly waited for her to make some mistake? She could handle any test he devised. To prove it, she turned her attention to the wagon, glancing up at the seat.

Following her gaze, Tucker stepped forward, "Here, ma'am. Let me help you."

"No, thank you," April replied. "That won't be necessary." She bent and with one hand gripped the hems of her skirt and petticoats, lifting them a discreet distance. She could do this, she told herself. With her free hand she reached up and grabbed the edge of the seat and carefully climbed the wheel to the wooden seat.

From her perch she looked down at the open astonishment on the male faces gaping up at her. "It's a long way to Kentucky, Tucker. I don't want to be a burden." She gave the old man a tentative smile, wanting him to understand.

Mr. McKenzie, on the other hand, had already replaced astonishment with his usual neutral expression. Without a word he turned on his heels and headed toward the rear of the wagon train.

April sat on the seat next to Tucker, hands clasped together in a semblance of calm. The waiting seemed to take forever. Mr. McKenzie's voice grew closer as he rode down the line of wagons, exchanging a few words with each driver. Alongside their wagon, he wheeled his horse around and stood in the stirrups. Waving his hat over his head, he shouted down the line of waiting wagons teams, "Wagons, ho!"

Chapter Four

April held her breath. With a jolt, the wagon began to rattle and bounce as it carried her out of Philadelphia. At last, she was finally on her way to her new, unconstrained life in Kentucky, the home of her heart.

The exhilaration of setting out soon faded, as traffic in and around the city kept the wagons at a slow pace. Mr. McKenzie and his mount disappeared ahead.

"Dan'll stay mostly to the front checkin' the road, watchin' for good places for nooning and night stops," Tucker commented. "Scotty'll be at the rear of the train, keepin' an eye on things, passin' messages up and down the line. We'll go at 'er six days a week, restin' the Sabbath."

Finally, the wagons left the well-populated areas behind. The land became a patchwork of wooded areas and open farmland, dotted with houses and barns as the road grew rougher. The bouncing and swaying of the wagon increased. At first she tried to sit up straight, but Tucker corrected her. "Ya gotta relax, ma'am. Don't go tryin' to fight the motion. Go with it." She observed the slackness in his body while he swayed back and forth with the motion of the wagon, then tried her best to copy him.

At evening, Tucker pulled the wagon off the road to the spot chosen. She couldn't believe how stiff and tired she felt.

Tucker climbed down, and tugging boxes and supplies from the rear of the wagon, he began setting up camp. Each step down from the seat brought a protest from her weary bones and muscles. A few moments later Tucker returned with an armful of firewood.

Efficiently, he set about building a fire and cooking the evening meal for the crew. He refused her offer of help and she was grateful. When supper was over, most of the men drifted off to smaller campfires that lit the line of wagons. Physically weary from the day's travel, she bade Scotty and Tucker good night and retired to the wagon.

~ * ~

Dan checked the picket line of horses for the second time, then sauntered toward Tucker's cook fire. He'd taken twice as long as usual currying his mare. With any luck, the Williamson girl would have turned in for the night. The woman was making him crazy as a caged wildcat.

This morning, he'd been planning to offer to help her up, thinking about his hands around her waist. Tucker beat him to the offer, but she'd climbed up on her own. The brief flash of petticoats and neatly shaped ankles lingered in his mind all day. As he approached the fire from the direction of the picket line, he was relieved to see only Tucker and Scotty.

"Kept some supper for you," Tucker called.

Dan sank down cross-legged and accepted the plate Tucker handed him. When he finished, he exchanged the empty plate for a cup of coffee. He held the cup between both hands, enjoying the warmth against the chill of the spring evening. "We made good time today."

"Near fifteen mile," Tucker said. "Now, reckon ya ken tell me about the ungreased axle? What's goin' on, boy?"

"Ye dinna think it was just an oversight?" Scotty asked.

"No," Dan replied. "I saw the hostler grease the axle."

Tucker frowned as Dan went on, "The British have promised the Indians they would help drive the Americans from the Northwest Territory. But Wayne's pushing so hard, the British are having trouble supplying themselves, let alone their Indian allies. The Redcoats could be trying to cut down on Wayne's supplies to even things up." Dan cast a warning glance at his companions. "Keep a sharp eye out. Like you did this morning."

Tucker glanced from Dan to Scotty then back to Dan, a worried look on his weathered face. "If'n there might be trouble, why'd ya bring her?" Tucker jerked his head in the direction of the wagon.

Before Dan could answer, Scotty snorted in laughter. "The lass coerced him into it. She holds a letter from General Wayne ordering Dan to escort her to Kentucky."

Tucker scratched his ear with a feigned blandness Dan recognized. "Feisty little filly then, ain't she."

"Yeah? You just keep an eye on her, Tucker," Dan returned. "Don't let her go wandering off by herself when we stop."

"I gotta let her 'wander off' once in a while when we stop," the teamster retorted, giving Dan a meaningful look.

Dan's split second of ignorance evaporated in a succinct swear word. Ignoring the amused looks of Tucker and Scotty, Dan told the teamster, "You tell her to wander on the north side of the wagons, and I'll tell the men to keep their wandering to the south side of the wagons." He rubbed his eyes with thumb and forefinger. "I knew she was trouble," he mumbled, before setting his cup aside.

He uncoiled his length from the ground and slapped the dust from the seat of his pants. "I'll post two men to watch. The rest of us better turn in. We roll out early."

~ * ~

Only half-awake, April slowly turned over. The protesting stiffness of her body jolted her into full awareness. Her eyes fluttered open and she remembered she was on the way to Kentucky. The pale canvas overhead hinted at dawn not far off.

Encouraged by the cool morning air to dress quickly, she dressed, braided her hair and pinned it up in her usual coronet style. Hoping she hadn't caused a delay, she climbed out of the wagon. A quick look around reassured her. Teamsters clustered around the fire drinking coffee. Tucker presided over a skillet and a Dutch oven that scented the morning air with the delicious aroma of sausage and biscuits.

Bedrolls still lay under most of the other wagons. Was she the only person sleeping inside? Of course, now she remembered,

Tucker had told her the other wagons were chocked full. With dismay, she realized that only when she retired to her wagon did the men have any privacy.

No one lingered over breakfast. Men moved to pack gear and harness teams. From her high seat, April scanned the wagon train. As they waited, she didn't see the tall, lean figure she told herself she wasn't looking for. She was considering asking Tucker where Mr. McKenzie might be when she finally spotted the man.

He rode toward the lead wagon, mounted on the same neatly made bay mare as yesterday. The mare had a delicate head set on a slim neck, a broad chest, her body close coupled. Man and horse moved as a true team, the man using only the slightest movement of rein or his firm thighs to guide her.

April watched as Dan McKenzie brought his mount to a prancing halt beside the wagon. He spoke to Tucker, without so much as a glance in her direction.

"Let's move." With a curt nod, McKenzie touched the mare lightly with his heels and they trotted down the line of wagons. Minutes later the wagon train rolled out on the second day of travel.

McKenzie's curtness didn't prevent her from enjoying the passing scenery. Every tree, plant, and early flower stood sharp and distinct, the grays and browns of winter giving way to the greens of spring.

The brief noon stop gave a chance to walk and stretch. As Tucker explained, the noon stop was to rest the horses, so they didn't bother to set up camp. "We'll build a fire just big enough to boil some coffee to wash down biscuits and bacon made this morning." After the nooning, April settled in to another session of Tucker's non-stop supply of facts, figures, and fables.

That evening as Tucker set up camp, April picked up an apron. Before she could tie it on, Tucker gently took it from her hands. "No need fer that, ma'am."

"But Tucker, I have to do something besides sit all day. You might as well show me what to do, because I'm going to help."

"Well," Tucker pondered, pulling on his ear. She put her hands on her hips and gave him her fiercest scowl, which caused him to smile. "Reckon I could use a hand at that."

Since she already knew how to wash dishes, that's what Tucker agreed to let her do. In the meantime, he sat her on a box and explained as he went along how to set up camp. Scents of supper began to fill the air. Before long, Tucker banged the ladle against the side of the coffee pot. "Come and get it!" and instantly a line of hungry teamsters formed.

April was doing the dishes when Dan McKenzie finally rode up. Scotty and Tucker went to meet him. Talking, the three of them walked toward the fire.

"The road's fine," McKenzie said.

Tucker snorted. "Ya'd never think it. What with ya stayin' out all day, ya'd think we never come this way before."

The remark made Scotty laugh and Dan say something under his breath. Just then, he caught sight of her. Instantly his dark brows drew together in a frown. "What's she doing?" He directed the sharp question at Tucker.

Tucker returned his scowl. "What's it look like?"

McKenzie turned his scowl to her. She raised her chin in his direction, daring him to say something as she picked up a tin plate, dried it, and set it on the stack of clean plates.

After a moment, he took off his broad brimmed hat and slapped it against his leg. "Oh..." Then he sighed.

April swallowed a giggle at his frustration.

"Just don't let her do more than she can handle." McKenzie gave a pointed look to Scotty and Tucker before turning and walking off.

She smiled as she finished the dishes. She'd managed two accomplishments today. Not only was she helping with the work, she'd managed to get some expression out of the Mr. Dan McKenzie.

~ * ~

As the wagon train traveled toward Pittsburgh, the days blended one into another for April. The familiar pattern of breaking camp, the noon stop, the evening camp, sleep, breakfast, and breaking camp seemed to be the only life she remembered.

Tucker gave her lessons on cooking without a hearth, telling her which wood to choose, and various ways to lay a fire. She even adjusted to the roll and bump of the wagon. But she liked best to sit and watch the road unfurl as they traveled west. Whenever they passed a farm, the people working in the fields stopped and watched them go by. Twice children came running to the roadside and waved while the wagons rumbled past.

Unfortunately, travel allowed plenty of time to think, and to her chagrin, she thought of Dan McKenzie often. Her eyes sought him out as the men gathered around the cook fire for supper. Her ears listened to his smooth, rich drawl as he spoke to the men. The more she saw of him, and heard about him from Scotty and Tucker, the more she was drawn to the tall frontiersman.

The wagon train put in a long day on Saturday. Dark had already claimed the day when the wagons pulled into the inn yard where they would rest on the Sabbath. After the luxury of an evening meal taken in the common room, April went gratefully to her pallet, looking forward to a day of rest on the morrow.

~ * ~

Weary after another long day in the saddle, Dan sat lounging against the wagon wheel and enjoyed a final cup of coffee. After supper most of the teamsters lingered in the common room for a few tankards of ale, but Dan preferred the fresher evening air. Even camped in an inn yard, Tucker had built a small fire and put on coffee for the evening watch.

With no immediate worries about tomorrow, Dan allowed himself to relax. As soon as he did, his traitorous thoughts turned to the Williamson girl. He'd meant to pay her no more mind than he did everyone else. The plan seemed to work on her, as after the second day he hadn't felt her gaze on him as much. But damn if he hadn't found himself mentally tracking her whereabouts, not relaxing until she disappeared into the lead wagon each evening.

What made it worse for Dan was seeing the way she fit in. She helped with all the meals, the setting up and breaking down of camp. She had looked like a city girl in her fancy green dress, but out here she didn't whine or fuss or ask for any special consideration. Scotty treated her like a younger sister. Tucker bragged what a quick learner she was.

Why was he thinking about her? She was just a passenger. Just business, nothing more. He couldn't let it be more, not with what he knew stood between them. Abruptly he stood, set his now cold cup of coffee on a box, and walked from camp.

Dan's sudden movement halted the conversation between Tucker and Scotty. Tucker watched Dan go, a frown adding more wrinkles to his old face. He turned to Scotty, "What's itching' his hide? He's bein' awful moody this trip."

"I dinna ken, for sure, but if it's what I think, it's just beginning." At Tucker's puzzled look, Scotty nodded his head in the direction of the wagon where April slept. A slow smile split Tucker's face as comprehension dawned.

~ * ~

"Ya ready to go, ma'am?" Tucker asked April Monday morning. The inn yard hummed with activity as the men readied the wagon train for the next week of travel. "Did ya enjoy havin' someone else cook and clean up for a change?" Tucker grinned.

She smiled in return. "I think I enjoyed the hot water more." Bathing in a tub of warm water instead of a sponge bath from a bucket had been a pure pleasure.

The innkeeper came around the corner. "Here you are." He handed Tucker a large split-oak basket, a layer of straw visible on top. "Three and a half dozen eggs." Tucker clinked several copper coins into the man's palm.

"I'll take those to the wagon," she offered. Tucker handed her the basket, and turned away to help the other teamsters. Skirts hitched in one hand, basket clutched in the other, she started across the yard toward the lead wagon, zigzagging to keep out the way of the busy men.

"Loose horse!" a man yelled.

April turned to see a panicked animal still half-harnessed, rush straight toward her.

Chapter Five

From behind, April felt two strong hands grasp her upper arms. She was pulled back against a hard, warm body. The horse dashed past so close part of the trailing harness slashed her skirt.

"You all right?" McKenzie's voice asked.

"Y-yes." Her heart thudded in response to the close call. Or perhaps in response to the hard warmth of the man against her back. For a second his hands tightened. She swallowed to bring her voice under control. He let her go and stepped in front of her. His blue-gray gaze swept over her, as if to prove it to himself.

Amazingly, she still held her skirts and the basket of eggs. She held out the basket for his inspection. "Even the eggs made it."

Her remark sparked a momentary gleam of humor in his eyes, then he spoke his usual one-word reply. "Good."

The horse made several circuits around the yard trailing the broken lines. Teamsters either scurried out of the way or made a grab for the reins.

"Everyone stay back," McKenzie ordered. Within a minute, the lathered animal came to a halt. McKenzie approached the gelding, speaking softly, and grasped the dangling leather. He crooned to the horse and stroked his neck for a few moments before he called one of the men to re-hitch the animal. She noticed a grim look on his face as McKenzie set about checking the harnesses on all the wagons.

"What's he looking for?" April asked Tucker, as the hubbub settled down.

"Just checkin', I reckon. Mebbe somethin' wrong, mebbe not."

Within a few minutes, McKenzie appeared with a broken harness. "What do you think?" he asked Tucker.

She watched Tucker turn the harness over and over in his weathered hands. With a sigh, he gave it back to Dan. "Stitchin' gave way." He pointed to the place where the leather pieces had ripped apart. "Could be just natural wear, could be it had a little help. Cain't tell, really."

McKenzie nodded. "Double check your gear from now on. I'll tell Scotty." He looked around at the now calm yard. "Bring 'em along when they're ready."

A few minutes later, just as she'd climbed to her seat, April saw McKenzie ride out of the inn yard. For the first time since leaving Philadelphia he carried his flintlock rifle in a scabbard, powder horn and bullet pouch tied behind the saddle. A tingle of apprehension shivered down her back.

The next afternoon the wagon train approached the Susquehanna River at Wright's Ferry. Along the river bank near the ferry teams and wagons milled about. Shouting drivers and nervous animals added to the din. From her seat next to Tucker, April saw McKenzie make his way to the ferrymaster. The men talked, nodded, then shook hands. McKenzie walked back along the line of their wagons giving commands and instructions, bringing order in the midst of the confusion.

The man certainly had the gift of leadership, April noted as he approached the lead wagon. He jumped up, balancing on the hub of the front wheel, and spoke to Tucker. "You'll cross on the first trip. Once you reach the other side, go about a mile and a half down the road. You'll see a stand of box elders to the right. Start making camp there. The rest of the wagons will be along in time for supper."

Excitement seemed to hover in the air. "What can I do to help?" she asked eagerly, looking past Tucker to the dark frontiersman.

He glanced in her direction. "Stay out of the way." Without another word, he jumped down from the wheel and strode off.

April blinked back the tingle behind her eyes. Even though he was probably right, his tone still hurt. She had proven her worth on this trip. Both Tucker and Scotty had said so. Why did the dismissal of someone who went out of his way to overlook her hurt?

An hour later, she stood on the deck of the gently swaying ferry. At the last minute, Scotty volunteered to remain behind to direct the departures and Mr. McKenzie and his mare joined the lead wagon to take charge on the opposite side. He talked to Tucker while they calmed the team of skittish horses.

After the commotion at the landing, she enjoyed the contrast of the cool, quiet river. The gentle lap-lap of the river interplayed with the creaks and groans of timbers and ropes as the ferry made its way across the Susquehanna. Holding the rail and with feet apart to keep her balance, she swayed in time with the sounds.

She spied two boys in a clearing on the opposite shore. She continued to watch as she heard the soft sounds of Mr. McKenzie's moccasins on the planking as he came to stand beside her.

Unable to resist the temptation, she asked "Am I in the way here, Mr. McKenzie?" She glanced sideways at him.

"No, you're not in the way."

Amused that a more overt apology seemed unlikely, she said, "We seem to be making good time."

He merely nodded. She turned to see where he looked with so much concentration, and found him watching the same clearing she'd noted earlier. "What do you see?" she asked.

"A young buck coming down to the river."

Following his gaze she saw a deer emerge from the woods and walk with dainty steps along the edge of the clearing to the riverbank. The deer stood for a moment, then lowered its antlered head to drink.

"There were boys in the clearing earlier," she remarked.

"Still there," Dan said, pointing to the other edge of the clearing.

She searched the area, finally spying the boys hidden from the deer's sight on the far side of the clearing. One boy raised a rifle.

Suddenly the deer bolted. The rifle belched a puff of smoke and a second later the sharp crack echoed across the water. Beside her, Dan snorted. The breeze blew the gun smoke over the meadow, thinning the dense white puff to blue-gray streaks. That's it. She turned to look into the blue-gray eyes of the man standing beside her.

"Your eyes are the color of gun smoke," she blurted.

His head jerked and a startled look flashed across his face. Appalled she'd said something so personal, she started to stammer an apology.

He waved her words away. "I've been told that before." With a shrug, he excused himself, leaving her to wonder if she had or had not offended him.

Dan walked back to join Tucker. Unconsciously his hand rubbed the front of his shirt, feeling underneath the buckskin the beaded medallion he always wore. She'd seen why the Shawnee named him Man With Eyes Like Gun Smoke, even though she didn't know. He made no secret of his heritage, and eventually she'd find out. Being a breed was like being a bastard—neither characteristic likely to come up in polite conversation, but the fact would always come out.

When it did, with her reason to fear and hate Indians, he'd see those emotions reflected in her eyes every time she looked at him. He wasn't in any hurry for that.

Realizing his palm still rubbed the medallion under his shirt, he swore and dropped his arm. He'd only wanted to apologize to April, to take away the hurt look in her eyes when he'd snapped at her earlier.

Instead she'd reminded him why he'd been keeping his distance. He couldn't have her, but it didn't stop him from wanting her. And he wasn't in any hurry to see the light in her eyes die when she did find out.

The day after crossing the river, the wagon train set out early as usual. April observed the tall frontiersman ride ahead while Tucker remarked how well Dan had handled the ferry crossing. Then in a nostalgic note, the old teamster started to recount disasters and mishaps of other river crossings.

April yielded to her curiosity about Dan McKenzie. She jumped in at Tucker's next pause. "Have you known Mr. McKenzie long?" she asked, watching the mounted figure ahead become smaller.

"Dan?" Tucker's eyes squinted as he thought. "Knowed him since he was in shirttails." Turning his attention back to the road, Tucker continued, "He may be kinda young an' all, but there ain't no better hand in the woods than Dan'l Boone McKenzie. Don't you worry none. He'll get you safe to Kaintuck."

She blinked. "Daniel Boone McKenzie?"

Tucker gave her a surprised look. "Ya didn't know? Well, that's his full name, sure 'nough." A faraway look came into Tucker's eyes. "Me and Dan's pa, we hunted some with Dan'l Boone. 'Course that was back afore Kaintuck were a state. We was just part o' Virginie back then.

"Like I said, me and Dan's pa used to hunt with Dan'l. Fact is, 'twas Boone hisself what knowed Dan's pa first. Boone always did judge a man by how well he done in the woods, and Dan's pa was right good. Boone respected that. Reckon that's why Dan's pa named him after Dan'l. Guess ol' Dan'l would be proud of his namesake." Tucker heaved a sigh, apparently for the "good old days."

Several rare moments of silence gave April the chance to ask "Why would Boone be proud?"

"Huh? Oh, 'cause like I said, ain't none better in the woods today than Dan McKenzie. 'Course, he come by it natural, spendin' all those years in the woods."

"Why did Mr. McKenzie spend time in the woods? I thought he lived in Oak Point."

Tucker shifted on the wooden seat, a sign she happily recognized as his settling in for a long tale. "Ya see, Dan's pa, he married him a widder woman, already had her a daughter by her first husband. Like a lot of Dan'l's Yadkin county neighbors, they'd upped stakes and went to Kaintuck with ol' Dan'l. Dan's pa took over the widder's little homestead 'round Boonesboro. But Dan's pa was too much like me and Dan'l. Never able to stick close to home and all the work. We was forever going off huntin' or just plain explorin'. Only me, I never had no woman to leave behind.

"We'd been out for three, four months once. When we got back, found out Dan's ma up an' died right after we left."

An old, deep sadness welled in April. She remembered how, as a child, her world turned upside down at the loss of a parent. "Neighbors had taken the two younguns in. Dan's pa, well, he just never got over his wife dyin'. Dan would've been about eight, mebbe nine then, I recollect. Anyway, Dan's pa left the girl with neighbors and he took Dan."

Had that loss affected Dan as deeply as it had her? Her empathy almost caused her to miss Tucker's next words.

"Dan and his pa traded amongst all the tribes."

"They were Indian traders?" she asked, aghast. She shuddered at the thought of a young Dan obliged by his father to trade and travel among the fearsome Indians who had destroyed her happiness and home. When Indians killed her father, her mother had taken her and left Kentucky.

"Yeah," Tucker agreed, thankfully not seeming to notice her shock. "Hear they done good, though I didn't see neither of 'em again for nigh on to seven, eight years. Then Dan and his pa had a fallin' out for some reason, so Dan traded on his own."

She concealed another shudder.

"Then 'bout ten year ago, just out o' the blue, Dan turns up in Oak Point to see his sister. Course, she'd married up with Scotty by then. Dan and Scotty got on good, so they went into business. Scotty, he set up the store. Dan, he done the tradin'. When Wayne called for frontiersmen to scout for the army, Dan volunteered. That's how they got into the government contractin' business. Two years running now, they've taken supplies out to Wayne."

The wagon lurched, and Tucker shouted, "Buck! Jack! Pull together!" He turned his attention to guiding the team through a particularly rough stretch. Once the road smoothed, he commenced a story of one of his early hunting trips with Daniel Boone.

April watched the road, listening to Tucker with half an ear. Now she knew how Dan came by his skill as a woodsman. And why General Wayne relied on him as a scout. But at what a price.

That evening after the dishes were finished, April put on the first coffee pot for the night watch as Tucker set a pot of water on the fire to heat. Why they needed hot water after the dishes were done no longer puzzled her.

The second evening of the trip, April had watched as after dinner, Tucker had given Scotty, and later Dan, a small pot of hot water. Puzzled, she asked Tucker why.

"Fer shaving," he'd replied.

"Why are they shaving now, not in the morning?" She had asked. Richard had always shaved before breakfast.

"Too much to do in the morning," Tucker replied. "'Sides, sweat runnin' down your face stings if ya just shaved. Best to wait 'til evenin', shave the same time ya clean off the day's dirt." This made sense, as she, too, in the confines of the wagon, washed as best she could each evening.

So now she thought nothing of it as Tucker heated water for the men who might want to shave. As soon as the coffee boiled, and each teamster had a cup, April retired to her wagon. In her canvas-covered home, she dozed, relaxed but not fully asleep. The sound of splashing water close by brought her awake. The dim interior of the wagon told her it was still evening, though late. She poked her head out of the wagon to find Dan washing by firelight.

Chapter Six

He hunkered down, facing the fire as he splashed and washed his face from a bucket. Transfixed, she watched the muscles of his bare back and shoulders ripple with movement, making her aware of the latent power in his lean body. His queue made a dark slash between his shoulder blades. He ran a damp rag over his shoulder and across the back of his neck. Fascinated, she watched a trickle of water trace down his spine to the small of his back where it disappeared into the waist of his clothing.

He stood to take the piece of linen Tucker offered him, and she smothered a gasp.

Usually covered by the long tail of his shirt, his breech cloth was secured around his waist by a belt-like leather strap. The leather leggings weren't like trousers, but rather simply tubes that reached to only a few inches above his knees. A thong secured the outside edge of the leggings to the waist strap. Her breath caught in her throat as the fading firelight painted deep shadows over the exposed muscles of his thighs.

As a child, she'd seen her father and other men dressed in breech cloth and leggings, but this was different. When he handed the towel back to Tucker, she smothered another gasp at the realization she'd continued to watch. Her face warm, and her heart pounding, she ducked back inside the wagon.

Once again the wagon train made a long push on Saturday to reach the inn where they would rest. Sunday was a repeat of the previous one, making April feel like an old hand. She did laundry and washed her hair with the violet-scented soap that had been a parting gift from Mary and Martha.

~ * ~

The next morning dawned perfect. The rain earlier in the week finished turning the landscape green, causing the plants to burst forth in a final fury of spring.

Unfortunately, the travel that allowed plenty of time to think, and to her chagrin, she thought of Dan McKenzie often. Her eyes sought him out as the men gathered around the cook fire for supper.

She noted the way he had with the men. They obeyed his orders without question, even the older men like Scotty and Tucker accepted his authority. Yet he had an easy manner of command, never needing to shout an order. A good hand with horses, he took care of his bay mare personally. According to Scotty, Dan was a crack shot with the rifle he now carried constantly.

Three days after the Sunday rest, the wagon train stopped early to take advantage of good grass and water. Finishing the dishes, April gazed around the circle of wagons. Not yet fully dark, the spring evening slowly fading faded to night.

"Think I'll go for a little walk," she told Scotty and Tucker.

"Not too far," Tucker warned.

"Be back before it gets full dark," Scotty added.

She nodded, feeling as if she had two big brothers.

Keeping their admonitions in mind, she crossed the road from the camp ground and strolled down the other side, where the fragrance of the spring flowers from the meadow opposite lingered. Home, was only a month or so away. Where the road curved, she turned and ambled back toward the camp, coming up on the picket line. At the end of the line she spotted Dan's bay mare.

Speaking softly, she approached the horse. The mare regarded her with a calm eye. April stepped closer. "Hello, girl," she said, and reached to pat the mare's cheek before running her hand down the sleek neck.

"Good girl," she murmured. "What does he call you, pretty girl?"

"I call her High Stakes."

Dan stepped forward from the deepening twilight and walked to where April stood next to his mare.

"I... I hope you don't mind my petting her?" she asked.

"No. She's friendly." Dan scratched the bay under the chin. He'd told himself it was only because of possible trouble he kept track of April's movements. What a liar he was.

"She's very nice. Why do you call her High Stakes?" April asked.

"Because I won her in a bet."

"A bet?"

"Last summer, on the fourth of July." Dan thought of all the reasons why he shouldn't stand talking to her in the twilight.

She took a step closer. "And?" she prompted.

He drew a deep breath and explained. "We have a celebration in Oak Point. Speeches, contests, a dance. There's a shooting match as well. George Wyckford—he's the lawyer in Oak Point—he claimed the man working for him was the best shot in Kentucky. Wyckford bet against me. His man and I tied the first round. Tied the second round. Finally Wyckford said the winner could have the pick of his string of horses." He remembered with glee the fury on Wyckford's face after the deciding round.

"And you won," she supplied when he didn't continue.

He nodded. "On the third round. Wyckford fired his man on the spot. He expected the winner to take his big chestnut gelding. Wyckford could've spit nails when I chose High Stakes instead. Offered me the chestnut and another horse to get her back." He gave the mare a final pat. "She'll be the backbone of my own herd as soon as I find the right stud." He stopped, wondering if it was proper to mention breeding horses to a city lady.

April reached out to stroke the mare's forehead. "I'm sure she will."

He gave an internal sigh of relief. Without thinking he said, "How're you getting on? Any of the men bothered you?"

She surprised him by giving a small laugh that sounded like delight. "Mr. McKenzie, the only man on this wagon train who has made 'improper advances' is you."

For a moment Dan had no idea what she was talking about. Then the memory of his offer that night on the inn porch came rushing back. He hoped the gathering darkness hid the flush creeping up his neck.

"And if you remember, I'm able to take care of myself," she teased in the same light voice. She made a fist, and gently placed it against his belly.

His gut tightened under her hand and his sharp intake of breath whistled between his teeth. He waited, thinking she would take her hand away. But she just stood there. She was so close he caught the light scent of violets from her hair.

Unable to resist, Dan slowly brought his hands up and gently grasped her shoulders. She didn't move, but her breathing deepened as if she were waiting to see what would happen next. His hand glided up over her shoulder, up the side of her neck, and under her chin. His heart thudded, but he moved carefully, allowing her the chance to stop him. This time, when he tilted her face up to his, she let him. For a brief instant he gazed into her eyes, trying to see expressions hidden by the darkness. His blood surged as she swayed toward him, her hands came to rest on his waist. He breathed her name as he gently covered her lips with his. His hand moved from her chin to her back to hold her against him. Her soft, warm body felt better than he remembered, tasted better than he had imagined.

After a long moment, he reluctantly released her, though he kept his hands at her shoulders. He should be furious with himself, shouldn't have kissed her, shouldn't have taken advantage of her not knowing he was a 'breed. Later he might feel lower than a snake's belly, but just now he didn't care. He wanted to hold her and kiss her again. It didn't help that she gazed at him with half-closed eyes, her moist lips slightly parted. He clenched his jaw, preparing to let her go.

Then she said his name in a long, whispery sigh.

He pulled her to him while her arms wrapped around his neck, the length of her body pressed against his as he kissed her again, her soft breasts tight against his chest. Any minute now, she would stop him.

When she didn't, he cupped her buttocks, pressing her hips and stomach against his. Even through her skirts she must have felt him, hard and rigid, for she gave a small gasp. Taking advantage of her open mouth, he deepened the kiss. She stiffened slightly at the invasion, and he gentled his hold, but continued to caress the inside of her mouth with his tongue. Any minute now she'd pull away. Any minute now.

"Dan! Dan!" A shout pierced the night.

He released April so abruptly she staggered. The voices calling from the campsite grew in volume. "Wait here," he ordered, giving her a glance. When she nodded, steadying herself with one hand against a tree, he turned and ran toward the swelling commotion.

Dan burst into the middle of the circled wagons where the shouting men formed a circle. He discovered Scotty and Tucker in the midst of chaos, dodging blows while they struggled to separate two teamsters. The men were dirty, their clothes torn. Blood ran from Scotty's nose.

"All right, stop it!" Dan's command carried over the raised voices. He grabbed the shirtfront of the man Tucker held around the waist, giving the man a hard shake. He turned and glared at the man Scotty held. The fighting sputtered to a halt.

All voices stilled, the mob becoming once again a group of men. Dan released the man he held, gesturing for Scotty and Tucker to do likewise. Chests heaving, the men stood still while they caught their breath.

Holding his anger in check, Dan looked around the now quiet circle of men. "What the hell is going on?" His hard voice slapped the silence.

No one spoke. The two brawlers hung their heads.

Tucker, still breathing hard, answered, "Johnston accused Miller... of stealin'. Johnston's tobacco... pouch is missin', demanded to look in Miller's gear for it. Miller said 'Hell no.'"

"Aye," Scotty added, "All the men fell to checking their gear, and..." His explanation died away as from the picket line they heard the horses stamp and neigh.

Scotty's question of "Where's the lass?" came at the same moment April's cry of "Dan! Scotty!" rang out.

Dan moved before the cry ended. Anxiety tore at him as he ran. Half-way to the picket line he saw her. April ran toward the camp, gripping her skirts in her hands. Relief that she was safe swamped him as he seized her by the arms when she stumbled to a halt in front of him. "Are you all right?"

She nodded and gripped his forearms for support. "Someone's after the horses," she managed to gasp. She looked back toward the picket line. Horses neighed and brush crashed.

"Stay with Scotty," he ordered and ran on toward the line. The rest of the teamsters ran by, following Dan into the night.

Scotty sat by the fire, complaining while April bathed the blood from his face. Dan returned to camp a few minutes later. Both turned as he approached. He accepted a cup of coffee from Tucker. "Someone cut loose most of the stock. Only about a quarter got away. With any luck they won't wander too far. The men are out looking for them."

Dan grimaced at the disheveled campsite, then looked at Scotty and Tucker. "You two all right?"

"Yeah," Tucker replied, "Just ain't as fast as I used to be, is all. Scotty and I would've sorted 'em out."

"Speak for yoursel'," Scotty answered.

Finally, Dan allowed himself to turn his attention to her. "April?" he asked, her name coming naturally to his lips, "What about you?"

April looked up. The sound of her given name in his deep voice, caused a flutter somewhere deep inside her. At the look of concern in his eyes, the flutter became a pulse. She remembered the wonderful sight of him running toward her, the concern he didn't hide when he asked if she was all right.

"I'm fine." Dragging her attention from Dan, she took one final swipe at Scotty's face. "There," she said, "that will do."

"Thanks, lass." He smiled in her direction, but his expression quickly became somber as he looked toward Dan. "This was nae accident."

"No accident," Dan agreed. To April's surprise he said nothing further. She watched Dan and Scotty exchange glances. From the distant night, she heard voices calling back and forth as the men hunted for the horses.

"Miller's in charge of getting the horses back," Dan said as he squatted by the fire. "Is there more coffee, Tucker?" Men! They weren't going to volunteer any information. Exasperated, she would have to ask. "Why would someone want to run off the horses?"

Dan's answer was reluctant and she felt him watching for her reaction. "Reckon someone doesn't want us to get to Pittsburgh."

"I see." Anything that threatened the wagon train threatened her goal to get to Kentucky. The firelight flickered over Dan's form, and she remembered his strong arms around her, his warm mouth covering her. Danger to the wagon train suddenly seemed nebulous and far away. Any danger to her was likely to come from the man staring at her. Or, she thought honestly, her reaction to his kiss, and her desire for another.

"Don't you worry, you'll get there safely," Dan promised, his voice tight, and eyes on his coffee cup.

The thought leapt into her mind that perhaps he, too, was thinking about the kiss.

Chapter Seven

"Well?" the blond gentleman with the aristocratic face questioned Moose and his companion. Seated in a crowded tavern, practically indistinguishable from the one where their first meeting took place, he considered the noise from the other patrons made their conversation a private one.

"That McKenzie, he's a real hard one to sneak up on." Moose complained. "We cut the harness, but the fool horse busted it gettin' hitched up. Would've made more trouble if'n they'd been on the road."

"That's right," Jonesy added. "McKenzie started keeping a watch posted right then."

"That, gentlemen," a sneer evident in the blond man's voice, "is your problem. I pay for results."

"They was held up half a day after we cut the picket line," Moose said. "Would've been longer, but how's we to know that girl'd give the alarm so soon? Didn't see her astandin' there in the dark."

"What girl?"

"McKenzie's got a girl traveling with 'em. Rides on the lead wagon with the old man."

"Now why," the blond wondered aloud, "would McKenzie carry a passenger? And a woman at that?" A speculative light came into his blue eyes as he caressed his signet ring. Then his face and eyes became hard, the transformation startling to Moose and Jonesy. "You men have last one chance to stop McKenzie. Don't fail again."

~ * ~

In the days after the attack on the picket line Dan filled his waking hours with the routine of travel, topped with the constant guard against possible attack. By his order every man now traveled with a rifle or pistol at his side. And everyone, except Tucker and

April, took turns standing a four-hour guard each night. Around three o'clock in the afternoon another spring rain shower blew up. Fortunately, the brief but drenching rain stopped an hour before the evening halt.

After supper Dan sat on a box by the fire. He ran a weary hand over his face and flexed his shoulders against the fatigue. Long days in the saddle and short nights were beginning to catch up with him. Fortunately, only two more days to Pittsburgh. Then he could relax for a bit.

"Another cup of coffee, lad?" Scotty asked as he refilled his own cup.

"No." Dan glanced over to where Tucker and April joked as they finished the dishes. When the clean up was finished, April would return to the fire. He stood and stretched, feeling like a fraud. "Time for me to check the picket lines and the night guards."

He did have to check the picket line and the night guards, but he did it now to avoid the temptation of April's company.

When he returned she had retired to her wagon for the night. He took his bedroll from Tucker and spread it out under the lead wagon. Then he took off his hat, stripped off his tunicshirt and moccasins, and stretched out in his breechcloth and leggings, his rifle close to hand. The morning watch came early, and he was tired. But as usual, once he rolled into his blanket at night his thoughts turned to April. How, in spite of the threat hanging over the train, she remained cheerful, helping Tucker and making the men smile.

A faint rustling noise came from the wagon above him, and he pictured her rolling over on her pallet. With a gusty sigh he remembered how she felt all soft and warm and willing, stretched against him. He didn't know whether to curse or bless the fight among the men.

He rolled to his side, pulling the blanket around him. He knew she wasn't the type to let just any man kiss her. And he was the wrong man for her. And if she knew the whole truth about him, she'd never speak to him—be justified in hating him. Even after thirteen years, he couldn't think about that day without pain. He crushed the memory. Fortunately, neither she nor anyone else had much chance of finding out the worst about him. The few who knew weren't likely to say anything.

Eventually April would find out about his Indian blood, though. He despised himself for wanting to hold her again before she found out.

~ * ~

April was dreaming. She knew the nightmare, but she couldn't escape it. She smelled smoke, heard men yelling. Once again she was a four-year-old, her head buried in her mother's lap, trying to escape the horrors of Indians as they attacked the fort. The smell of smoke grew stronger. A gunshot caused the dream to jerk and change. The vision drifted and she was eight years old, standing beside her mother in the cabin doorway. She saw her father's body draped over the back of his horse as they brought him home. "Papa!" she screamed.

She bolted awake, to find Scotty shaking her shoulder.

"April!" he shouted, shaking her again. "Wake up! Get out of the wagon!" Fighting the nightmare, she tumbled out of the wagon, pulling her cloak over her chemise. The smell of smoke and the shouts continued. They were horribly real. Scotty dragged her clear of the wagon, and pushed her down beside the box next to the cook fire. "Stay here," he commanded.

Total confusion reigned. Billows of acrid smoke drifted across the circle of wagons. It stung her eyes and bit deep in her lungs. She coughed while she pushed her trembling hands through the plackets to fasten her cloak. Breathing shallowly, she wiped her eyes and looked around. Half-dressed men ran and shouted. A gust of heat turned her around. Flames engulfed the canvas top of the wagon just two away from hers. Men beat at the blaze with shirts and blankets.

Horrified, her gaze traveled on around the circle. At each wagon, men fought the fire. Scotty grabbed the bucket that had been her bath water. He threw the water on the flames beginning to lick at the rear of her wagon. The red tongues of fire dissolved, leaving a smoldering section of canvas. Scotty bent double, his breath wheezing.

April ran to his side. Grabbing his arm, she led him back, seating him on the box. Another quick glance showed most of the fires now under control. "Where's Dan?" she asked, hearing the tremble in her voice.

Scotty shook his head, still unable to talk. A teamster limped up, his face streaked with soot, his clothes filthy. "Dan and Tucker took out after whoever done this. He musta' lit that wagon first," the teamster pointed to the wagon with the most damage, two places before April's wagon in the circle, "then set fire to the others. Had to have been another man takened an ax to the wheels." The teamster wiped a dirty hand over his face, smearing the soot.

"Here, sit down," she told the teamster. "Are you all right? Are you burned?"

"No ma'am," he answered.

The teamsters began to drift over to the remains of the cook fire. April looked at the ring of tired, dirty faces. Lifting her voice, she addressed the men. "Is anyone hurt?" A quick survey revealed amazingly few injuries, only a couple of burns and scrapes. She washed away the dirt and smoke, doctored the cuts and burns.

A rifle shot sounded in the distance and all heads snapped in its direction. No one moved for several seconds.

"Bet Dan got him," a voice commented.

She began to shiver. Please, please, she prayed, let Dan be safe. She pressed a hand to her stomach, which began to roll over and over.

Scotty, turning from the sound of the shot, glanced her way and hurried to her side. He led her to the box to sit down. "Dinna worry, wee lassie." His burr was stronger than usual. "Danny can take care o' himsel'." He looked around and spoke to the men. "All except the watch, turn in. There'll be plenty of work for everyone in ta morning."

Within a few minutes, only Scotty and April were left by the fire. Scotty took two pinches of tea from the canister, and dropped them in the small pot of boiling water. "A cup o' tea'll put ye aright, lass."

"I'm sure it will." Her insides still shook and she huddled inside her cloak.

~ * ~

Dan's pace slowed from a run to a fast trot as he came up on the camp. He swallowed hard, trying to slow his rapid breathing. The sight of burnt canvas on the lead wagon tightened his gut. A few more steps brought him to where he could see between wagons for his first glimpse of the camp fire.

He saw April and the tightness in his gut eased. A smudge of dirt stained one cheek and several strands of hair escaped the long mahogany braid that lay over one shoulder.

Overwhelmed with relief, he stepped through the ring of wagons and into the light of the campfire. His movement must have caught her eye, for she turned and saw him. Her body jerked. With a strangled cry of surprise, she dropped the cup she held, her eyes going wide with fear. Her reaction struck him like an arrow and he stopped dead.

He had a quick, mental picture of himself. He'd rolled out of his blanket wearing only a breech cloth and leggings, his hair falling over his shoulders. She hadn't said a word, but she might as well have screamed "Indian!" He lowered his rifle until the stock rested on the ground next to his bare feet, the powder horn and bullet pouch still swinging from his other hand.

"Dan!" Scotty exclaimed, "ye're back!"

At his name, Dan saw April's shoulders slump in relief. The hand that had been at her throat dropped to her lap. He started forward again, conscious of his nearly naked thighs, covered only by the narrow flap of the breech cloth and a few inches of his leggings. Besides his knife, he wore only his beaded medallion, a tattoo encircling his left arm, and a knife scar curving along his left side. The only thing missing, he cynically told himself, were the feathers and the paint. And he'd worn the feathers and paint a time or two.

He forced himself to walk toward the fire. He tried to focus his attention on Scotty, though all he really noticed was the embarrassed smile April gave him. She hadn't realized the truth in her reaction. And she was entitled to the truth, or at least this part of it. His feet led him to stand before her. He bent to pick up the fallen cup.

"Danny-ma-boy," Scotty exclaimed as he moved between Dan and April to clasp Dan about the shoulder. "Where's Tucker?"

"He's with the man we caught. The man's wounded. I came to get help to bring him in. How's everything here?"

Scotty took the cup from Dan's hand and moved to the fire to refill it. Dan followed Scotty and turned away from April feeling reprieved. His first responsibility was the train, the safety of the crew and supplies.

"We were verra lucky, escaped major damage. Just a few burns, nae anyone hurt badly. Ye can see the damage, burned canvas, wheels destroyed."

"I need a couple of men to help Tucker."

Scotty nodded, then handed him the cup. "I'll take care of the men. Ye take tea to the lass."

Resignation settled low in Dan's belly. He walked the few steps to where April sat. Still without a word, he handed her the cup. She cradled the cup between her hands as if she needed the warmth. He ground his teeth against the bitter taste in his mouth.

She gave him a warm, open smile that tightened the knot inside him. "You scared me when you came out of the darkness like that. I thought you were an Indian."

"I am."

Her smile wavered, then disappeared. Her brows drew together.

Wanting the waiting over, he said flat out, "I am an Indian."

She looked at him as if she'd never seen him before. He watched her gaze scan his loose hair, his bare chest, his tattoo, his scar, and finally, his naked thighs. Her puzzlement faded into dawning knowledge, knowledge that seemed to leave her bewildered, stunned. A knife twisted in his gut.

At the sound of footsteps behind him, April's glance flicked over his shoulder. With relief he turned to find Scotty approaching with two men. Dan slung the powder horn and bullet pouch over his shoulder and hoisted his rifle. "See that she gets some rest," he ordered Scotty. "Let's go," he said to the two teamsters. He turned and walked away without a backward glance.

Chapter Eight

April watched Dan and the two men stride between the wagons and disappear into the night. Her chest felt tight, her lungs incapable of getting enough air. Dan an Indian? It had to be some kind of horrible joke. "Scotty?" she said, not sure of the question she asked, frightened of the answer she read on his face.

"Aye, lass. 'Tis true, or at least true enough." April's stomach clenched and she closed her eyes, but Scotty's voice continued. "Dan's father was a half-breed. Dan tells me some folks consider that even worse than being full-blood Indian."

Her heart thudded in her chest. "Why didn't someone tell me?"

The Scotsman shrugged, looking slightly embarrassed. "Never occurred to anyone, I guess. Everyone close to Dan knows. 'Tis the fact he's part Indian and the ten years he spent living among them that recommended him to General Wayne as a scout."

Someone should have told me, she thought with a sudden flash of anger. Wayne should have told her, or Colonel Barker, or... She recalled the scene in Barker's office. Now she knew the reason the colonel treated Dan in an abrupt and condescending manner. The understanding brought a flicker of compassion, but she pushed the softer emotion away, wanting anger to block the hurt, the fear.

"Lass?"

She looked up, not knowing how long she'd been staring into the cup in her hands.

"Ye need rest, lass. All will look better in the morning."

Too tired, too upset to deal with anything just now she handed him the cup. With effort, she stood and trudged to the wagon.

~ * ~

The morning's light revealed damages the dark of night had concealed. Dan surveyed the camp. The canvas has burned completely away on the wagon where the fire had started. Each wagon farther from the first one had less fire damage. Thank God the man with the torch had chosen to start where he did. If he'd torched the lead wagon first, it would have been doubtful April could have escaped unharmed. The thought made him sick.

Besides the charred canvas and blackened traces, three wagons had a wheel with one or two of the lower spokes chopped through. The weight of the cargo had splintered more spokes, leaving the wagons listing dangerously.

His assessment completed, he returned to the cook fire to find Scotty up and drinking coffee. With a groan of fatigue, Dan sank cross-legged to the ground next to him, taking the coffee his brother-in-law offered.

"Could've been worse. Three wagons out of commission. Only a few supplies lost." Dan took a sip, the bitter coffee matching his appraisal of the damage to his wagon train. Thoughts of April continued to nag at him, the danger she'd been in, the way she'd jumped when she caught sight of him, the look in her eyes before he'd walked away.

"How's April?" he asked, glancing toward her wagon.

"The lass is fine. She pitched right in, treating the men's burns an' all, dinna start shaking until it was all over." Scotty paused. "She worried some about ye."

Dan grunted in reply. Let Scotty decide what it meant. Dan stood and threw the remains of the coffee into the fire with an angry gesture. "I'm going on to get some help. Spencer's wagon has the lightest load. Have the men put it on blocks, use those wheels to fix the other wagons. When you're ready to roll, leave Spencer here on guard. I'll get back soon as I can."

"Aye, we'll get it done." Scotty paused, his gaze going to the two new graves at the edge of the clearing. "What about the men that did this?"

Dan swore in disgust. "Wish Tucker wasn't so quick to shoot. They can't tell us who hired them, if they even knew. Unless you or I have some enemies we don't know about, the British must be behind this."

"Aye, 'tis most likely," Scotty agreed. "I'll wake the men." He laid a hand on Dan's arm, "Be careful. There could be more than just those two. Mary'd nae forgive me if I let anything happen to her baby brother."

"I'll be careful," Dan replied, as he picked up his rifle. "You do the same." He walked off to catch up his mare, and then headed for Pittsburgh.

The sound of someone riding out of camp woke April with a start. Last night came back with a rush—her nightmare, the fire, her worry about Dan, then Dan's voice, hard and cruel, saying, "I am an Indian."

Sunlight filtered through the canvas cover and voices called good-naturedly to one another. Perhaps the reason things generally looked better in the morning, April speculated, was morning proved life and time went on regardless. The whole camp was up and working except her.

"Scotty!" she called as she sat up. "Why didn't you wake me?" Work would fend off thoughts of last night.

"There's nae hurry, lass," Scotty's voice answered. "We'll nae be a moving for a time. Stay there. Tucker will bring ye a bucket of hot water. Ye may want to clean up a bit this morning."

Tucker, bless him, brought her two buckets of warm water. "Here ya go. Take your time, if'n ya want. Dan's done gone ahead to Pittsburgh for help. We won't be ready to go 'til after dinner most likely."

As she washed away the grime, she wished she could wash the confused thoughts and feelings from last night. Her long-time fear of Indians and the nightmare made her shudder. Was Dan part of that nightmare or the man who'd kissed her in the twilight? What would she say, what would she feel the next time she saw him?

Because of the late start, the wagon train covered less than ten miles that day, far short of the usual fifteen to seventeen miles. The next morning, the sun barely up, they broke camp and started down the road, needing a good start on this last, long day to reach Pittsburgh by nightfall.

At mid-morning, Dan came into sight, accompanied by a wagon and a mounted soldier. April's stomach fluttered and she clasped her hands together. What would she say to him? What would he say to her?

Tucker pulled the team to a halt. Scotty rode up from the rear of the train, stopping next to the lead wagon. Dan kicked his mare into a trot, pulling ahead of the army wagon as he came to meet them. The flutter in her stomach increased its rhythm.

"Howdy," Tucker called out. Dan waved a greeting and reined in his mare alongside Scotty's gelding.

"You're making good time," Dan greeted Scotty.

"Aye, ye, too."

"Yeah. Got the spare wheels," Dan said, as he jerked his head in the direction of army wagon lumbering up the road. "We'll get Spencer's wagon fixed and join you at the fort." He glanced back at the wagon and soldier as they came on. "Major Sinclair sent the captain, there," Dan indicated the mounted soldier with a nod of his head "to escort you on in to the fort."

While Dan talked, April noted lines of fatigue pulling down the corners of his mouth. He hadn't shaved and looked like he hadn't slept in at least twenty-four hours. Dan put his heels to the mare and trotted off down the road to take up a position slightly in front of the army wagon.

Tucker clucked to the team and the wagon rolled forward. April sat, dumbfounded. Dan hadn't spoke to her, hadn't even looked at her. Like a silly school girl, she imagined something between herself and an Indian. How stupid, she reacted so to a kiss that obviously meant nothing to him. She squared her shoulders and looked down the road to Pittsburgh. Her goal was getting to Kentucky, and she was almost at the halfway point.

Scotty rode up with the army captain.

"Mrs. Williamson, Tucker, 'tis my pleasure to introduce Captain Foley. He's to be our escort on ta the fort."

The soldier swept off his hat. The morning sunlight danced along the row of brass buttons holding back the red facings on the captain's blue coat and glinted off the oval brass plate on his white crossbelt.

Captain Foley rode next to the lead wagon all morning. At the noon stop, he solicitously helped April down from the wagon seat. She hadn't the heart to tell him she'd been climbing up and down by herself all the way from Philadelphia.

The sun set just as they reached the outskirts of Pittsburgh. Scotty and Captain Foley rode ahead to announce their arrival to Major Sinclair.

Several wagons parked in front of a blacksmith's shop partially blocked the roadway. "How large is Pittsburgh?" she asked Tucker while they waited for a wagon from the flour mill coming from the other direction to pass the smithy.

"Well, cain't say rightly," Tucker said, his forehead wrinkling in concentration. "Couple of thousand, mebbe." A smile brightened his face. "Enough folk to support six taverns, though. This has been a mighty thirst provokin' trip."

April laughed, having a feeling it wouldn't take the old teamster long to find one of the taverns. "Well, I for one, am looking forward to a bath in something a little larger than a bucket."

Once the road cleared, the wagons continued toward Fort Pitt in the thickening twilight. Off to the right through scattered trees, the Monongahela River rolled along, dark and smooth. She mentally followed the river downstream. A few miles more and the Monongahela joined the Allengeny, the fort stood between their converging banks. Together, the rivers formed the Ohio, the watery highway that would carry her to Kentucky. Three weeks ago in Philadelphia, Kentucky had been a dream. But the Ohio River was a tangible link to home.

~ * ~

Lounging against the door frame of a well-appointed inn, an elegantly dressed blond gentleman watched the battered wagons rumble toward the fort. So that was the girl. He stared at the small figure next to the old man. More importantly, he noted the burned canvas, the charred wagon beds, the tired slump of the teamsters.

One. Two. While part of his mind counted the wagons as they slowly lumbered past, he planned his next move. Three. Four. Later this evening, he'd call on a pompous captain he'd been cultivating. Five. Six. Over a few tankards of ale, the captain could be trusted to share any gossip. Seven. He'd find out exactly how bad the McKenzie train had been hurt. Eight. Damn! Only one wagon missing. His hirelings had been only moderately successful. When neither of the two riffraff turned up for final payment, he'd wondered.

The last wagon passed, and he returned to his table in the corner of the common room. As usual, he would use his superior intelligence, his guile, his cunning. Taking a drink from his tankard, he mentally smiled in remembrance of the damage done to the wagons. He preferred stealth to a straight-forward attack.

He'd learned the value of a roundabout strike early. The only son of a wealthy planter family, he'd been indulged, pampered, allowed to have his own way. As was his right. He was eight when he and a slave boy fought over a toy top. Although smaller than he, the black boy pushed him, throwing him to his knees. He considered running, crying, to his mother. That would have gotten the slave a beating. But, using his intelligence, he thought of a better way.

He crept into his mother's room, took a brooch from her jewelry box and hid it in the slave boy's pallet. For thievery the slave was banished from the townhouse and sent up river to their country home. Instead of one quick beating, over and done with, the slave had spent the rest of his life working long hot hours on the rice plantation.

Still smiling at the old memory, the gentleman stood. He threw a small coin on the table, and strolled from the common room. He stopped on the porch and pulled a gold watch from his pocket, checking the time. Yes, he would soon find the talkative captain at the tavern. Closing the watch with a snap, he tucked it back in his pocket. Maybe he'd only caused minimal damage to McKenzie this time, but he wasn't finished.

~ * ~

Feeling refreshed from a night of sleep in a real bed, April entered the Sinclair kitchen. She'd been surprised last night when Tucker had pulled the wagon up before a small frame house. Scotty had ridden up just as the front door of the house opened and introduced April to Major John Sinclair and his wife Rachel. While Tucker and the wagon train went on to the fort, the Sinclairs had given April and Scotty dinner and a place to sleep.

"Did I oversleep?" April asked.

Busy kneading bread at the end of the table, Rachel Sinclair smiled and shook her head. Her sleeves were rolled up to her elbow and a bibbed apron covered her dress. She'd pinned her wavy light-brown hair into a neat chignon at the nape of her neck. "You didn't oversleep. Help yourself to some tea." She nodded toward the cozy covered pot.

When the tea in April's cup was almost finished "What can I do to help?" she asked.

"Just sit there and keep me company until I get this bread finished. Then I thought you might like to do your laundry. I need to do washing too. And, as long as we're heating water, we can wash our hair. We have to get ready for the celebration tonight."

"Celebration?"

"Guess you wouldn't know," Rachel replied with a light laugh. "The commanding officer of the fort has been promoted, so the whole fort is celebrating with a potluck supper and a dance. I've already got two pies in the oven." She formed the loaves and put them into the bread pans. "The major and Scotty have gone over to the fort to take care of business. They won't be back until this evening to escort us to supper and the dance. We have the whole day to ourselves."

Chapter Nine

Dan and the repaired wagon arrived at the fort around mid-afternoon. He found Scotty and John Sinclair at the sutler's store.

"Arrangements for the trip down river can wait," John Sinclair said, slapping Dan on the back. "Come to the stable. I want to show you the horse Father sent for me from our plantation in Virginia."

"This animal more important than a drink or a bath?" Dan asked, tiredness making him half-amused, half-annoyed at John's enthusiasm.

John's smile could almost be called a smirk. "It's a stallion. Wait 'til you see him."

"He'd better be a damn fine animal," Dan replied, as he followed John and Scotty toward the stable.

John's stallion was indeed a damn fine animal, but Dan kept his approval understated. A plan began to form in his head and there was no sense in making John any more enthusiastic than necessary. The horse duly admired, the three men returned to the sutler's.

In addition to offering all types of dry goods for sale, the sutler also sold beer, ale, and whiskey at the back of the store. The men each took a tankard before going to sit at a wobbly round table. John said, "I told Rachel we'd be back in time to take them to the dance." He cast an eye over Dan's travel-stained figure. "You better get cleaned up."

Dan leaned back in his chair. The wagons were safe for the time being and the company of friends made him relax. He gave John a fabricated scowl. "Who was so anxious to visit the stable? Otherwise, I'd have had a bath by now."

John ignored Dan's look and comment. "There's a bath-house out back. Go get cleaned up. They're setting up supper over at the parade ground. I'll go on home and fetch the womenfolk and meet you two there."

Two hours later, Dan and Scotty walked toward the light and the music. Both turned out in their good clothes. Scotty wore his broadcloth suit, silk shirt, and stocking and buckle shoes. Dan added a broadcloth coat over his linen shirt, buckskin breeches, and top boots. Flexing his shoulders, he told himself it was the confines of the coat that bothered him. Hell, he might as well admit it; he wondered how April would treat him. With luck, maybe she'd just pretend not to see him. But his mind kept picturing how she shrank back in fear when he told her he was Indian.

The trading partners strolled across the parade ground where torches lit the area in front of a large barn. In the stretch of clear ground outside the barn, tables held ham, cornbread, light bread, pots of beans, side by side with cakes, pies and puddings. Off to one side, the remains of a side of beef still hung on a spit, the fire now just embers.

The torches' flickering light washed over the steady flow of people as they ate and drank. At the end of the tables stood barrels of cider, and over to one side, half a dozen men gathered around a whiskey keg. Music drifted out of the open barn doors.

Following Scotty, Dan entered the large barn and stopped just inside the door to survey the crowd. The majority of the men were military. They dominated the gathering in their dark blue coats with red-facing sashes and epaulets marking their rank. Women spilled a mass of color across the floor as the dancers swept to and fro. Dan's gaze ran over the crowd and unerringly settled on April.

She danced a reel, part of a group which included Captain Foley as well as John and Rachel Sinclair. Green and white ribbons wound through her braids, and her dark green skirt swished as she laughed and twirled, giving him a glimpse of her trim ankle now and then. God, she was a pretty little thing. He refused to acknowledge the internal wince of something that could only be called regret.

The tune ended. In answer to Scotty's wave, the dancers headed in Dan and Scotty's direction.

While Major Sinclair introduced everyone, April studied Dan out of the corner of her eye. He looked slightly wary, as if he, too, felt unsure.

Scotty turned from the group to give Dan a nudge. "Look who's here," the Scotsman half-whispered, nodding to a point beyond April's shoulder.

"What's he doing here?" Dan whispered to Scotty in a fierce undertone. April turned to see the fort's commanding officer introducing a gentleman to John Sinclair.

The gentleman cut an elegant figure in a suit of deep blue, his embroidered silk waistcoat glittering with gold buttons. Blond hair, tied back with a queue ribbon that matched his vest, fell with studied elegance over his ears, framing his aristocratic face. Handsome, she decided, but dressed more for a Philadelphia ballroom than a dance held in a barn.

Major Sinclair escorted the gentleman across the room toward them. Proceeding around the circle, the major introduced George Wyckford, who gave a charming smile to the women and a handshake to each man. When Wyckford first saw Dan and Scotty, his eyes registered surprise, followed by another emotion quickly concealed. April blinked, unsure of what she'd seen. Then she remembered—Wyckford had owned High Stakes.

Wyckford shook hands briefly with Scotty. The same courtesy stopped short with Dan. They merely exchanged curt nods. As Wyckford and Dan stared at each other, a definite chill settled over the gathering. With a quick intake of breath, she realized Wyckford had acted the same as Colonel Barker—refusing to shake hands with Dan. She reflected on Dan's wariness when he'd entered the barn and wondered if he expected such behavior from her.

In an attempt to cover the strained silence, Major Sinclair addressed the gathering. "Mr. Wyckford is a lawyer, presently living in Oak Point, as do Mr. Murray and Mr. McKenzie."

"Your business brings you to Pittsburgh?" April asked Wyckford, partly to assist in Major Sinclair's effort and partly out of curiosity.

"I'm looking into old army records. I have several clients with conflicting land claims." Once again Wyckford exhibited a charming smile. "Are you and Mr. Williamson living in Pittsburgh?"

"I'm a widow. My husband and I lived in Philadelphia, but I was born in Kentucky, so I understand the problem with land titles." Though she held her father's original deed, she knew many early settlers had lost title to their land because of the conflicting colonial, state, and federal laws.

"I'm on the way to Oak Point myself. Mr. Murray and Mr. McKenzie have been kind enough to provide me with transportation."

"I was in Philadelphia only last month," George Wyckford commented. "Such a pity we did not meet there. I shall look forward to seeing you in Oak Point."

She produced a noncommittal smile in reply.

Scotty cleared his throat. "How long will you be staying in Pittsburgh?" he asked Wyckford.

"I don't know, Mr. Murray." He turned to April. "But it will be long enough to ask this lovely lady to dance." He took her hand as the band struck up another tune. She hesitated a moment, but decided that dancing with him was one way to end the conversation. She allowed him to escort her to the dance floor. The Sinclairs and others followed Wyckford's lead.

Left standing with Scotty and Captain Foley, Dan watched Wyckford effortlessly lead April through the intricate steps. So focused on the couple, Dan almost didn't hear what Foley said.

"Glad to see you and the wagon finally made it." The captain slapped Dan on the back. "Great party," Foley commented, looking over the dancers.

"Great," Dan agreed, rankled that Foley, too, seemed to be watching April. His sarcasm must have shown, as both Foley and Scotty glanced his way.

Captain Foley sighed and said, "Well, the party's over for me. I have to report to duty. See you tomorrow."

"Let me walk you out," Dan said. Seeing April dancing with Wyckford irritated the hell out of him.

Dan returned a few minutes later to find Scotty still in the same spot, watching the dancing. His brother-in-law gave him a sideways glance and Dan answered the unspoken question. "It's not as smooth as Kentucky whiskey, but that 'Monongahela' will warm your belly."

"How much did ye have?" Scotty questioned, amusement in his voice, his attention still on the dancers.

"Not enough," Dan muttered under his breath.

All afternoon Dan had avoided asking anything about April. Even when Scotty related how attentive Captain Foley had been to her on the ride to Pittsburgh, Dan hadn't taken the bait, though he'd been almighty glad to see Foley leave. Compelled by an intensity he didn't want to think about, Dan's gaze followed April's green dress as she circled the room with Wyckford. At least she wasn't smiling at the bastard like she'd smiled at Foley.

Maybe he didn't rightly know how he felt about April, but he sure knew how he felt about Wyckford. The lawyer had been a burr under his saddle ever since he'd come to Oak Point. Although he managed to hide it, he felt the sharp sting Wyckford intended every time the lawyer looked down his aristocratic nose and publicly referred to Dan as 'breed.

At least, Dan thought, he had ten years of living white to learn how to deal with people like Wyckford. Disregarding the scorn of the likes of Colonel Barker and Wyckford irritated them as much as their prejudice grated on Dan.

The music stopped and the Sinclairs, April and Wyckford walked toward where Dan and Scotty stood.

"Not dancing, Scotty?" Major Sinclair asked lightly.

"Nay, ye already have the two prettiest lassies," Scotty smiled at April and Rachel. "Perhaps I'll claim the next dance. As long as no one tells ma wife when we get back to Oak Point."

After the chuckles died down, George Wyckford turned to April and asked, "How long do you plan to visit us in Oak Point?"

"I'm not visiting. I plan to live there."

"Surely you jest," Wyckford replied. "The frontier is no place for a delicate lady such as yourself."

Amazing. Apparently there was one point of agreement between him and Wyckford.

Dan brought his attention back in time to hear Wyckford say, "As I told several colleagues in Philadelphia, I feel the Indians are still a serious menace. They have the backing of the British army and I'm not convinced now is the time for the aggressive policies of Wayne. From a business standpoint, we cannot afford to offend either the British or the French. We simply must make peace. Leave the Ohio Valley to the savages for the time being."

"Come now, you must have more faith in the army than that," Sinclair interjected.

"It's not a question of faith, but of power and strength. We cannot defeat the British and the Indians." Wyckford turned from Major Sinclair to face April. "You must have some concern about Indian attacks, Mrs. Williamson?" His voice turned harsh. "Or do you have no idea how truly savage they can be?"

Dan watched her pale. She knew all right. She hid it well, but he heard the underlying fear in her answer. "I know, Mr. Wyckford. I was four during the siege of Harrodstown. When I was eight, the Indians killed my father at Blue Licks." April drew a breath, making Dan aware he'd been holding his. "But that was a long time ago. I think perhaps you are over dramatizing the present problem."

"In any case, shall we talk of something else?" Rachel interrupted, "There are no Indians here tonight."

Wyckford looked from face to face around the circle, a lazy smile coming to his lips. "Not precisely true," he said, letting his gaze drift derisively over Dan.

Knowing what was coming, Dan braced himself. With a strength of will, he kept his eyes on Wyckford, refusing to look at April.

Wyckford's voice dripped sarcasm. "Perhaps the ladies are unaware McKenzie here is an Indian."

Dan returned Wyckford's derisive look. "It's no secret my grandmother was Shawnee."

"Really, Mr. Wyckford," John Sinclair said, "I doubt Dan is much of a threat. I'm sure you realize he spent most of the past two years as a scout for General Wayne and the Legion. He was even wounded last summer."

Wyckford switched his attention to the major. "He goes back and forth between the Indians and the Legion, correct? Who can tell which side he's really on?"

Dan heard shocked gasps from the women. His fists clenched at his sides.

Wyckford looked down his nose at Dan and spit out the words, "McKenzie's either a spy or a traitor."

Dan's temper boiled. He surged toward Wyckford. Scotty took a quick step sideways, blocking Dan's forward movement. John Sinclair stepped in front of Wyckford, who hadn't moved.

Struggling for control, Dan allowed Scotty to bring him to a halt. From the corner of his eye, Dan saw April and Rachel, both pale and wide-eyed. Several other people turned to look in their direction.

In the stunned silence, April's heart thudded. She released the breath she held when the tension drained from Dan's body, his fists relaxing.

"Mr. Wyckford," the major spoke in a firm, low voice. "Mr. McKenzie is here as my guest. I suggest you apologize or leave." There was a small silence, as the major looked from Wyckford to Dan. People on the outskirts of the confrontation began to turn away, the excitement apparently over.

With a frosty smile, Wyckford turned toward April and Rachel. "Ladies, I sincerely apologize for upsetting your evening." He gave a small bow. He faced the major. "Good evening, gentlemen." He turned and sauntered nonchalantly away, disappearing into the crowd.

April looked at Dan. The wooden expression on his face gave nothing away, only a faint flush marked his high cheekbones. Surely his insides must be churning as much as hers.

Wyckford's slur accomplished one other thing. When he'd called Dan a traitor, she had felt Dan's pain. And she'd hated Wyckford. Dan's Indian heritage hadn't change the way she felt about him—but how could she tell him? Lost in thought, she jumped again when Scotty spoke.

"Now that he's gone, perhaps we can return to enjoying ourselves." Scotty's inflection was light, but his tone brooked no argument. "John, why don't you dance with your wife?" He shooed them toward the dance floor.

Scotty took Dan by the arm and led him to her. "Dan, take April and get the lass a cup of cider." While giving the order, Scotty tucked April's hand in the crook of Dan's elbow. He hesitated, but she gave his arm a small squeeze.

Dan led her across the floor and out into the soft summer evening. They crossed the yard, less crowded now than earlier. He took her beyond the tables to where a log, its upper edge adzed smooth, served as a bench. At one end a soldier and his girl sat side by side lost in their own quiet conversation, the man's arm around the girl's waist. Seating April at the other end of the log, Dan said, "Wait here. I'll get the cider."

April watched his long legs carry him toward the supper tables. With a sigh, she smoothed her hands over her skirts, then twisted her fingers together. Her whole body had been aware of the warmth and strength of him as they walked arm in arm.

Dan returned, holding a tin cup in each hand. "Here's your cider." He didn't sit, but instead hunkered down by the end of the log, so that both of them looked out over the supper yard. Sounds of music and laughter drifted on the night air. A full moon hung low in the sky. In the quiet, April felt a kind of peace settle around them.

Beside April, Dan rested his forearms on his knees. As he lifted his cup to his mouth, she caught a sharp pungent odor and she smiled to herself. He brought her cider, but the contents of his cup came from the whiskey barrel.

After a moment he made a noise halfway between a snort and a laugh. "Didn't think Wyckford and I would ever agree on anything, but he was right about one thing. The frontier is no place for you."

With a small shake of her head, April matched his soft tone. "We've had this conversation before. Life in Kentucky can't be that difficult. After all, other women live there."

Still looking out over the yard, he made the non-committal noise he was so good at, making her smile. After a moment, still not looking at her, he said, "When I was in Philadelphia, your friend Mrs. Allen told me how terrified you were of Indians. And you'd already told me about... about Blue Licks."

He turned to look at her. He drew a deep breath and went on, "If you're so afraid of Indians, why aren't you afraid of me?" The question hung between them in the darkening night.

Chapter Ten

"I... I don't know why," April stammered, as she raised her head.

With Dan crouched beside her, their eyes were almost level. She took heart from his seemingly relaxed pose. She might as well admit the truth. "I guess the reason I'm not afraid of you is that I know you. Had I known you were part Indian, I certainly would have hesitated to ask you to take me to Kentucky."

Dan shifted his weight and took a small sip from his cup, feeling the warmth of the whiskey slide down his throat to settle in his belly. He wondered if the warmth would untangle the knot that had formed there when she'd squeezed his arm and looked at him without fear. He brought his attention back to the journey to Kentucky. "Getting there is one thing, living there another."

He let out a long sigh, and started to talk. The words seemed to be drawn out of him. "You haven't seen what life on the frontier can do to a woman. There's too much to do, too much to endure. When I was just a tad, my ma would sing while she worked, used to read me stories of an evening. Even taught me to read a little." He balked at telling her that by the time he returned to Oak Point at eighteen he'd forgotten how. His sister spent that winter re-teaching him.

"As I got older, the singing, the reading, gradually stopped. She was just too worn out. Pa was never much of a hand for keeping to a job. If he decided to go hunting, he went. Didn't matter if he left the field half-plowed or no firewood chopped. Sis and I did as much as we could, but it was never enough." No need to tell her how his mother once smelled of starch and soap when she hugged him, but by the end she didn't change her dress for days on end.

"I watched her work and worry herself to death. One morning she just... didn't wake up." He gripped the cup tight in his hands, afraid to look at the woman beside him, afraid of what he might see on her face. He swallowed to clear his throat.

"After that Pa took me to live with his Indian kin. His pa was dead, but his ma was still alive. We generally spent the winters with her and the rest of the time we traded back and forth between the Indians and the whites."

He hesitated, then undid several buttons and pulled the beaded medallion from inside his shirt. "Owl Woman, my grandmother, gave me this. She made it for grandpa McKenzie. He died before I was born and when we went to live with her, she gave it to me." He pulled the leather thong over his head, and handed the medallion to April, pleased her fingers naturally touched his as she took the beaded badge.

"Grandfather McKenzie told her about thistles in Scotland, so that's what this is supposed to be."

He watched her fingers caress the nubby pattern. Purple and green beads on a white background gave the impression of a thistle, if not the actual image.

After a moment, she handed the medallion back to him. Clearing her throat, she said, "It must have been hard on you and your father, being pulled both ways."

"Yeah." Dan heard the hard edge in his voice, but shrugged it away. "Sometimes I think that's what made the old man such a bastard at times. He never knew what he was." He took another small drink from his cup. Glancing up at the woman beside him, he detected no scorn, no pity. Might as well tell her most of the rest of his story, he decided—but not all of it.

"When I was fifteen, Pa and I had a parting of the ways. For the next three years I lived as a Shawnee brave. I traveled with Standing Bear, an Indian cousin a couple of years older than me. We went all over the territory—Fort Detroit, down the Ohio to the Mississippi, all over. Trading, trapping, stealing from other tribes, living wild and free. But it wasn't..." he paused, searching for the words. "...wasn't right for me." That was as close as he could come to explaining. "I had to return to the white world. See how Sis was doing."

How could he explain what he only understood, but was unexplainable, even to himself? He only knew what he felt. He paused a moment. "Being Indian and white pulls me both ways, too. Some of my blood may be Indian, but I learned my mind lives in the white world."

He shifted again, setting the whiskey to sloshing in the half-empty cup. "Wyckford, damn him, is right about another thing. I do feel like a traitor when I spy on the Indians."

"Why do you do it then?" she asked softly.

He jerked his head up, then stood with an abrupt movement. "I have to, don't you understand? I have to." He ran his hand through his hair and paced back and forth. "The British are only using the Indians. They give them guns and ammunition. Send them out to kill and raid. When we fight back we kill Indians. Between us we're killing them—people I know, people I lived with for seven years." Hearing the anguish in his voice, he stopped.

Once under control, he continued, "When push comes to shove, the British will never support the tribes. If Wayne can win a major battle, the tribes will realize that. Then they'll have to agree to peace terms. The sooner the Legion is successful, the sooner Indians stop dying."

Dan looked down at April, her head bent as she studied the cup of cider in her hands. Wanting to see her face, he hunkered down in front of her. The muted light from behind him was enough. Unbelievably, he saw understanding and compassion which helped rinse away the pain of being called a traitor and a spy.

April watched Dan set his cup aside. Hearing about his past, she understood his feelings about women on the frontier. Conditions had changed in the last twenty years, but this wasn't the time to remind him.

He crouched in front of her, one hand on a buckskin clad knee, his other forearm rested on his thigh, his hand dangling, relaxed from his wrist. The beaded medallion, suspended outside his half unbuttoned shirt, trembled slightly with each breath. Her face warmed in the strength of his gaze.

She'd come outside with him to let him know how she felt. He'd amazed her by sharing parts of himself she knew he'd shared with few others. She drew a deep breath, and let it out. Now she must tell him her feelings.

"You asked if I was afraid of you. Maybe I was for a brief time, but not anymore. It doesn't seem to make any difference how I felt. You're just you. Dan McKenzie." Obeying some deep need, she reached out and laid her hand against his cheek. His skin was warm, with only the faintest scrape of whiskers under her fingers as she trailed her hand down the line of his jaw. Her fingers drifted across his lips and she felt his breath, warm and moist.

He tensed under her touch and his eyes blazed, shooting blue-gray sparks. "I'm not afraid of you, Dan." Her voice sounded breathless.

The blaze in his eyes intensified. Embarrassed, she started to pull her hand back, but he caught her wrist, holding her in an iron grip. Straightening to his full height, his hand still locked around her wrist, he drew her to her feet. The cup of cider fell unnoticed to the ground. He pulled her roughly against him. "Maybe you should be," he warned.

Captured in his embrace, she looked up into his eyes feeling his heart beat with steady power, his chest rising and falling with each breath. "Maybe I should be afraid," she agreed softly. She moved her captured hand up his chest and he let go of her wrist. "But I'm not," she concluded. Her hand moved to the back of his neck. His face came down toward her and his warm lips found hers.

A giggle sounded off to the right. Startled, April broke the kiss. The soldier and his girl at the other end of the bench both wore knowing grins.

Flushed with embarrassment, April tried to pull away. But Dan's arm still circled her waist and kept her there next to him as he responded to the soldier's grin with one of his own. Delight fluttered through her at the sight. She'd never seen him smile, really smile, before.

"Try over behind the quartermaster's," the soldier suggested, nodding in that direction.

"Thanks." Dan dropped his arm from her waist and took her hand instead. "Come with me?"

She nodded her assent and he led her across the yard. The music from the dance floated on the air, a counterpoint to the sharp crunch of Dan's boots and the swish of her skirts.

The quartermaster's storehouse was barely twenty yards away, but once they rounded the corner of the building they were alone in the shadows. Dan stopped and swung her around to face him, his hands warm on her waist.

"Now," he said, his voice soft and teasing, his smile flashing in the dim light, "tell me again how you aren't afraid of me."

"I'm not afraid of you," she whispered, as she slid her hands up his arms and wrapped them around his neck. He gathered her to him until her breasts pressed against his chest. His lips came down to meet hers. His kiss demanded her response, claimed possession, overwhelmed her with pure heat. His mouth opened, his tongue running lightly across her lower lip. This time she knew what he wanted. Yielding, she opened her mouth to accept his intimate caress. She caught the sharp taste of whiskey as he explored her mouth with his tongue.

When he finally broke the kiss, both struggled for breath.

His kiss left her lightheaded, and she might have fallen had he not held her up. Awash in feelings and desires, she couldn't think. Didn't want to think, just continue to feel.

Holding April close, Dan struggled to get his breath. The touch of her soft hands on the back of his neck made desire flame through his body. He wanted this woman. He took two steps forward, pressing her back against the plank wall of the building.

He leaned against her, pressing her to the wall, wanting to feel all of her as he captured her mouth again. No longer supporting April in his arms, his hands were now free to caress her. She breathed in small gasps, her eyes closed. He brought up one hand to touch her face, his fingers tracing the shape of her brow, then down her cheek. She gave a long sigh, turned her head. Her warm, moist lips kissed the palm of his hand. His stomach flipped over. "God, April," he groaned.

He reached back to cradle her head. In the faint light he made out the ribbons threaded through her braids, and the sharp, sweet fragrance of violets enveloped him. He wanted to tug out the pins and tangle his hands in her hair but some still sane part of him kept him from doing so. He kissed her again while he slowly brought his hands down her neck and across her shoulders. Lifting his head for a breath, he leaned back and looked at her.

The square-cut neckline of her dress revealed the beginning swell of her breasts. They rose and fell in invitation with each rapid gasp, her nipples outlined against the fabric. Gently pushing her shoulders back against the wall, he planted a line of kisses along her collarbone, feeling her rapid pulse under his lips when he paused at the hollow of her throat. He dropped his hands to her waist. His thumbs almost touching, he slowly slid his hands up her rib cage until he cupped a breast in each hand.

April gasped aloud in surprise and pleasure. His touch as he stroked and caressed her breasts partially satisfied the nameless longing she felt when he leaned the length of his body against hers. Waves of warmth washed through her. Needing to touch him in return, she brought her hands inside his coat, running them up his chest, until she encountered the gap of his half-buttoned shirt. With only a slight hesitation, she slipped her hands inside to the warm planes of his chest.

Dan rewarded her boldness with a quick intake of breath that quickly became a groan of masculine pleasure. She marveled how he could feel soft and hard at the same time, like a layer of warm satin over solid granite. He was warm, alive, powerful. His hands drifted over her hips, and then around to her buttocks, holding her to him. He gently rocked his hips back and forth. Even with the layers of petticoats muffling the sensations, tingles of desire shot sparks through her.

April wrapped her arms around his neck, and he kissed her once again. She wanted him closer and couldn't think how.

His hands clutched at her skirts. When he moved his lower body away from hers, she moved her hips forward to follow him. He mumbled, "No, wait," and with light pressure, pushed her back against the wall.

There was the rustle of cotton fabric and when he again leaned forward against her, the material of her skirt and several petticoats were bunched up around her waist. Only the buckskin of his breeches and one petticoat separated them. His hands on her hips burned through her single petticoat. The tingles of passion shot through her, running together to collect at the juncture of her thighs. He moved against her, drawing a sigh from her, and a satisfied murmur from him.

The sigh of pleasure barely escaped April's lips, when Dan's body stilled. Only then did she hear a voice calling his name. He let out a breath in a long shuddering sigh, warm against her cheek. He took a half step backward, withdrawing his hands from her. With a sound like falling leaves, her skirts settled around her ankles.

Someone called his name again. April removed her trembling hands from his neck. Their breath still came in ragged gasps, but he cleared his throat and answered, "What, Scotty?" amazing her with how normal his voice sounded.

"The dance is almost over," the voice replied. Fortunately, Scotty was being discreet, staying where he couldn't see them. His disembodied voice continued, "You and April be back to Sinclair's in ten minutes." The statement was little short of an order.

"We'll be there," Dan answered. He rotated his shoulders as if willing his body to relax.

April leaned against the wall, her breath slowing to normal. Still lightheaded and dizzy, she wanted to shout and she wanted to weep.

Shout because she felt so wonderful.

She hadn't known the way a man and woman could make each other feel was so powerful, so compelling. She now understood remarks she'd only vaguely understood before. Sly remarks about men and kisses and beds, and other things which brought giggles and blushes in the sewing circle. Shaken and in awe of the power of what she and Dan had experienced together, she wanted to shout because she loved Dan McKenzie.

And she wanted to weep because she loved Dan McKenzie.

She was in love with him though there was no guarantee he could ever love her, ever accept her as anything other than a city girl. She felt suspended between glory and despair.

He breathed her name and she opened her eyes. The dim light revealed the concern on his face. A reflection, she hoped, that the last few minutes had moved him as they had moved her.

He buttoned his shirt. She smoothed down her skirts and put a hand up to check her hair. They looked at each other, both awkward and uncomfortable, not knowing what to say or what to do.

Finally Dan cleared his throat, "We'd better go. Scotty will be waiting." He hesitantly offered her his arm, and she hesitantly took it, as they started back to the Sinclairs'

~ * ~

The Saturday morning sun shone through the window of the Sinclairs' back room, while April dressed and put up her hair. Of all the people in the world, why had she fallen in love with him? Regardless of how she felt, she thought with a sigh, nothing had changed. She still was determined to finish the journey to Kentucky and prove to herself she was capable of living on her own.

What, she wondered, did you say to a man who'd had his hands under your skirts the last time you saw him? She smiled to herself as she secured the last hairpin. By now she knew him well enough to recognize she needn't worry. Just like after the first time he'd kissed her, Dan would act like nothing had happened.

She made her way to the kitchen, relieved to see only Rachel standing at the end of the table slicing a side of bacon. April picked up a large cotton apron lay over the back of one of kitchen chairs and tied it over her dark blue dress. "What can I do to help?"

"Why don't you start the bacon," Rachel said, laying aside the knife. "I'll mix up the hotcakes. The men went down for a quick check of the flatboats, but John said they would be back in a few minutes." By the time Rachel and April had breakfast ready for the table, the men returned.

"Sure smells good," John said, giving his wife a small hug of greeting as the three men entered the kitchen.

April's heart beat just a little faster as Dan came through the door. She smiled to herself at the way he didn't look at her. Unless she missed her guess, he would be scowling at her in a couple of minutes.

John Sinclair sat at the head of the table. Rachel set a plate of bacon and hotcakes before each place. April put a crock of butter and a pitcher of syrup on the table and poured each man a cup of coffee.

Dan pulled up a chair, sitting at John's right; Scotty took the place by his side. Keeping his gaze on John, Dan fixed his thoughts on the flatboats.

"It will be Tuesday, then?" John asked him.

"Tuesday's fine." That would give him time to finish his other business with John Sinclair.

What Dan didn't want was time to think about April. Watching her moving around a kitchen, getting his breakfast, made his insides unsettled. It looked too comfortable. And the feeling made him uneasy. At least she didn't seem to be paying him any special attention. Come to think of it, he wasn't sure he liked that either. He scowled as she put a cup of coffee by his plate.

After the meal, Dan excused himself. Between his business with John and errands for McKenzie and Murray, he managed to stay away from the Sinclair house for the rest of the day. Pleading business, he slept at the fort that night.

But Sunday afternoon, Dan found himself walking up the path toward the Sinclairs' kitchen door calling himself a fool every step of the way. He expected the woman to run when she found out he was part Indian, but had she? How could a man ever figure out a woman?

She may have been born in Kentucky, he reminded himself, but she'd been brought up a long way from the frontier. She knew all the words to the hymns they'd sung in church this morning, when he'd only been in a church a handful of times. He'd sat on the hard wooden pew, unable to pull his gaze from the back of her head, wondering what he was doing there. Now he was purposely seeking her out, and he felt a fool for doing so.

Through the open door he saw April seated next to the table. A cherrywood box with brass corners lay open on the table, a square of linen, pair of scissors, and paper of pins next to it. He halted on the step and leaned against the door jam, studying her. She didn't look up, her attention on the needle that flashed in and out as she mended a dress. Hesitantly, he cleared his throat.

April jumped. With a gasp she turned, one hand to her heart. Seeing him, she let out a deep breath. "Will you stop doing that!"

"Doing what?"

"Scaring me half to death. You move so silently, I never know you're there."

Thankfully, she sounded more amused than scared or angry. "Sorry." He cocked his head to one side, fighting the urge to grin as he said, "I thought you weren't afraid of me?"

A blush spread over her cheeks. "I said I wasn't afraid of you, not that you didn't scare me," she replied before studiously returning her attention to her sewing.

"Men learn to move quietly on the frontier, or they don't survive," he said quietly. Dan pushed himself from the doorway and entered the kitchen. He hung his hat on one of the pegs just inside the door. Twisting around the chair next to April, he straddled the seat and folded his arms across its back.

His eye caught the square of linen on the table. "What's that?" he asked, gesturing with a nod.

"A sampler." April pushed the sampler toward him. He smoothed out the cloth, running fingers gently over the cross stitches. He'd watched his sister sew enough to appreciate the time it took to make something this intricate.

A vine, done in three shades of green, sprinkled with small white flowers, wound its way around the linen square to form a border. The top of the sampler contained the alphabet in capital letters, while the lower-case alphabet decorated the bottom. All the letters were done in a neat, deep blue cross stitch. He'd seen other samplers, all with borders and the alphabet, but this one was different. Detailed in tiny stitches in the center of the sampler was a log cabin. A puff of smoke came from its stone chimney, several trees shaded the background. Under the cabin read the legend, "My Kentucky Home, April Fletcher, 1782."

"You made this a while ago," he commented, not knowing what else to say.

"I was seven and spent the whole winter working on it. Every stitch that wasn't exactly right had to come out and be done over again." She glanced at the sampler, then up to him. "It's one of the few things left of my childhood. I hated Philadelphia when we first went to live there. I slept with this sampler under my pillow the first few years we were in Philadelphia. I hoped it would act like a good luck charm to take me back to Kentucky."

Folding the sampler along the creases in the linen, he handed it back to April, conscious of her fingers touching his as she accepted it. He stood abruptly and slid the chair under the table. "Looks like it worked."

Seeing the sampler and hearing her talk convinced him of the strength of her commitment to live in Kentucky. Yet he knew commitment alone did not guarantee success.

Maybe she could accept what he was, just as Scotty, the Sinclairs, and others had done. But no one, not even himself, could accept what he'd done that horrible day. He was wrong for her. He took a deep breath and let it out heavily. He should walk away, but knew he wouldn't. "Would you like to walk down by the river?" he asked. "I'll show you the flat boats. Since it's Sunday, we'll not be interrupting the workers."

She flashed him a smile. "Yes, I'd like that."

A few minutes later Dan led them down the well-worn pathway that meandered through scattered maple and dogwood trees along the river bank. Sunlight glinted off the Monongahela to their left. A quarter mile ahead, Dan pointed out several docks running out into the river behind the businesses lining Water Street. Further distant, where Fort Pitt guarded the junction of the two rivers, a flicker of red, white, and blue waved over the corner blockhouse.

The path was wide enough for him to walk at April's side, but narrow enough for her skirts to brush against his boots with every step. They walked from shade to bright sunshine and back again as they followed the path. He watched the bright sun strike flashes of red from her hair. Hair, he remembered only too well, that smelled like violets.

"Tell me about Oak Point," April said as they strolled along.

"It's just a town. Grown a lot in the last ten years, though." They stopped beside several large boulders.

Leaning against one of the sun-dappled gray stones, April asked, "Do you live in town?"

"My place is about five miles out, but it's sort of run down now. Haven't spent much time there lately. The last couple of years General Wayne has kept me busy." He absent-mindedly rubbed his left side, feeling the scar running along his ribs. "Been easier to stay with Sis and Scotty whenever I was home.

"We have a good size store in town. Built right onto the house. Four years ago we built a second story, since they needed more room for the boys."

"Boys?"

"Sis and Scotty have three sons."

"Your business has been successful then?"

"We had one of the first real stores in central Kentucky. Scotty put up all the money to get us started ten years ago. He insisted on putting my name first, since it was better known. It was a struggle at the beginning, but contracting for the government these last few years has helped. I'll have enough money to finish paying Scotty back by year's end. Then I can get on with my own business while Scotty runs the store."

"What business is that?" she asked.

He paused to look out over the river, thinking how he'd convinced John to put High Stakes to his stallion. "When all the fighting is over, I'll be able to stay in Oak Point, get the farm going the way I want. Someday I'll raise the best horses in Kentucky."

Dan shifted his shoulders against the rocks. The early summer heat had only warmed the outer layer of the granite, and the spot he'd been leaning against was no longer warm. They'd better get to the flatboats. They should be on their way. He studied April as she watched the river. His eyes went to her feet.

"Those shoes you're wearing," he gestured at her feet, "they have leather soles?"

"Yes, they do. But why?"

"They're too slick. I forgot once, wore these boots on the flatboats and nearly fell overboard," he explained. "Come on," he said, "I know where we can get you a pair of moccasins with nice soft soles. One of the Indian scouts at the fort always has some trade goods."

~ * ~

That same afternoon a well-dressed gentleman mounted on a chestnut gelding rode out of the city. He held a small bouquet of flowers in his right hand. Anyone who cared to notice would assume he rode to meet a lady friend. Several miles out of town, he flung the flowers aside. He then spurred the chestnut down the road, watching for the small bit of yellow cloth tied to a branch.

After twenty minutes, the rider spotted the bit of cloth and jerked back on the rein. The chestnut half-reared at the sudden command to halt. The gentleman swore, cutting the horse with his whip, as he turned him on to the faint track marked by the scrap of yellow cloth.

He guided the gelding along the path, going deeper into the heavy woods, ducking now and then to avoid low-hanging branches.

After perhaps a mile, the woods thinned, and the horse and rider stepped into a small meadow. The two men waiting in the meadow arose from their seats on a fallen log.

The two men stood as the gentleman rode toward them. A uniform coat, folded inside out to conceal its scarlet color, lay on the log. This was the third time the gentleman had met the British captain, his contact from Fort Miamis.

Chapter Eleven

"Afternoon, Colonel," the captain greeted George Wyckford.

"Afternoon, Captain," George Wyckford said.

Captain Markham stood at attention. He knew the colonel insisted on military correctness at all times. Wyckford's glance swept over him and went to the man by Markham's side.

"And what might this be?" Wyckford asked.

"Le Corbeau, sir. He's one of our scouts," Markham explained. The scout, dressed in typical frontier buckskins, was short and stocky, his dark greasy hair hanging loose.

"The Raven, eh," Wyckford translated looking the 'breed up and down. "Looks like it, too," he said to the captain. The captain gestured to Le Corbeau who took Wyckford's horse and led it to where the other horses were tethered. The two British officers walked to the log which held Markham's coat.

He waited for Wyckford to sit. Only when Wyckford waved permission did Markham seat himself.

"What's the news from Fort Detroit?" Wyckford asked.

"The same. Our government in London is greatly concerned with the French. The commander's afraid we'll run out of time." Markham noted Wyckford's frown, but continued. "The Indians need a major victory against Wayne soon if we are to hold the Ohio territory."

"We will win," Wyckford snapped in reply. The whole fort knew of Wyckford's deep hatred for both the Americans and the Indians. The colonel seemed almost unreasonable in his determination to see a British victory.

Wyckford looked out over the meadow and mumbled, "We gave up too soon ten years ago. We won't do it again. The Americans must pay for what they did." He paused, looking to Le Corbeau tethering his horse. "All we need do is keep these savages stirred up. Let the Americans and the Indians kill each other. The less of each the better. In any case, we still hold Canada, and we can hold the Ohio Valley as well. We must keep to our task, Captain Markham."

"Yes, sir," Markham replied, keeping his tone respectful. He didn't know how Wyckford could be so sure they would win. Back at the fort, every British soldier seemed certain the government in London no longer cared about North America. The threat of war with France dominated British concern.

Markham shifted uncomfortably and cleared his throat. "Colonel, the commander asked me to remind you not to give the appearance of favoring the British takeover of the Ohio Valley."

To Markham's relief, Wyckford simply snorted and said, "Tell the general not to worry. I parade myself as a conservative and cautious individual. The Americans are too naïve and unsophisticated to suspect anything." Wyckford shifted on the log. "I spoke to several Representatives when I was in Philadelphia last month. As a concerned citizen, of course. There are those who believe if the 'Legion,' as General Wayne so grandly labels the American army, is recalled, there will be peace on the frontier."

"I'll report what you say to the general," Markham agreed, nodding his head as the Indian scout returned. Le Corbeau seated himself on the ground next to Markham.

"Now to the business at hand," Wyckford said. "The flatboats with Wayne's supplies will leave Pittsburgh early Tuesday morning. I trust that will give you time to arrange something?"

"Yes, sir," the captain replied. "Le Corbeau is in touch with his people. They'll keep the supplies from reaching the American army."

"Good." Then, as if a thought struck him, his eyes narrowed. He spoke to Markham, "There will be a bay mare on one of the boats. Have him," he waved toward the Indian, "tell his men I'll pay extra if she's returned to you. That bastard McKenzie stole her from me."

"McKenzie?" Le Corbeau spoke, frowning. "Big man, un grand homme? Shawnee? Man with light eyes, like smoke from rifle? Scout for Americans?"

To Markham's surprise, the colonel spoke directly to the Indian. "You know him?" Wyckford leaned forward.

Le Corbeau glanced at Markham, who nodded for him to continue. "This man much trouble, trop facheux. He too good scout. Tell Wayne where we hide, where we camp. He say he friend of Indians. Say British bad. Tell Indians not to fight." Le Corbeau shrugged. "Some, they listen to him, not fight against Americans."

Markham watched the colonel's face darken as Le Corbeau spoke. After a moment of hesitation, an unpleasant smile spread slowly over Wyckford face. He leaned back, glancing at Markham, then back at Le Corbeau. "Tell your men I will pay, Le Corbeau. I will pay a bounty to the man who brings me McKenzie's scalp."

~ * ~

Along with Scotty, April headed toward the wharf. Excitement churned in her stomach like the last time she and Scotty walked toward the beginning of a journey. Her new life in Kentucky loomed half a journey closer. And Dan's presence presented a sweet complication the likes of which she'd never known.

This time she wore a navy blue dress and one petticoat. On the trip out she had learned wearing the proper number of petticoats made movement difficult, and adopted the frontier expedient of wearing only one. Here in Pittsburgh, she'd worn three, but today went back to one in preparation for the flatboat.

For her luggage she'd wrapped two spare petticoats around her sewing box, and placed them along with a spare chemise and toilet articles in a clean flour sack. Her other possessions had been repacked into one of the trunks and carted to the flat boat. The flour sack would double as her luggage and pillow, and once again, her cloak would be her blanket.

The damp, pungent smell of the river increased as they approached the landing. Thirty or forty people scattered in small groups on the shore, waiting to watch the boats launch, gave the docks a festive air.

Men bustled around carrying ropes and poles. The content of the wagons, now stacked and covered by canvas crisscrossed by ropes, sat on each boat.

"Each flatboat is forty-five feet long and thirty feet wide," Scotty said. "The logs have been tied together with rope and with planks nailed across the top of the logs to provide us with a floor. The sweep," he pointed to the large steering oar at the stern, "is used to guide the boats. We'll be letting the current do the work to take us down river."

Scotty led her toward the third boat. "We'll be riding this one." Slightly different from the first two, the canvas-covered supplies were not shaped in a square, but L-shaped, leaving one open corner toward the rear. The open rectangle was fenced off to form what looked like two stalls, the floors covered with straw and separated by a waist-high row of boxes,

Scotty had warned the flatboats would have less room and less privacy than the wagons. Fortunately, they would only be on the boats for a week at most.

Standing on the wharf, she wiggled her toes in the moccasins, still not used to the soft, but snug and comfortable way they felt. As April's surveyed the crowd once again, Dan appeared around the corner of the dry goods store, leading High Stakes. Her flutter of excitement increased at the sight of him, once more in frontier garb of linsey-woolsy shirt open at the neck, belt at his waist carrying his knife. The shirt stopped at mid-thigh, revealing his long legs, encased in leggings and moccasins on his feet. The way he walked, his movements smooth and easy as he led beside the bay mare, drew her eye.

"There ye are," Scotty hailed him. "We're ready when you are."

"Let's get started then," Dan replied.

Dan turned to Tucker, "You got your supplies loaded up?"

"Sure 'nough."

"Let's go then. Give me a minute to load High Stakes, then Scotty can bring April on board."

That man, April thought in exasperation, mentally shaking her head. Every time she met him, it was like starting their whole acquaintance over again. Maybe someday he'd actually smile first thing. Then she'd probably faint dead away.

~ * ~

Dan stroked the mare's neck and whispered in her ear. As if agreeing, High Stakes bobbed her head, and as though she did it every day, the mare quietly followed Dan up the gangplank.

"Pure amazing," Tucker commented. "That man sure 'nough has a way with horses."

Clutching her flour sack, April followed Scotty up the gangplank. The stack of supplies for Wayne were so tall she could see over them only if she stood on tiptoe. About twelve feet of open space separated the canvas-covered supplies from the rear of the boat.

Dan led High Stakes into the outside stall. He tied her halter to one of the ropes securing the canvas bulk that formed the front end of the two stalls. He gave the horse a final pat and left the stall, tying a rope across the open end.

He turned and looked at April. She smiled, but he didn't return the greeting. He rubbed his hand over his jaw, and then with what sounded like an exasperated sigh, gestured to the second stall. "This is the best I could do."

"Do for what?" she asked, confused.

"This is where you'll have to stay."

Understanding dawned. "It doesn't look so bad."

His expression lightened a little.

She walked forward to get a closer view. A box ten feet deep and four feet wide, the floor of her stall was covered with a deep layer of straw.

"We put this solid row of boxes between the stalls," Dan explained, pointing to the three-foot-high barrier that separated High

Stakes' quarters from hers. "We could throw a strip of canvas over the top rail, close everything off, if you want. And," he stooped to pick up a folded blanket just inside the stall, "we'll put this over a rope so you'll have a door of sorts."

"I'm sure I'll be fine." Maybe she had the same accommodations as the horse, but the stall was clean and neat. And it seemed silly to expect anything more. Especially when she saw no accommodations, of any sort, for the men. "I'll have more room here than in the wagon."

She sensed Dan relax beside her. He shook his head. "April, I..." he started. He reached out and briefly touched her shoulder. "I have to go. I'll be on the lead boat; Tucker will tell you anything you need to know." He strode down the gangplank.

She sighed, willing her heartbeat to return to normal. Would she ever figure out what went on behind those blue-gray eyes? With a shrug she put down her bag.

Tucker hurried up the gang plank. She put aside her thoughts of Dan as the boats made final preparation to leave. The cry of "Cast off!" brought a rough "hurrah" from the crowd.

The flatboats drifted down the river. Each sweep needed two men to keep the boats centered in the current. The city gradually faded, the voices, the rumble of wagons, the sound of hammers, the smell of smoke and dust gradually replaced by the lap of water, the occasional command, and the heavy, moist scent of the Ohio. With the first bend in the river, Pittsburgh disappeared from sight.

"We'll tie up to the south shore for nooning, an' every night," Tucker explained.

"At least this part of the trip won't be as dusty as the wagon train," she commented, thinking it fortunate, as her change of clothing was so limited.

The swaying of the boat made April slightly queasy. She tried to refuse the bread and cold meat Tucker served at noon, but he assured her she would feel better if she ate. And he was right. By late afternoon she began to feel more comfortable.

Just before sunset, the boats put into the south shore to tie up for the night.

Tucker returned from shore with an armload of wood. Now April understood the reason for a box of dirt about two feet square built on the open space at the back of the boat. Here Tucker built the fire, and slung an iron kettle from a tripod to cook a dinner of bacon and beans.

As on the wagon train, each man collected a plate and ate wherever he found a seat. Dan and Scotty joined her and Tucker on the rear deck.

The familiarity of fixing supper, sitting with the plate in her lap, made her feel she'd slipped back into her traveling role as the first two days of travel passed.

~ * ~

The twilight lingered with the lengthening summer evenings. Dan sat cross-legged, leaning against the supplies while he watched April dry the dishes as Tucker put on the traditional pot of coffee for the evening watch.

He should go gather the wood he'd promised Tucker for the night's fire, but he'd do it later. Right now he'd rather sit and watch April. He liked the way her skirts swished as she turned and stooped.

He'd stay away from her once they got to Oak Point. He'd have to report back to Wayne before too long. Once she was out of sight, he'd put her out of his mind.

Sure you can, a voice teased as he watched her pour a cup of fresh coffee and bring it to him.

"Here," she offered with a smile that knotted his belly.

"How many more days to Cincinnati," Tucker asked, pulling Dan's thoughts back to the conversation.

Dan had to think a second. "Three, maybe four."

"Been a good trip." Tucker looked at April. "Bet you're real anxious to get to Oak Point."

"Oh, yes. I dreamed of coming home for so long when I was in Philadelphia, sometimes I can hardly believe I'm almost there." Dan noticed she couldn't hide the fervor in her voice.

"That's right," Tucker said, "you was born in Kentucky, weren't ya?"

April smiled and nodded.

"Never thought to ask afore, but if'n ya are so all fired determined to go back, why'd ya leave Kentucky in the first place?"

Dan's heart began to pound. The bitter taste of dread crept up the back of his throat as all the dark reasons he thought he'd pushed aside came rushing back.

His legs seemed made of lead as he stood. He didn't want to hear her tell Tucker how her father had been killed by Indians at Blue Licks. His belly burning, he walked down the gangplank into the soft summer twilight.

That night Dan lay on his blanket, looking at thousands and thousands of stars sprinkled over the velvet night sky.

Scotty's voice came out of the dark. "She surprised ye, dinna she."

"What?"

"I dinna ken why ye were so stand-offish with the lass at first. Ye expected her to run when the subject of yer Indian blood came up. She surprised ye and dinna run." When Dan made no comment, Scotty goaded, "Am I right?"

"No," Dan kept his voice low. "She didn't run." He let out a deep sigh. "But she should have." The despair must have shown in his voice for Scotty raised up on one elbow to look across at him. "What's wrong?"

Dan shrugged. "It doesn't matter. It... just wouldn't work out, that's all." Feeling utterly weary, he rolled over turning his back on Scotty. "Now, leave me be and go to sleep."

Scotty lay back down. But after only a few moments of silence he softly called, "Dan?"

Dan lay still, hoping Scotty would leave him alone, but his brother-in-law called again. Dan rolled over and looked at him. "What now?"

Scotty, his voice betraying his embarrassment, asked, "Ye didna, ah, the night of the dance, ye didna, ah, force yersel' on her?"

"For christssakes, Scotty!" Dan sat bolt-upright and glared at the older man. "What do you take me for?"

"Sorry, Danny-me-boy."

Dan sat on his blanket, his arms crossed and resting on his upraised knees. Damn, he shouldn't have been so short with Scotty. But he'd have to tell Scotty something if only to make him stop match-making.

"I couldn't hurt her, Scotty. I'd take her right back to Philadelphia tonight, if she'd agree. She belongs somewhere civilized, not out here. Someone who can give her a good life." He looked over the dark water. "She sure as hell doesn't belong with me." Not him, never with him.

Scotty sat up. "Why not ye?"

Dan felt his brother-in-law's questioning gaze, and knew he had let the pain show in his voice.

The old fear and old guilt rolled over him. He took a deep breath. When his words came they were half-sigh, half-moan. "Scotty, I was at Blue Licks."

Scotty frowned. "Where April's father was killed? Did you know him?"

"I wasn't fighting with the settlers." The next words felt like broken glass in his throat. His heart thudded and his skin grew tight and sweaty, just like it had that day. "I was with the other side. I was one of the Indians when they killed all those settlers at Blue Licks."

Dan lowered his head, resting his forehead against his folded arms. "Pa and I'd been out hunting, I was fifteen. We'd just come back to Kentucky from over on the Mississippi. We knew the British were directing the Indians against the settlements because of the war, but never thought anything more about it.

"We ran across a small party of Indians around ten in the morning. I knew right off something was wrong. Said Pa and I should join their 'hunting party.' Said what they were hunting was better game than we were hunting. This game would 'show the color' of our blood.

"I couldn't believe it when we reported to a British officer. Now I look back, I think Pa must have suspected what was going on, but I was too raw to know any better."

He'd been so surprised when he saw the British officer in his red coat, he'd started to protest, but his pa'd slapped him so hard he split his lip. "Keep quiet, and keep your scalp, boy," he'd ordered.

Dan raised his head, looking out over the river. He didn't look at Scotty. "The Indians, mostly Shawnee with some Wyandot and Delaware, had just attacked Bryan's Station. They'd burned the outlying cabins and crops, but the British couldn't get them to hold a siege at Bryan's. The war party was pulling back toward Ohio territory when we ran across them. By that time the settlers got the militia gathered to help Bryan's Station, so they decided to go after the Indians.

"I still don't know if it was the British officer's or Indians' idea to set an ambush for the militia at Blue Licks. Found out later Daniel Boone warned those hotheads that it could be a trap. But the militia divided up into three groups and crossed the Licking River, heading right into the ambush.

"The first volley caught the center group of the militia by surprise. Then all hell broke loose. The rest of the Indians, Pa included, burst out of hiding, yelling and screaming, chasing the remaining militia. God, I was scared." The remembered fear made his stomach crawl.

"I hadn't fired and tried to hang back, but it wasn't any use. They dragged me down the hill." Seeing his reluctance, a British officer had clubbed him in the ribs with the butt of a rifle. While he gasped for breath, two warriors had dragged him stumbling down the hill and into the battle.

"After the first shots, both sides used tomahawks and knives on each other. I fought just to stay alive. By the time the remains of the militia straggled back across the river, only about half of them were left." He remembered crouching on his hands and knees, trying to drag air into his burning lungs, amazed he was still alive.

"I can still see it, Scotty," he whispered. "What they say is true. The Licking River ran blood-red that day." A shudder shook him. "You know the funny thing? The Indians were right. That's the day I found out the color of my blood."

The boy he'd been was still gasping for breath after the battle when a Wyandot warrior came up to him. With fingers bloody from the hand-to-hand combat, he'd wiped four red streaks across Dan's cheek. "What color your blood now, boy?" he'd asked.

Dan stared at the dark night sky. Telling the story seemed to have left him as weak as the battle itself. "I felt ashamed. I'd betrayed the white part of me and felt I couldn't ever live white, either, not after what I'd done.

"I went up to Chillicothie." Dan glanced at Scotty.

Scotty nodded, telling Dan he recognized the name of what had been the principal Shawnee town.

"Met up with Standing Bear, an Indian cousin of mine who was seventeen, and the two of us took off together. For three years I tried to be all Indian, to forget I was part white." He realized his right hand rubbed the tattoo circling his left arm. "But it didn't work. So I came back to Oak Point."

He glanced at Scotty. "You should have seen your face, Scotty, the day I showed up."

"Ye were a sight to be sure, lad," Scotty chuckled. "All that long hair loose, no shirt, riding bareback right through the center of town."

Dan gave a hollow laugh in return. "I was damn lucky someone didn't take a shot at me, the way I looked."

"Dan? Who knows ye were at Blue Licks? Does Mary know?"

Dan shook his head. "No." He rubbed the back of his neck. "Guess no one knows, except the Indians I was with."

"Then who's to tell April? You know I would na."

"It's enough I know I was there," Dan replied sharply as he lay down, turning his back to Scotty. "Let's get some sleep. Morning will come just that much earlier if we don't."

Chapter Twelve

Crack!

The sound of a shot jerked April awake. She scrambled into a sitting position in the gray dawn, hearing the men's shouted alarm.

"Indians! Indians! Canoes on the river!"

"We're under attack!"

Cold fear darted through her. She crawled to the open end of her stall in time to see Tucker plop his rifle along the top of the supplies. At the click of flint striking steel she tensed, but still jumped at the loud bang. Acrid, pale blue-gray smoke drifted across the boat.

"Stay down!" Tucker shouted. He pulled the ramrod out and began to reload. Close by, High Stakes snorted, hoofs thudding against the wooden planks.

April pulled on her moccasins, her fingers trembling as she secured the laces. From the two boats moored ahead came the sounds of battle—gunshots and men shouting, the thunk of bullets hitting supplies, the twang as arrows struck. None of the noises drowned out the fearful beating of her heart. The clamor seemed hideously at odds with her sternward view from the last boat. She saw only the peaceful river, its surface like gray silk in the dawn light.

Dan's voice roared, "Push off! Get the boats on the river!" Her heart thudded in her throat. She peered through the railings toward the shoreline. Dan sprinted down the river bank. Wearing only breechcloth, leggings and moccasins, he gripped his rifle in one hand, his knife in the other.

"Cassedy! Edwards!" Dan yelled toward April's boat. "Push off!" He stooped, his knife slashing. The bow mooring line parted with a faint twang. The two men pushed against the river bank with long poles. Secured by only the stern line, the boat slowly nosed out onto the river.

Dan ran along the bank and stooped to cut the stern line by the gangplank. "Get back up front!" he ordered the two men as he took the gang plank in two leaps. The men dropped their poles on the deck and dashed to join the fight at the bow. Dan's foot struck the deck as the gangplank splashed into the slowly widening gap between the river bank and the boat. Two more steps brought him to her.

"Get down!" He pushed her down by the shoulder, even though the solid wall of crates protected her. He propped his rifle against the supplies next to Tucker. Stripping off his powder horn and bullet pouch, he dropped them at Tucker's feet. "Here, you may need extra shot."

Tucker nodded, not bothering to answer as he continued to load and fire.

April watched Dan run aft and grasp the sweep. She felt frozen, unable to move while her mind worked at double speed. In the same split-second, she thought if she knew how to load a rifle, she could help Tucker, and then had time to marvel at her own thoughts.

Dan pushed against the sweep, steering the boat further from the bank. His shoulder and chest muscles bunched as he strained against the sweep that usually required the brawn of two men. April jumped when Tucker fired once more. She glanced around. The shoreline retreated. The boat moved into the river.

A double splash came from the river side of the boat. She snapped her head around. Fear clenched her stomach, rendering her speechless. An empty canoe bobbed away and an Indian heaved himself out of the water onto the boat. He crouched on his hands and knees on the deck. Water streamed from long black hair. Terrified, she watched while his companion pulled himself from the river onto the planking beside him.

The first Indian's gaze darted over Tucker, still loading his rifle. She glanced around for a weapon of some sort. With rising horror she saw the Indian smile when his gaze moved past Tucker and fasten on Dan's unprotected back. Ignoring the older man, the brave rushed Dan, knife glittering in the early morning sun.

"Dan!" she screamed.

Without glancing over his shoulder, Dan let go of the sweep and ducked. The pressure of the river swung the sweep over his head. Spinning, Dan straightened. He slammed the sweep into the Indian's chest, knocking him to the deck. Dan kicked the knife from the Indian's hand and whirled to help Tucker, who struggled with the second Indian.

The stunned Indian lay on the deck. Then he rolled over, gathering himself to get up. Without making a conscious decision, she jumped to her feet, clutching the flour sack containing her sewing box and petticoats.

She dashed to the fallen Indian, now on his hands and knees. With all her might, she swung the sack. She shuddered at the solid 'thunk' and stepped back as he slumped to the planks. He lay still. Blood trickled from his temple. She stared, horrified, her heart thumping.

A loud splash tore her stare away from the Indian at her feet. Dan caught Tucker as he swayed. Gently, Dan lowered the old man to a sitting position, letting him lean against the wall of supplies. Dan quickly crossed to her. Kneeling beside the unconscious Indian, Dan grunted his approval. She registered the diminished sounds of the battle—fewer shouts, the gunshots farther apart—as Dan began to roll the Indian over and over toward the stern.

In sick fascination, April followed the trail of bloody red splotches left on the deck. Her stomach rolled in concert with each turn of the Indian's body. She clasped one hand over her mouth. Her other hand, still clutching the neck of the flour sack, pressed against her stomach. Fighting the rising nausea she took slow, small steps backward, unable to look away from the horrible sight.

Dan shoved the Indian off the edge as something rolled under her foot. One of the boat's poles. Lurching, she stumbled backward—and stepped off the side of the boat.

She hit the water with a sploosh, her skirts billowing around her. The cold water soaked through the fabric, her skirts grew heavy. She'd learned to swim as a child and memory guided her body. She righted herself, struggling to tread water.

Dan ran across the deck, yelling, "Make for the shore! Quick, before your skirts drag you down!"

The boat had already drifted out of reach. Air hissed and bubbled as it escaped through the fabric of her clothes. She started to sink. A hurried glance over her shoulder showed the river bank only thirty feet away. She twisted toward the shore, hearing a splash behind her. A heartbeat later, Dan's head and shoulders popped out of the water in front of her. He shook the water from his eyes. Turning on his back he stretched out his hand.

"Here," he gasped.

She latched onto his outstretched hand and kicked as hard as she could. Dan swam on his back, tugging her through the chilly water, his legs kicking beside hers. Dan suddenly stood, the water only hip deep. He jerked her upright, then pulled her through the water to the shore.

He dragged her up the gentle slope, and they collapsed on the bank. She half-sat, half-lay on her side, astonished to see she still clutched the dripping flour sack. Beside her, Dan knelt, hands braced on his thighs, his bare chest heaving as he drew deep, gasping draughts of air into his lungs.

She coughed, gasped for air and coughed again. Dan took the flour sack from her. "Come on," he said. He took her hand and pulled her protesting body to her feet. "That raiding party... may send someone... looking for us."

"But, the b-boats," April stammered, anxiety tightening her throat. She looked to the flatboats. Deep on the river, the three boats glided away.

Dan waved, waiting only until Tucker waved in return. "They have to go on." He pulled her into the underbrush, heading south, away from the river.

Dan set a quick pace. He carried her sack in his right hand, pulling her along in his wake with his left, his long legs taking them swiftly through the forest. She ran to keep up.

He forged straight through the bushes and brambles. Branches and twigs scratched her hands and face, tugged at her hair. Her wet skirts wrapped themselves around her legs, hampering every step. Finally, with an exclamation of exasperation, she pulled her hand from Dan's. She stopped, gathered up her skirts, and threw them over her left arm, leaving her legs unencumbered from the knees down.

He took her hand again. Within minutes, she gasped for breath, as did Dan. The mid-morning sunlight dappled the hot, still woods. The river's dampness gave way to perspiration. Moisture beaded her forehead and upper lip. Sweat ran down Dan's naked back as he guided them through the woodland. Still they went on. She thought of nothing, aware only of the labor of her lungs, her legs, the dryness of her throat, as she trotted behind Dan.

"Dan," she finally gasped.

He looked back, slowing a bit. "Just a little farther. Can you make it?"

She simply nodded, not really sure.

Dan led her around a berry bramble, into a large swale where ferns grew thick between the trees. Much to her relief, instead of pushing his way through the mass, Dan followed a narrow deer trail that criss-crossed the tract. At the far side of the fern swale, a small stream gurgled its way toward the river.

"We'll rest here." He let go of her hand. She dropped to the ground. The sound of their heavy breathing mingled with the buzz of insects in the heavy summer air.

After a few moments, Dan shifted toward the stream, scooping up the clear water to drink from his hands. April followed his example.

"Go easy," he cautioned. "Too much'll cramp your stomach."

The water tasted cool and sweet. She held a mouthful, letting the wonderful wetness seep down her dry throat. She splashed the water over her face, and ran her hands around the back of her neck.

Dan watched April as she rinsed her face in the stream and then took another small swallow of water. Reassured by her actions, he splashed water over his own face, chest, down his arms. The sudden contrast of temperatures made him shiver. Moving back from the stream, he settled himself against a tree. He let out a deep breath, running his hand through his hair.

"Damn, that was close." He sighed, closed his eyes and rested his head back against the bark. Mentally checking their position against an internal map, he realized they were within a few miles of a perfect place to hide and rest for the night.

His breathing eased almost to normal. He'd let her rest a while longer, then they'd go on. He tilted his head forward and opened his eyes. "April..." His voice died away.

She crouched on her knees, still beside the stream. Her hands covered her face, her shoulders shook with the force of her silent sobs. He scooted to her side and put his arm around her.

"It's all right. We're safe now," he lied. Her tears were a natural reaction, but they burned his heart. He knew how a person could be too damn scared at the time to feel, and how later on the fear surged back. He pulled her to him as he moved back to the tree.

With his back braced against the solid trunk, Dan tugged her across his lap, resting her head against his chest. Her arms encircled his waist, accepting the comfort of his embrace. She hid her face in the angle between his neck and his chest, her tears warm and wet on his bare skin. He stroked her hair with his free hand, smoothing the mahogany strands away from her face. He brushed his lips lightly against her temple.

"Don't cry, honey," he entreated. "Everything is fine. We're safe." He prayed it was true. The intensity of the protectiveness he felt for her astonished him. He closed his eyes, refusing to give a name to the emotions which seized his heart. Gradually, her sobs lessened and died away. Her body relaxed and her breathing became slow and steady. Cradling April in his arms, he shut his mind to all but the immediate problem of their survival.

April blinked, climbing out of the daze into which she'd fallen. Her cheek still snuggled against his chest, she found herself looking directly at the dark-blue curved, intertwining lines that encircled his upper arm. The design looked like an ink drawing of a braid. Without thinking she ran her finger across the dark-blue lines.

"It's a tattoo," Dan's voice rumbled in her ear. His arms relaxed and she sat up. "Indians regard tattoos as body adornment."

Fascinated, she watched the design as Dan flexed his arm, struck once more by the uniqueness of the man she loved. At a total loss for what to do or say, she brushed a lock of hair back over her ear.

He gave her a half-smile. "Better?"

"Yes." He must think her a weak, weepy fool. "Sorry I cried so."

He shrugged. "There was reason enough." He moved her off his lap, stood up and stretched. Retrieving the flour sack, he placed it next to her. "I hope this is important."

She heard a faint teasing note in his voice and looked up in surprise, as he made light of the situation to distract her from their problems. How could she not love him?

"This is my sewing box, wrapped in my spare petticoats and chemise."

With a half-smile he looked down at her. "Odd weapon, but it sure worked. Bet that Indian's headache will last into next week."

She remembered the Indian charging Dan's unprotected back and suppressed a shudder.

The memory must have shown on her face, for his smile faded. He helped her to her feet, his expression serious. "Can you make it a little farther? I know a perfect spot to stay tonight."

April sighed. Her legs ached, she itched from brushing through the ferns, and she hadn't had breakfast. She remembered that night on the back porch of the inn, when she'd told Dan women could do what had to be done, just as men did. "I can make it," she said.

This time they walked instead of ran. Before long, she got her second wind and walked steadily behind him until they reached the place he had in mind.

"It's a rockhouse," Dan said.

Nestled in the side of a hill, several large boulders lay jumbled together. One huge, slab-like stone rested at an angle against the others. The open triangular space between them created a wide, shallow, rock-lined area.

"A rockhouse," April repeated. It looked like a place a child would choose for a playhouse. A spring flowed from a tangle of stones nearby, trickled across the rocks, and within a few feet formed a small pool. From the pool, the stream flowed across the meager meadow and into the woods.

Dan put April's sack down. Drawing his knife, he walked to a nearby box elder tree and cut a leafy branch. Re-sheathing the knife, he handed her the branch.

"Use this to sweep out. I'll go over yonder," he waved across the stream, "and cut more branches to make a bed for you."

She swept out the leaves and pebbles which had accumulated on the floor. Dan returned with an armload of maple boughs. The leaves tossed with each step he took, the bottoms flashing gray-white against the dull green tops.

Dan dropped the branches and wiped his hands against his leggings. He looked at the sky, then back the way they had come. "I have to check our backtrail. Cover any tracks we made."

Apprehension gripped her at the thought of being alone. He must have read her fear.

"We probably weren't followed, but I have to make sure. The attack on the flatboats was by canoe. Chances of them following us on this side of the river are slim as we're only about three, four days from Oak Point." He gestured south-southwest. "I'll be back before dark. You'll be all right here."

She read the concern on his face. Somehow, she said the words she knew he needed to hear, whether or not they were true. "I'll be fine."

He nodded. A heartbeat later he lifted his hand and brushed the backs of his fingers along her cheek. Dread clogging her throat, she took hold of his hand, giving it a squeeze as he stepped away.

When he reached the edge of the clearing, he turned and raised his arm. The gesture seemed to be as much a salute as a wave, then he turned and disappeared into the woods.

When she was certain Dan was gone, she sank to her knees. Without his presence, exhaustion and fear swept over her. She wrapped her arms around herself. Think of something else. She swallowed the lump stuck in her throat and blinked her eyes against the tears. Think of how you've made it to Kentucky. Her heartbeat slowed, the tension seeped from her body and her breathing steadied.

Dan counted on her. She drew strength from his reliance. With a groan at the stiffness of her legs, she rose and stretched.

Bending over the pool for a drink, she gasped at the image in the water. She looked like a wild woman, her face smudged with dirt and her hair a tangled confusion, the braid loose. Making a face at her reflection, she drank deeply, then washed her face.

To keep herself too busy to think, she unpacked the damp flour sack, spreading the contents out to dry. To her surprise the contents of her cherrywood sewing box were hardly damp, she'd been in the river such a short time. In the small pool, she rinsed the flour sack, the spare undergarments, her muddy, ripped dress, spreading the garments over several large rhododendrons bushes close to the rockhouse. Finally, she rinsed her hair, then bathed in her chemise as best she could.

By the time she finished, the warm summer sun had dried her other chemise and petticoats. Exchanging her wet chemise for dry undergarments, she chose a small boulder to serve as a chair. Sitting on the "porch" of the rockhouse, she brushed her hair, carefully working out the tangles. She used a green ribbon from the sewing box to tie her still damp hair at her nape.

A glance at the sky showed the sun still well above the tree tops. How far would he go? she wondered. Was he all right? To keep her mind and hands busy, she turned to her sewing box. Needle and thread and thimble to hand, she began to mend the rents and ripped seams in her dress. The needle may have trembled slightly, but her finished stitches were small and even. Be safe, Dan, she prayed with each stitch.

~ * ~

With his arm, Dan wiped the sweat from his forehead. He'd retraced his and April's trail through the fern swale, erasing the signs of their passing.

He squinted at the sun. He'd have to hurry to get back before sunset. The thought of her, alone and frightened at the rockhouse, gnawed at his gut. He pushed the worry away and concentrated on the problem at hand.

Something about the attack nagged at his subconscious. At the edge of the swale, he paused as it came to him. During the ambush, he'd heard the attackers yelling. Squatting to rest for a moment he rethought the attack, searching his memory.

Thinking back, did he comprehend some of the words—the words "bounty" or "reward" with the word for "scalp." He'd also heard his Indian name. He was known as Wayne's scout, so he could easily understand the British were offering a reward for his scalp. He stood and took a deep breath.

He'd found no sign of pursuit thus far, and he began to hope he'd told April the truth when he said there would be none. Easing carefully through the undergrowth, he headed in the direction of the river until he came to a well traveled trail. Deciding to take a chance since his tracks would lead toward the river, he moved onto the trail, walking briskly. One quick inspection of the river then he'd head back to the rockhouse. He stepped up his pace to a trot.

As he did, the bushes to his left erupted. Instinctively, he dodged sideways, drawing his knife. A blur of motion caught his eye a split second before he felt a sting along his side. Fighting for balance he spun to face his opponent. The momentum of the Indian's slash had carried him through a half-turn, his knife in his far hand. Dan sprang forward. He thudded into the brave. Bare, sweaty torsos slipped and strained. With a powerful shove, the Indian pushed Dan away.

Panting, the men faced each other, both in a half-crouch. The Indian's knife glittered in the afternoon sun. During their brief struggle Dan had sensed a strength fresher than his own.

Still circling, Dan drew a deep breath. He had to win this fight quickly or he wouldn't win at all. His opponent lashed out. Dan jumped backward, avoiding the lethal blade. The Indian smiled slightly, feinting as Dan backed away. One more time, Dan thought, as the two men circled. Another thrust. Again Dan leaped back.

Preparing for another lunge, the Indian drew his hand back slightly. Dan sprang forward, inside the flashing arc made by the Indian's blade. His own blade slashed wildly as their bodies slammed together, arms grappling. For a long second Dan thought he'd missed. Then the Indian howled. His grip relaxed and he fell to his knees.

Gasping for breath, Dan stepped back, his blade up. There was no need. His wild slash had laid the Indian's forearm open. As Dan watched, the man's knife fell from his fingers into the dust of the trail.

A questioning yell from the direction of the river jerked both men's heads up. The remnant of the raiding party was on the way.

Chapter Thirteen

Dan turned and slipped into the trees. Fifty yards down the trail, he ducked into the undergrowth, weaving his way deeper into the forest. As he ran, he pressed a hand to his side to prevent leaving a blood trail. He pushed through the undergrowth heading southwest, parallel to the river. If they followed him, he would lead them away from the rockhouse. His lungs burned. The thought of April alone kept him going long after his aching muscles cried for rest.

Within minutes, he stopped by a small stream to drink and splash water on his face then down his side. He'd been lucky. The blade hadn't bitten deep. The long, superficial cut lay just above the knife scar he already carried.

Beginning to hope the Indians had given up, he looked around. Less than a hundred yards south stood an ancient oak, several massive branches dipping groundward. An easy scramble to the top branches gave him a view of the river bank. There, just at a bend in the river, a canoe rested on the sandy bank. Seconds later two braves appeared, one supporting the other. They climbed into the canoe and set out for the Ohio side.

~ * ~

The sun dipped behind the tops of the trees across the small meadow while April repaired the last rip in her dress. Something caused her to look up from her work. Dan entered the meadow. He strode across the clearing toward her, two rabbits dangling from his hand.

Relief swept over her and she pushed the mending from her lap. She rose and hurried toward him. She caught sight of the thin, red line along his side.

"Oh, you're hurt," she gasped. She reached out, toward the bright red tear weeping from the beginning edge of the wound, but she drew back. She clutched her hands together to keep them from fluttering, the urge to touch him, to make him feel better nearly irresistible.

Dan looked down at his side. With the heel of his hand, he swiped away the blood. "Must have opened up when I stopped to wash up a mile or so back."

April tore her gaze from his side and quickly surveyed his form. His dark hair was damp, his skin free of dust and sweat. Her gaze returned to his wound. "Doesn't it hurt?" she blurted.

"No." His smile turned self-conscious and he shrugged one shoulder. "This one," his thumb traced the wicked scar that curved along his bottom rib, just beneath the new red streak she'd asked about, "this hurt like the devil. A souvenir of the first summer I spent scouting for Wayne."

She suppressed a shiver of sympathetic pain and used the back of her hand to push a loose strand of hair out of her face. A hundred questions swirled in her mind, but before she could ask, he hurried on, "I made it all the way back to the river. Everything looks fine. Even managed to catch something for dinner." He gestured at the rabbits, now lying by his feet.

"I'm glad you're back," she said simply.

Dan gave a sigh and opened his arms. Without hesitation she stepped into his embrace. A deep contentment filled her as he held her close, rocking her gently back and forth.

After a long moment, his hands moved to her bare shoulders and in that moment, she became aware of their near nakedness. Her chemise not only left her arms and shoulders bare, but the low neckline only half-concealed the swell of her breasts. She had come to his arms for comfort. But warm comfort flared into hot desire.

He tugged her close, holding their lower bodies in intimate contact. April looked up into his pale eyes, now darkened in passion. Again she was caught up in the incredible feeling that being in Dan's arms invoked, the way they responded to each other.

She breathed his name and ran her hands slowly up his bare chest, enjoying the chance to touch his smooth, warm skin. Her hands on the back of his neck, she kissed the underside of his jaw. She felt, as well as heard, a growl rumble deep in his chest.

He felt so good, so solid when he hugged her tightly. Her breasts, shielded only by her chemise, pressed against the hard muscles of his chest. His hand made slow, lazy circles on her back, pressing her to him. She thought she might melt, her muscles and bones dissolving under his caress. Wanting to give him pleasure, to share what she felt, she kissed the angle of his jaw once more.

Another groan rumbled in his chest and his lips found hers. She welcomed the invasion of his tongue as his hand roamed over her body, caressing her neck, stroking her breast, cupping her buttock, pulling her hard against his arousal.

A compelling need for air finally broke the kiss. Her chest heaved. Her breath came in ragged gasps. His breathing echoed her own. As if searching for control, he gently pushed her away.

"April," he said, his voice rough and low, "if we don't stop now, I won't be able to."

April blinked. With sudden clarity, she understood what he was saying. Part of her urged her not even to think, to just go ahead and let it happen. But another part urged caution.

What she knew of the physical aspects of love she had learned from him.

And love him she did. She loved his strength, his gentleness, his loyalty to what he believed was right, his determination, his steadfastness. She loved him with her heart and soul. The desire to complete that love with a physical union was overwhelming.

"Don't stop," she whispered, looking into the blue-gray fire of his eyes.

He closed his eyes as a shuddering groan rippled through him. Then reaching behind her, he untied the green ribbon at the nape of her neck. She shivered as he threaded his fingers through the strands, cupping the back of her head and tilting her face up to his. He kissed her, slipping his tongue between her parted lips and pulled her against him once again. Abruptly, he picked her up, holding her high against his chest and carried her toward the maple-leaf bed in the rockhouse.

At the entrance he set her on her feet. Without a word he fetched her dress and extra petticoats and spread them over the leaves. He returned to her side and to her surprise, picked her up once more, kissing her while he held her in his arms. Then walking the few steps to the bed, he knelt and gently put her down.

Late afternoon shadows filled the rockhouse. The fading light served as a balm to April's apprehension. With half-closed eyes she watched Dan as he bent and untied the blue beaded thongs around the knees of his leggings. Straightening, his hands went to his waist. Her heart did a double beat. Before she could decide whether or not to watch, he slipped off his moccasins and pushed his leggings down, leaving only his breech cloth. He stepped out of the leggings and her gaze traveled down the long, lean length of him.

The glow of the setting sun turned his body bronze. Clad only in his breechcloth, each muscle, each vein, each sinew, stood defined and refined by hard work, until only the pure essence of maleness remained.

Without thought she reached for him and he lay down beside her. A warm lassitude swept over her as he kissed her. His hand moved between her breasts where he began to undo the small buttons of her chemise. She gasped when his warm, rough hand glided over her naked breast, his fingers teasing the peak. Still trying to absorb the sensation, she gasped when his mouth found her other breast. The gasp became a moan and her back arched, trying to get closer to the feelings he created.

He ran his hand up her leg, pushing the petticoat up to mid-thigh and she quivered beneath his touch. Under her bunched up petticoat, he ran his hand over her belly. Wanting and dreading, she felt his fingers glide into the nest of curls at the top of her legs. When he found the warm moistness of her most intimate place he murmured approval. A nameless need consumed her. She jerked and writhed under his hand, his mouth.

She gave a breathless cry when he rolled away from her. Before she could wonder why, he rolled back, the breechcloth gone. He was hot and rigid against her. He ran his hand down to her knees and back up, urging her to part her thighs. She willingly complied. Her hands clutched his back, feeling the ripple and flow of his muscles as he brought his body over hers.

His body between her legs, he kissed her. Instinctively, she arched her hips in invitation. Bracing himself on his elbows, he slowly entered her. Then with an ardent thrust, he came fully into her. The sharp, burning sensation made her gasp. In reflex, her body tensed and her eyes flew open.

In the shadows she felt, as much as saw, Dan's questioning gaze. He breathed her name.

"April?"

She didn't want to answer his unspoken question. The brief pain had already passed. The longing and emptiness gone, Dan's body gave her the completion she needed. With a sigh of contentment, she slipped her arms around his neck.

"Please, Dan," she whispered in return, pulling his lips down to meet hers.

He moved within her and she thought she would perish from the pleasure. She rocked her hips, moving with him. The pleasure mounted, consuming her. Sensations built and multiplied to engulf her body and soul. For a moment she feared she would disappear altogether. Clutching Dan, she followed where he led. Intense, rippling waves washed over her, carrying her higher and she cried out in surprise and wonder.

She vaguely heard Dan gasp, felt the shudders shake his body. They collapsed together, bodies slick with perspiration, struggling to drag air into their lungs. After a few moments, he slid his weight off to one side, pulling her to snuggle against him. He threaded his fingers into her hair and nestled her head against his shoulder.

April felt a wordless contentment. In this place where neither time nor trouble existed, caresses and murmurs served better than words. She lay close to Dan and the world was complete.

~ * ~

She awoke slowly as one by one her senses brought her to consciousness. A tantalizing aroma wrinkled her nose. Dusk had given way to true dark. Flickering lights played against the granite side of the rockhouse. She stretched, the leaves rustling softly beneath her.

Once again she caught the inviting smell of food. Her stomach growled. She sat up, pushing her loose hair back from her face, and glanced toward the entrance of the rockhouse.

Halfway between the pool and the rockhouse entrance, Dan crouched beside a small fire, roasting two rabbits on spits. While her stomach urged her to go and eat, her heart wasn't in such a hurry.

He must have sensed her gaze, for he turned and glanced toward the rockhouse. His momentary glance and the stiffness of his posture reflected her own uneasiness at facing him. How could talking to a man she knew intimately be so difficult? Her stomach growled again, a reminder she did have to eat.

She pulled on her dress, thankful the dark green color helped disguise the mass of wrinkles it had become. She stood, her body stiff and shaky. Hoping for composure, she walked from the rockhouse to the fire.

"Don't burn yourself." Dan handed her one of the rabbits. She swallowed her nervousness at the total neutrality of his tone and took the proffered spit.

She sank onto a rock a few feet from where Dan sat cross-legged on the ground. Hunger curtailed any conversation while they both attacked the warm meat.

She tried not to notice the peculiar way Dan watched her as if trying to see into her thoughts. She had the awful feeling that what they had done together was somehow evident on her face. She thought of the Widow Martin, how the older woman seemed to know there had been no intimacy with Richard.

A glance across the fire showed Dan's gaze still riveted on her. Unable to bear the weight of his stare any longer, she was suddenly angry. "What?" she snapped, glaring at him.

Dan blinked, as if coming out of deep concentration. He shifted his gaze to the fire, and said in a soft voice, "Why didn't you tell me?" He drew a deep breath. "Did you lie about being a widow just to get to Kentucky?"

Stung, she replied, "I didn't lie. My husband died last November."

The frontiersman's eyes narrowed. "Then what the hell was wrong with him?" he fairly shouted.

"Nothing was 'wrong' with him," she shouted back. Then just as quickly as her anger flared, the emotion died away. Throwing a handful of rabbit bones in the fire, April watched the sparks shoot up then die back.

"The year after mother and I returned to Philadelphia, she married William Williamson, a man much older than she. I think William felt sorry for me because his parents had also died while he was young and he'd been raised by his older brother.

"When the cholera came in '89, all three of us took sick. Mother and William died within a day of each other." She paused for a moment. The memories were no longer painful, simply sad. "Just before she died, mother told me to be a good daughter to William and do as he asked. William knew he was dying too, and he asked his older brother, Richard, to take care of me.

"Richard took me straight from the cemetery to the preacher's house, and we were married. I was only fifteen, and he was fifty-six. I believe he always thought of me as a little girl, his brother's child, for that's how he treated me the five years we were married.

"I didn't lie to you," she said. "I am a widow, if you can be one without truly having been a wife." Not knowing what else to say, she rose from her seat and walked to the pool to wash her hands.

Dan watched her walk toward the stream. Her husband hadn't loved her, he thought with sudden intensity. He couldn't have loved her and not touch her. Not if he'd loved her the way he loved her. His chest hurt, his breath stuck in his throat. But he loved her.

He loved her. Not just wanted her, but loved her. He shouldn't, not with his past—but he did. He swallowed, hoping the despair would lessen. He scrambled to his feet and walked toward the woman he loved. April knelt beside the pool. She ran her damp hands over her face.

Dan halted beside her. He touched her shoulder briefly, denying himself the longer contact he wanted. "Sorry I accused you of lying. I was just... surprised is all."

She shrugged and pushed her hair away from her face, a gesture he found pleasing. With only a slight hesitation, she placed her hand in his, and he helped her to her feet.

"Come back to the fire?" He made it a question.

She nodded, and they walked toward the dying flames.

He sank, cross-legged, and watched April fetch the brush from her sewing box. Sensing he made her uncomfortable, he transferred his gaze back to the fire.

"Shouldn't keep the fire going much longer," he said just to be talking. "No need to take chances."

"Do you think Scotty, Tucker and the boats got away?"

He nodded, then added, "The Indians were withdrawing. With luck, the flatboats will land in Cincinnati tomorrow or the next day, so I doubt the Indians will give them any more trouble." Especially, as he now suspected, he'd been as much a target as the supplies.

Out of the corner of his eye, he watched April brush her hair. She'd pulled part of the heavy mass over her shoulder and each brush stroke started a little higher up as she set about working the tangles out.

Dan picked up a few pebbles and tossed them into the fire. "There's no way we can catch the flatboats, so we'll cut overland to Oak Point. Tucker saw us get to shore so that's what they'll expect us to do. We'll go southwest," he gestured in that direction. "It should be only three or four days."

He stood. The journey to Oak Point would be rough. Alone, he judged he might make the trip in two days, easy, but he'd gone without food and slept in the open before. He kicked dirt into the fire. "We have to put this out, now." The flames died. He stirred the dirt around with a stick and the coals dimmed. He added more dirt and the light and the heat disappeared. In the sudden dark, April hugged herself. Dan came to her side.

"Are you cold?" he asked.

She shook her head. The darkness shadowed her face. He put his hand on her shoulder and felt her shiver, but she didn't pull away.

Dan helped her to her feet. After a second's hesitation, he gathered her into his arms. She came willingly, her cheek against his chest. Looking over her head, he saw the rockhouse, the white splash of her petticoats marking the place where they had been one. She'd come to him truly innocent. He felt no shame for what he'd done. Instead, he remembered the fierce surge of exaltation as he realized he'd been the first.

Encouraged by the willing way she'd come into his arms, he had to ask. "Did I hurt you?" His hands cradled her face, turning it up to his. The rising moon cast enough light for him to see her slightly parted lips, eyes that glistened, the rise and fall of her breasts as the tempo of her breathing increased. The desire he saw unleashed the passion which he'd been trying to control since he'd felt her eyes sweep over him.

"Ah, God, April," he groaned. "I never wanted to hurt you. I only wanted to love you."

She answered in the same ragged whisper. "You didn't hurt me, Dan. I wanted to love you, too."

He kissed her and her arms wrapped around his neck. His mouth still holding hers, he took slow, short steps, walking her backward, their bodies moving against each other with every step. After a dozen steps, he broke the kiss. Taking a deep breath, he rasped out, "Come'ere," and swept her up in his arms to carry her the remaining distance to the rockhouse. Deep shadows filled the space between the granite walls where he gently dropped her to her feet.

She unclasped her hands from his neck and began a shy exploration of his body. He stood stock still as her hands ran slowly over his shoulders, around and down his back. He shivered and gave a heavy sigh of pleasure telling her he enjoyed her touch.

Encouraged, she traced the waist of his breech cloth, drawing her hands from his back around his hips to his stomach. He sucked in a breath, his muscles tightening under her hands. With a sigh of her own, she glided her hands up his chest. He shuddered and started to breathe again. Whispering her name, he pulled her hard against him and she willingly surrendered her control. Her dress rejoined the petticoats on the maple leaves, followed by her petticoat, leaving her clad only in her chemise.

Dan stepped back to untie his leggings and breech cloth. Naked, he pulled her down beside him on the rustling leaves. Lying on their sides, he undid the buttons of her chemise, while they exchanged small, breathless kisses. Go slow, Dan told himself. He remembered the sudden jerk of her body and knew he had caused her pain. This time he wanted her to feel only pleasure. He'd give back the joy he'd experienced.

He rolled to his back, pulling her over him. He slid his hands over her hips and buttocks, finding the hem of her chemise. His hands glided up the backs of her smooth thighs.

"Sit up," he instructed in a ragged whisper. He gently pushed on her shoulders and then ran his hands down her side to guide her knees to the ground on either side of him. With a few gentle tugs, he pulled her chemise up and over her head.

Her dark, thick hair hung around her shoulders like a cape, her body pale ivory in the dark shadows. "You're beautiful," he whispered. He drew her hands to his lips, kissing each palm. He pulled her forward and, even better than his imagining, her hair fell around them, spilling over her shoulders, tickling his chest, locking them together in a world of their own.

His breathing deep and ragged, he tangled his hands in her wonderful hair. By his guidance, she leaned forward, resting her hands next to his shoulders, her body exposed for his exploration. His mouth teased, nipping and suckling at her breasts. She moaned and moved in response, making him throb in reply. But he held back. He wanted her to be ready, oh, so ready that there wouldn't be, couldn't be, any pain.

Almost before he finished the thought, she cried out and tremors shook her body. He quickly rolled her beneath him and entered her in one slow, smooth, thrust as she clung to him. Panting and gasping his name, she moved her hips against him and his control shattered. He thrust into her, the warm waves built and engulfed him, also. A long, shuddering sigh shook him and his body released its hot life into her.

Chapter Fourteen

With a jerk of his arms, Dan flipped the trout out of the stream. The morning sun sparkled off the trailing arc of water as the fish thumped on the bank. He waded from the knee deep water and pulled on his leggings and moccasins. He gutted the three trout he'd tickled from the stream before stringing them with one of the wild sweet pea vines that grew thick upon the bank. Fish in hand, he started back to the rockhouse and April.

April. When he had awakened this morning, they had been lying together, April snuggled in the crook of his body, his arm holding her close. In the predawn light she'd looked washed out and exhausted. No wonder, he thought with a stab of guilt. He'd run her through the forest and then made love to her twice. As he'd disentangled himself, she'd stirred.

Coming back into the clearing, he saw the fire he'd kindled earlier that morning had burned down to a bed of coals. Panic flashed briefly at the sight of the empty rockhouse, but subsided at the sight of a damp chemise on a bush by the pool.

"April?" he called.

"I'm here." The muffled reply came from the brush beyond the pool. She pushed through the bushes into the clearing. She made her way across the clearing, balancing a strip of curled bark in both hands. As she drew closer, he saw the faint lines of fatigue on her face and a slight stiffness in her movements.

Guilt jabbed him. Not because he'd made love to her. Never for that. But guilt for what his love was already doing to her, wearing her down, using up her slender strength. She didn't belong out here and he knew it. He should keep his hands off her and send her home to Philadelphia.

"I picked some blackberries." She indicated the piece of bark heaped high with berries.

He heard the false cheerfulness in her voice, and he damned himself again.

"I see we're having trout for breakfast." She nodded at the fish dangling from the vine.

"I was lucky." He placed the trout directly on the coals. "When they're done we can peel the scales and skin right off."

Sitting by the fire, they ate the blackberries, sweet-tart and still damp from the morning dew. By the time the berries were gone, the trout was ready. He used the berry-stained bark for a plate while they ate the flaky fish with their fingers.

During the silent breakfast, Dan decided on his course of action. He had to get April safely to Oak Point, and that safety had to include protecting her from himself. So he'd keep memories of last night, locked away, along with his love and his guilt. He couldn't be anything to her but a guide. At least he was a damn good guide and scout. She'd reach Oak Point.

Throwing the bones in the fire, Dan stood and looked around the clearing. Shaking out her skirts, April followed suit.

"We'd better be on our way," Dan said. "Once the sun gets high it'll be a hot day." He glanced to where her clothes were spread over the bushes. "Gather everything up. There's something I want to check. I'll be back in a few minutes." When April nodded, Dan turned and left the clearing.

Once he was out of sight, April slumped back down on the rock. She still felt tired and hungry. When she awoke this morning the events of yesterday had flashed through her mind like a dream that had happened to someone else, long ago. The Indian attack, the run through the woods, being with Dan. For a brief moment she could think she had imagined it all, but her stiff and sore body and the small dark brown stain on her chemise confirmed its reality.

What had happened between them in the rockhouse was either the best thing or the worst thing in her life. She was sure of only one thing. She loved Dan McKenzie.

Even after breakfasting together, she still didn't know what to say, how to act. As she packed, she decided to take her lead from

Dan. She finished placing her clothing and sewing box in the flour sack when Dan returned.

"Our luck is holding," Dan said, as he held up three more rabbits, victims of the snares he'd set. "We'll have something to eat tonight." He glanced around the clearing, then turned to her. "You ready?"

"Yes." She gestured to the flour sack.

Dan dropped the rabbits by the sack and crossed to the rockhouse. He gathered up the maple leaves, tossing them into the brush behind the granite boulders. After smothering the remaining coals, he used a stick to scatter the still warm rocks that had ringed the fire. With another branch, he swept and scattered the evidence of the fire.

April watched Dan erase every indication they had been there. In spite of the warm sun, she shivered, her throat tightening. Unaccountably, she felt Dan was wiping out all traces of what had happened between them.

Dan stooped to pick up the rabbits and shouldered the flour sack. "Let's go," he said, his voice quiet, as if sensing her discomfort.

April followed him out of the clearing, looking back at the rockhouse, which now seemed cold and empty. She fastened her eyes on his broad shoulders as he led the way.

Gradually, the morning sun warmed her back. She inhaled deeply, drawing in the warm, heavy, damp-green scent that was Kentucky. As she followed Dan through stands of trees, she named them to herself—basswood, oak, maple, ash, hickory. Over the muffled tread of their moccasins came the chatter of squirrels and the songs of birds.

She let out a deep sigh. She was home.

Dan walked slower than his normal pace to accommodate the woman behind him. He'd seen the sadness in her face when they prepared to leave the clearing. He heard her soft footfalls following.

When he glanced over his shoulder, he was relieved to see the sadness gone from her face. Partly as an excuse for easy travel and partly as an excuse for conversation, he began to point out animal signs to her.

"See," Dan squatted beside the trail, "here's where a fox went by. See how the track of his hind foot falls almost directly over the track of his front foot? Now look up yonder." He stood and walked a dozen paces up the trail. "This is where he started to trot, see how the tracks change. The prints are separate, one right behind the other."

He stopped to point out the fresh tracks of the deer that had preceded them down the trail. Farther on, he showed her the tracks of a muskrat; how his scaly tail made a wavy line between the tracks of his feet as he'd ambled along the muddy stream bank.

By noon, when a blackberry thicket provided the meal, Dan felt the strain between them had lessened. Glancing toward the sun, he squinted. "Let's find a shade tree and rest for a couple of hours. Over there is good." He indicated the shade of a huge oak.

A few hours later, refreshed by her nap, April walked steadily behind Dan along a twisting deer trail. The gurgle of a nearby stream brought thoughts of a cool drink. Her mind thus occupied, she almost ran into Dan when he abruptly stopped. Reaching back, he pulled her down to squat next to him. Fear sparked along every nerve ending.

"Stay here, stay quiet," he whispered as he put the flour sack and rabbits next to her. He melted into the forest. Goose bumps covered her. She shivered in the hot, humid summer air. Each beat of her heart marked the passing seconds. The quiet stretched on forever, though only a few moments passed before he called.

"April, over here."

Breathing a prayer of thanks, she snatched up the sack and the rabbits and hurried toward Dan's voice.

She entered the clearing where Dan knelt looking over his shoulder in her direction. As soon as Dan saw her, he turned back and with horror April realized the form at Dan's feet was a man. She rushed to Dan's side. Close up, the harsh red of the man's sunburned back made her wince. The poor man wore only knee breeches, his shirt, stockings and shoes gone. Dan carefully rolled him over. His battered face came into view and April gasped.

"Dear God! What happened to him?"

"Someone beat him. Robbed him, took his clothes."

"Is he alive?"

The stranger's one eye was swollen shut, the other stuck shut by the crusted blood from the cut above it. His lips were dry and cracked. Dan ran his hands along the man's arms and legs, then traced the man's chest. When he felt over the man's left side, the man winced and groaned.

"Probably broken ribs," Dan observed. The man's stomach looked like one large bruise. "He's been bleeding some inside. I'll move him to the shade." He gestured toward a stand of redbud trees, whose many branches cast deep shadows.

April scrambled to her feet and hurried to the shade. She pulled open the flour sack, yanked out one of her petticoats and spread it on the ground to make a bed. Grabbing her spare chemise, she said, "I'll get some water." She hurried toward the sound of the stream, and pushed through a tangle of umbrella leaf and wood ferns. She dipped the chemise into the happily gurgling stream.

Holding the sopping garment before her, she made her way back to find Dan had the man stretched out on the makeshift bed.

"I'm going to take a quick look around," he said as she approached. "Be back directly."

She barely had time to nod before he disappeared into the woods. Kneeling beside the hurt man, she gently wiped his damaged face, removing dirt and dried blood. Reversing the chemise to the clean end, she squeezed the water from the material, letting water drip onto his cracked lips, watching his throat to see if he swallowed. When he did and she was satisfied he wouldn't choke, she squeezed harder, giving him a small trickle. He swallowed, coughed, and groaned.

"Rest now," April told him, carefully stroking his hair from his forehead. Dan reappeared "Will he be all right?" she asked, looking across the man to where Dan knelt.

"Probably."

April made numerous trips to the little stream. Slowly she kept giving the stranger water, as well as sponging his body, trying to relieve his badly sunburned back. He drifted in and out of consciousness, but never became coherent.

While April tended the stranger, Dan once again scouted the area. He found the trail where the robbers had headed north, but nothing else. He set several snares, planning to check them tomorrow morning. On the way back to camp, he found a stand of cattails at the bend of the stream and dug up the roots, arriving back at camp just as the sun set.

As Dan kindled the fire, the injured man groaned. Dan moved to April's side as the stranger's eyes flickered open. His gaze wandered, then steadied on them both kneeling at his side for a moment before his eyes closed again. He took a deep, obviously painful breath. He exhaled slowly and mumbled, "Samaritans, I trust." After that he slept.

Dan roasted the rabbits he'd snared that morning. After the fire died down, he put the cattail roots in the coals. "There. Come morning, we'll have breakfast." With the flames out, the warm dark settled around them.

Noting the droop of April's shoulders, he crossed to her and sank cross-legged by her side.

"You're tired. Go ahead and rest, I'll keep watch."

"All right," she agreed. Now that she'd eaten, he noted she fought to keep her eyes open. She shifted positions, as if to rise and move away. Unable to resist his need to touch her, his need to take care of her, he put his hand on her arm. "Stay?"

When she didn't resist, he breathed a sigh and pulled her to him, nestling her against his side. After a moment she rested her head on his shoulder. The warmth of her body, her steady breathing made him want more. Blood flooded his loins, making him hard, and he cursed to himself. She was already exhausted, and now they had a new problem. He glanced at the injured man.

Dan knew the physical demands the next few days would require, and he worried about her slender strength. He felt her body relax, her breathing deepened and he guided her down, her head pillowed on his thigh. He glanced at the injured man, grateful for his presence. Dan forced his mind to plans of survival.

~ * ~

April looked up from her station beside their casualty, wincing at the ripping sound. Dan tore her petticoat into long, wide strips to make a stretcher. Kneeling beside the injured man, Dan wound another strip around the man's chest binding his arms to his ribs. The man mumbled and twisted while they rolled him onto the make-shift stretcher.

His skin burned from fever. He drifted in and out of consciousness, allowing them to give him water and small bites of food this morning. Dan took another strip and tied the man to the make-shift stretcher. The last strip of petticoat he draped across her shoulders, knotting the ends around the poles so they were level with her hands.

"This will act like a yoke," he explained, "help you take the weight of the stretcher." Even though Dan set an easy pace, the staggering physical drain of carrying the stretcher soon consumed April. Whenever the terrain allowed, Dan told her to put her end down and he would pull the stretcher as if it were a travois until the ground became too rough. The end of the day found her too tired and sore to think.

She sat in an exhausted heap while Dan set up camp, started supper, and took care of the man. Dan's stamina amazed her. Admiration filled her as she watched the man she loved go so competently about taking care of them. Today took all her energy. Too tired to think beyond her love for Dan, she slipped gratefully into sleep.

The next two days became a blur. She and Dan spoke only of the necessities of walking, eating, sleeping. Her only conscious thought was to put one foot in front of the other. Each night she fell asleep as soon as they stopped. Dan would wake her to eat, then after tending the injured man, she quickly dropped into sleep again.

Mid-morning of the third day Dan stopped so suddenly April stumbled, the injured man groaned as the stretcher bumped against Dan's back.

"We made it. Look." He gestured with his chin, his hands still gripping the stretcher.

Over Dan's shoulder April saw a split rail fence and only fifty yards away, a log cabin. Smoke drifted from the chimney.

"It's the Ferguson's place. Only a few more steps. Can you make it?" he asked, glancing back at her.

April felt an absurd urge to laugh, but only said, "I made it this far."

Dan led them along the fence line toward the house.

"Hello the house!" He shouted when they drew near. "Hey, Ferguson, you in there?"

They entered the yard and stopped to put the stretcher down in the shade of the porch. April swallowed her groan of relief, flexing her aching shoulders. As she straightened, the front door opened and out stepped a young woman. In the crook of her arm was a rifle, held with great familiarity, her face calm and questioning, not frightened. Then her eyes widened.

"Dan? Dan McKenzie?" She propped the rifle against the wall and ran down the steps.

"Your pa home, Janie?"

"No, he's out hunting. What happened?"

Briefly Dan explained about the Indian attack and finding the man, while Janie's gaze went from the injured man, to April, and back to Dan. Dan finished with a quick introduction. "April, meet Janie Ferguson. Janie, this is Mrs. Williamson." April nodded to Janie. April judged Janie a year or two younger than her own twenty years, but she reacted to the situation with a competence.

"I'll hitch up the wagon and take you into Oak Point." Janie interrupted Dan's explanation. "Y'all go on in, sit down and rest."

"We'll be fine here on the porch," Dan said. He slumped down, his back resting against one of the porch roof supports.

Knowing she looked as bedraggled as she felt, April was glad Dan had chosen the porch. Besides, she didn't think she could walk one pace more than necessary. She sank gratefully onto the porch step.

With a shake of her head, Janie disappeared into the house, returning with a dipper and pail of water. A minute later she was back again with cold cornbread and buttermilk.

"Here, it's not much, but it was handy," she said, setting the food on the porch between Dan and April. With a whisk of her skirts, she surged down the steps. She knelt by the injured man and put her hand to his forehead for a moment before hurrying on to the barn to hitch up the wagon.

April shifted on the step, trying to find a more comfortable position for her sore muscles. She glanced at Dan. He looked as hot and tired as she felt. Perspiration streaked the dirt on his chest. Fatigue had etched deep lines around his eyes, now closed in weariness, as he rested his head back against the porch post. Dust and whiskers shadowed his jaw. Deep lines sketched from either side of his nose, down around his mouth to his chin.

Janie drove into the yard, and while Janie and Dan and loaded the injured man, April retrieved the dipper and pail from the porch.

"I'll take care of him," Janie said to Dan, "if you can drive."

"I can drive."

Dan helped April into the wagon bed. "Ride here, it's softer than the seat." He climbed on to the seat and gathered up the reins. He clucked to the horse and the wagon bumped out of the yard.

Chapter Fifteen

Dan drove the wagon in to Oak Point and April finally sighed with relief. The McKenzie and Murray general store stood on the south edge of town, a two-story building facing the dusty, unpaved main street. The bottom story, made of logs, was topped by a second story of finished lumber, a common frontier practice as the original log structures, built twenty or so years ago, were expanded with the product of local sawmills. The combination spoke of endurance and success.

A smaller, single-story log structure stood directly behind the store. A roof extended between the two creating a covered area between the buildings. Doorways from both buildings opened into this dog-trot, each standing ajar to the summer air.

Dan pulled into the large side yard, swinging the rattling wagon close to the dog-trot. Drawn by the noise, a curly-headed boy appeared in the open door of the main building. Looking back into doorway, he shouted, "Hey, Pa, Mama! It's Uncle Dan!" Bounding out of the doorway, he ran to the wagon and clambered up on the seat.

"Mama sure has been worried about you." Squirming around on the seat, the boy looked in the bed of the wagon. "Hiya, Miss Ferguson. Who's that man? What happened to him? Howdy, ma'am, you must be Mrs. Williamson. Pa said y'all would get here."

Seconds behind the boy, Scotty came through the doorway and hurried out into the yard. "Alexander," he admonished the boy, "give them a chance to tell us what happened." Dan climbed down and Scotty greeted him with a hearty hand clasp, slapping him on the shoulder with his other hand. "Danny-ma-boy, 'tis good to see ye."

Scotty circled to the rear of the wagon and gave April his hand to help her down. Once she was on the ground, he enveloped her in a brotherly hug. "Ye made it, lass. Welcome to Oak Point."

A woman appeared in the store doorway. She quickly crossed the yard and flung her arms around Dan, hugging him as he hugged her back.

Scotty, his arm around April's shoulder, led her toward Dan and the woman. "Let me introduce ye to ma wife. Mary, I am pleased to present to ye, April Williamson. April, this is ma wife and Dan's sister, Mary Murray."

Mary released Dan, turning to face them, giving April her first real glimpse of Dan's sister. April's mouth fell open. She'd expected a resemblance to Dan. Now it was obvious Mary must resemble their mother. Mary was of average height, but where Dan was dark, she was fair with blue eyes several shades deeper than Dan's, and curly blonde hair drawn back into a casual knot at the nape of her neck.

Overcoming her surprise, April murmured something appropriate. Glancing at Dan, his frown told her he had correctly interpreted her astonishment. Mary's appearance marked her indisputably as Dan's half sister, and not of mixed blood, while his own appearance constantly reminded those who knew him of his Indian lineage. As clearly as if they were printed on his forehead, April read Dan's thoughts as he wondered how she would react to this reminder of his mixed heritage. Now she understood why the Bible used the word "know" for what passed between a man and a woman, because she now "knew" Dan. Knew him physically, and knew his thoughts.

This reflection brought an ache to her breast. She loved him enough to know his mind, but she didn't know his heart. The ache brought home to her how deeply she had fallen in love with the dark frontiersman.

Mary's voice tugged her from her reverie. Waving her hand at the injured man, Mary said, "Scotty, you and Dan carry him into the spare store room. Alexander, honey," she addressed the boy, "run and get my medicine basket."

As the men moved to do her bidding, Mary turned to April. "I'll bet you're just about worn out, Mrs. Williamson."

"Yes, ma'am, just about," April agreed.

"Janie, go and put some water on to heat. I know Mrs. Williamson will feel much better after a bath." Mary led April toward the single-story log building. "This was the original cabin, but we've converted it into two storerooms." Dan and Scotty carried the injured man into one room, while Mary took April to the second doorway.

Mary pushed open the door, revealing a deep room, the back section stacked ceiling to floor with crates and barrels. The front half contained a large wooden tub of beech wood and a scarred table holding soap and several lengths of toweling. Next to the table stood an equally battered chair, a strand of wire twisted around a broken rung.

"Between Scotty, Dan, and the boys, it's easier to send the lot of them out here to get clean," Mary explained. "Scotty had your trunks brought from Cincinnati. I'll fetch you some clean clothes." Mary left just as Janie carried in two buckets of warm water and poured them in the tub.

April shed her petticoat and chemise. Stepping into the tub, she sank into the warm water with a sigh. Wonderful. She let the heat seep into her aching muscles. Leaning her head back against the beech staves, she closed her eyes for several long minutes.

The rest and relaxation gave her new strength. She proceeded to scour away the dirt and grime. She winced as the soap stung the palms of her hands, blistered and bruised by the stretcher. Finally, feeling clean and revived she stepped from the tub, dried herself, and put on the clean chemise and petticoat.

Janie returned and, taking one look at April's hands, she left and returned with a bowl of salve and bandages. With her hands bandaged, April gave herself up to the luxury of having Janie comb the tangles out of her hair. "That will to do for now. We can put it up after it's dry," Janie said as she tied April's hair with a ribbon at the nape of her neck.

From the small building, the two young women walked across the dog-trot and into the large back room of the store. The large room did duty as both kitchen and parlor. Arm chairs and a rag rug sat before the brick fireplace and inglenook that filled one corner. On the wall separating this room from the store in front, a stairway and banister railing led to the second floor. A large kitchen table took up the rest of the room. Dan and Alexander sat one of two short benches flanking each side. Scotty sat on a ladder-back chair at the head of the table.

"Come in and sit down." Mary opened the oven and the aroma of fresh baked biscuits filled the kitchen. April and Janie sat on the bench opposite Dan and Alexander. "It's just stew and biscuits," Mary continued, "but Dan said he could eat anything as long as it wasn't rabbit."

April glanced at Dan, but he avoided her gaze. He looked different somehow. The difference wasn't just hair, still damp, or his clean shaven jaw. A moment or two later it hit her—he was wearing a shirt. In the past few days she'd become so accustomed to seeing his bare chest it had seemed natural. She quickly looked down at the table top, embarrassed in retrospect by her acceptance of his nakedness.

While they ate, Scotty explained how the flatboats had arrived safely in Cincinnati. "Tucker was nae hurt near as bad as yon stranger ye two brought in. Swore all he needed was a glass or two of whiskey to put him right."

Dan chuckled. "Sounds like Tucker."

"Where did you find the man you brought in?" Janie asked.

"Out in the middle of nowhere, not by any of the trails," Dan answered. "Someone beat him pretty bad. Think he has a couple of broken ribs."

"Indians?" Mary asked skeptically.

Dan shook his head. "Indians most likely would have either killed him, or taken him prisoner, not just left him."

The talk around the table turned to the political news Scotty had brought from Cincinnati. "Colonel Dunlap said ta tell ye, Dan, if ye're still alive, ye donna' have to return to duty until the Kentucky militia is called to join the Legion."

Dan would be returning to the Legion in a few weeks. April placed her spoon on the table. Again she felt the ache of her love for him. She ought to be worried about what happened in the rockhouse, but she couldn't. She was just too overwhelmingly weary. She let the conversation swirl around her. Though hungry, her stomach warned her not to eat too much and her bandaged hand made it clumsy to handle the spoon.

The conversation became a dull buzz and she no longer tried to decipher the words. Her bandaged hands throbbed, her shoulders ached. The room began to blur as her eyes fought to stay open.

Dan finished his last bite of stew and, with relief, pushed the bowl away. His hunger had died the first time he saw April's bandaged hands fumble with her spoon. When her eyes blinked several times, Dan gently kicked Mary under the table to draw her gaze, then nodded in April's direction.

"Goodness!" Mary exclaimed, catching sight of April. "The poor woman's asleep sitting up, and us talking on and on." Mary stood and went to April's side. "We'll have to find you a place to sleep."

"Thank you," April murmured, as she, too, stood. When she did, the color drained from her face and she swayed. Dan cursed himself as he leapt around the table and caught her up in his arms. She felt lighter than a minute and there was no strength in the arms wrapped around his neck.

"I'll take her upstairs," he said. Without waiting for questions or comments, he carried her up the steps to the second floor.

At the top of the stairs, the familiar wide hallway stretched the length of the building where windows along the right side let in the afternoon sun. Without thinking, he pushed open the first door on the left. The sparsely furnished room contained only a narrow bed and a cane-bottom chair.

Crossing to the bed, Dan lay April on the patchwork quilt. Kneeling beside her, he smoothed her hair back from her still pale face. April's eyes fluttered open for a second and her lips sketched a brief smile in his direction. As her eyes closed she murmured, "I love you, Dan."

The words stopped his breath. He slowly withdrew his hand from her hair, stood, and strode to stare out the open window. Even if she thought she loved him, what good had it gotten her? Nothing but physical hardship. And social censure if people knew he'd made love to her. Warm air drifted through the room. He turned, seeing she was already sound asleep, her knees drawn up, one hand under her cheek. Her dark hair spread over the pillow and around her shoulders.

"Dan?" Mary's voice called.

He retreated downstairs. "I gave her my room," he said as he crossed the kitchen. "I'm going out to check on High Stakes."

Dan crossed the yard to the corral, where he leaned his forearms on the top rail. High Stakes nickered and trotted over to be petted. Willing his thoughts from April, he scratched the mare under her chin. He entered the corral, ran a hand down her neck, then over her withers and barrel, reassuring himself she was indeed healthy. High Stakes looked fine, her coat sleek, and eyes clear. He knew she was in foal since she hadn't come into season again since he'd put her to Sinclair's stud.

Dan talked to the mare, while he continued to pet her. "You take care of that Sinclair foal, now, you hear? You're carrying the future of our breeding enterprise. Once I can stop scouting for Wayne, we'll get the farm going, get some more mares to keep you company." He rubbed between her eyes, and High Stakes bumped her head against his chest. "Go on now," he said, "you're too spoiled. Go on." Giving her one last pat, he left the corral.

Dan closed the gate, watching High Stakes amble over to the water trough. He turned his back to the corral and leaned against the top rail. With a deep sigh, he let his head fall back. Getting out of the wilderness alive, taking care of the three of them, had filled his thoughts.

Thinking of April's bandaged hands made his gut ache. His own calloused hands were sore. Why hadn't he thought of how her hands would be? He imagined the bruises across her shoulders from the petticoat yoke. The blisters that must be on her feet.

More fierce was his anger for having wanted her. For wanting her still. This time, this woman was different. This time the possible consequences of having her haunted him. What if he'd made her pregnant?

Approaching footsteps interrupted his dark thoughts.

"Are ye all right?" Scotty asked. He leaned against the fence next to Dan.

Dan nodded.

"And the wee lass?"

"You saw her. What do you think? I half killed her getting her here." He didn't try to camouflage the bitterness in his voice.

"Ye got all three of ye here. Ye're too hard on yersel'."

Dan simply scowled at Scotty, willing him to change the subject. The Scotsman took the hint, for he made a dismissing motion with his hand and launched into a new direction.

"Do ye think Wayne will defeat the Indians?"

"Eventually." Dan nodded, thinking. "Wayne's worked hard. He kept the Legion moving closer and closer to the British forts supplying the Indians. Made a true garrison at Greenville. The Indians were short on food last winter, and the way Wayne's pushing them this summer, next winter will be tight. The army needs one good victory. Just one. Then the tribes will be ready to parley in about December or January when their bellies are empty.

"We're so close, Scotty." He paused, not having the words to express his deep feelings. "So close to having the fighting stop. It's got to stop soon." Before every Indian he knew or cared about was dead. He straightened from the fence. "I'm going to Cincinnati. Talk to Colonel Dunlap."

"But he said he dinna expect ye for three more weeks," Scotty exclaimed.

"I know." Dan paused a moment, then asked, "Scotty, did you hear of any other attacks when you were in Cincinnati? Indians attacking any of the other contractors?"

"Nae. We were one of the first ones in. Why do ye ask?"

"I think maybe the attack was aimed at us, specifically." Dan hesitated, then said, "One of the Indians called me by name. Said something about a reward."

Scotty's eyebrows pulled together in a frown. "A reward?"

"Another thing bothers me. This fellow we found." He started to pace. "I can see a thief taking his horse, maybe even his clothes, things of value. But everything? He even mumbled something about his Bible. Why steal a Bible?"

Dan stopped as he returned to Scotty's side. "I need to see if Colonel Dunlap's heard any rumors. If there's a reward for me, there's probably one for the other scouts. Maybe General Wayne as well.

Dan told himself he had to check with Dunlap, find out what was going on in the Ohio territory. And besides, he reluctantly admitted to himself, he wanted to be away from April for a few days. Maybe a trip to Cincinnati would help clear his head.

~ * ~

When April awoke in the morning, the strong sunlight streaming through the window told her she'd slept through breakfast. She rolled over, rejoicing that the feeling of weakness had dissipated with the long, restful sleep. Hesitantly, she came down stairs, wondering if Dan was up yet.

The large kitchen-parlor room was empty except for Mary, who sat in one of the chairs by the fireplace mending a shirt. Mary gave her a cup of tea and a biscuit left over from breakfast to hold her over until the noon meal. While she ate, Mary told her the injured man had come around this morning as she slept. To her amazement, he turned out to be Reverend David Carroll, the new Methodist circuit rider the town had been expecting.

"A minister?" April said. "God was certainly looking out for him. What did Dan say?"

"Well..."

Mary's tone coupled with a sideways look turned the biscuit April just ate into a rock in her stomach. "What's wrong?" she asked. "Is Dan all right?"

"Oh, he's fine," Mary hastened to reassure her, coming to sit by her side. "It's just that he left for Cincinnati last night. He'll only be gone two or three days. Said he wanted to check in with Colonel Dunlap."

Dan'd left without so much as a goodbye. For six weeks she's lived within the sight and sound of him. She simply felt numb. But, as the day went on, anger replaced the numbness. She wanted her independence, yet the first thing she did when she got to Kentucky was expect some man to take care of her. A man who, in any case, was leaving to join the militia in another month.

Tomorrow she would ask Scotty directions to the land office and march herself down there. Maybe she had needed Dan to get to Kentucky, but she could make a life here without him. She refused to listen to the internal voice that said maybe she didn't need him but she still wanted him.

~ * ~

Wyckford stomped around the campfire Markham had kindled earlier. The French half-breed, Raven, kept out of Wyckford's way, standing sullenly to the side. The 'breed had found the British officers ten days after they left Pittsburgh, as they traveled to Fort Miamis.

"He says the Americans beat off the attack," Markham translated. "He says the Man With Gun Smoke Eyes has a strong manitou, one that protects him. It will be very hard to kill him as you wish."

Wyckford looked at the 'breed, not bothering to conceal his contempt. "Oh, all right," he agreed with reluctance. "Tell him I will double the reward for McKenzie's scalp. Tell him I'll leave the money with you at the Fort."

Dismissing the Raven, Wyckford slumped down by the fire to watch Markham fix the evening meal. By rights Wyckford knew he should be more upset about the supplies getting through than about McKenzie's escape. But with McKenzie the war had become personal. Dan McKenzie summed up everything Wyckford hated and despised about America.

In America there was no sense of breeding, of class, of what was important. The Americans had stolen everything from his family—the plantation, the town house, the horses. For their loyalty to the crown, his family had been forced to flee from Charleston with the British fleet when the Americans had closed in. His family had returned to England, where the rest of the relatives had grudgingly taken them in.

Using his superior intellect to dupe and mislead the inferior colonials gave Wyckford great pleasure. Singling out McKenzie personally intensified the satisfaction. Not only was the 'breed a threat to the British alliance with the Indians, he was an insult to civilization.

Wyckford remembered how appalled he'd been, seeing people treat McKenzie as an equal instead of the baseborn bastard he was.

Oh-so-subtle hints and insinuations dropped here and there were working. He smiled, remembering how he'd seen several of the citizens of Oak Point snub McKenzie recently. Chipping away at McKenzie's reputation would do to entertain him until he had the 'breed's scalp.

Chapter Sixteen

The dawn light filled the dog-trot as April stepped out from the kitchen, a large white apron tied around her waist, a butter churn in her hands. Setting the churn beside the bench, she drew a deep breath of cool, moist morning air. She relished the moment of quiet on her third full day in Oak Point.

With a steady, unhurried motion she moved the dasher up and down. Matching the rhythm of the dasher to the words, she chanted:

"Come, butter, come.

Come, butter, come.

Peter standing at the gate,

For his buttered bread does wait.

Come, butter, come."

Hearing a horse come into the yard, April wondered who could be visiting this early. An instant later, Dan and High Stakes crossed in front of the dog-trot, heading toward the corral. Her heart thumped in her chest. She took a deep breath to calm herself and watched as Dan dismounted and looped the reins over the middle rail. He uncinched the saddle, taking it from the mare's back, then tossed it across the top rail.

As he casually swung the heavy saddle, she found herself admiring the grace and power of his movements before she reminded herself she didn't need him. Dan turned the mare into the corral with a pat on the rump. He picked up his rifle, powder horn, and bullet pouch and turned toward the house. And toward her.

Suddenly, she wished he hadn't returned so soon. She lowered her eyes and clutched the dasher, continuing the steady up-and-down movement.

Drawing to a stop a few feet in front of her, he rested the rifle butt on the ground. She looked up as he pushed his hat back from his forehead. His pale blue-gray eyes narrowed and his gaze leisurely raked her up and down. Her breath caught in her throat, and she tried to read the mixture of emotions in his icy-hot gaze. Annoyance? Desire?

Oh, yes. Desire. Whatever else was in his gaze, she read desire. To her confusion and embarrassment, her body responded to his gaze, her nipples becoming taut against the bodice of her dress. Her grip on the dasher tightened, and her chin came up. Long seconds passed. The dasher went up and down, up and down.

Shifting his feet, Dan let out a gusty sigh, and she watched him bank the fire in his gaze.

"Are you all right?" Before she could answer, he took a step forward and carefully tugged one of her hands from the dasher, turning it palm up. He lightly traced a circle at the base of her palm as he studied her healing blisters.

"Yes, I'm fine."

He nodded.

She withdrew her hand, and the silence stretched between them, broken only by the swish of the dasher as she searched for something to say.

"Did you ride all night?" she asked.

"No. I stayed at my place last night. It's only a few miles from town, that's how I got here so early."

From the kitchen behind them came the sounds of someone chunking wood in the fireplace. Footsteps crossed to the door and Mary appeared, rescuing April from Dan's nearness.

"Dan!" Mary said in surprise. Before she could move from the doorway, Alexander burst out of the kitchen.

"Uncle Dan!" he cried, as he caught Dan around the knees with a hug.

"Hiya, squirt," Dan tousled the boy's curls. "Here, Matt," he spoke to the tall twelve-year-old on Alexander's heels. "Take my rifle?"

"Sure thing, Uncle Dan." The boy took the rifle and turned to carry it inside.

"I'll take the rest," Mark said, reaching out for the powder horn and bullet pouch. Dan handed them to him, and Mark turned and trailed his twin brother into the house.

"Welcome home," Scotty said. He'd followed his sons from the kitchen and shook Dan's hand.

Mary's welcoming smile lingered as she said, "Well, no need to stand here all day. Come on everyone, breakfast is ready."

And although she wanted to deny it, honesty forced April to acknowledge that if the day now seemed just a little brighter, holding just a few more possibilities, she felt that way because Dan was back. Her independence was about to be tested.

~ * ~

Dan knocked on the door of the storeroom.

"Come in," answered a pleasant, cultured voice.

As Dan entered, the nightshirt-clad man on the bed sat up, his arm supporting his side.

"Reverend Carroll? I'm Dan McKenzie," he said, stepping over to the bed, offering his hand.

"My pleasure," the man replied, shaking Dan's hand. "My thanks for all your assistance. You saved my life. I'm—"

"It was nothing." Dan made a dismissive gesture with his hand.

The man started to laugh, but gasped and caught his side. Reverend David Carroll didn't look much like a minister, Dan thought as he took a seat. Only a year or two younger than himself, the reverend didn't wear either a self-sacrificing expression or the smug look of contentment of most clergymen.

As if he'd guessed Dan's thoughts, the reverend said, "Don't look much like a man of the cloth, do I?" He shifted, wincing. "But the Lord works in mysterious ways, as they say. I suspect I'm one of them."

Dan found himself smiling back, unaccountably liking the man. "Well, it wouldn't be far wrong to say it was a miracle we found you. What were you doing out there, Reverend?"

"I was lost," he admitted. "The Board of Missionaries in England assigned me to Kentucky. I tried to tell them I wasn't a good choice for the frontier, but they knew better of course. They insisted since I was a former colonial, I would be just the man. I was born in Charleston, but my parents sent me to school in England when I was eight."

He shrugged, the movement careful, as if testing his injuries. "In any case, I wandered off the trail, enjoying the countryside, then got lost. I ran across two men who offered to guide me to Oak Point. I'm sure you can guess the rest."

Dan nodded. "They beat you, stole all your supplies and your horse?"

"That's right," David agreed.

"How are you feeling now?"

"Fine except for these ribs. Mrs. Murray and Mrs. Williamson have taken good care of me. Could you do me one more favor? Do you think you could help me convince your sister I've recovered enough for her to let me get out of this bed?"

~ * ~

Dan entered the kitchen as Mary finished the noon meal dishes. He flopped into a chair, sideways, one arm draped over the chair back. "Thanks for giving the reverend a pair of Scotty's breeches."

"You didn't have to volunteer to help him move to the Elkhorn Inn tomorrow," Mary said. She turned to run the dish rag over the table. "Did I tell you, Janie will be staying with us for a few days? She and April have volunteered to sew the reverend new clothes."

His sister went on to talk about how well the garden was doing, and about the boys. She wasn't going to make this easy for him. "How's April doing?" he was finally forced to ask.

"She's fine," Mary answered, her skirts swishing as she returned to the table and sat on the bench opposite him. "You saw her yourself at breakfast. Her hands are almost healed. She's been a great help with the boys."

Dan nodded. On his way in he'd seen April walking along the path with Alexander skipping by her side, both of them carrying fishing poles.

He'd hoped a few days away from her would allow his feelings to cool off. Not a chance. One look at her this morning, and he could hardly walk straight. How would he keep his hands off her when she was right under his nose all day?

"How long is she going to stay here?" He made his voice sound as disinterested as he could, but Mary's smile told him he hadn't been successful.

"James and I told her she could stay until she gets settled. You did know she had a land claim?"

"Said it was the reason she wanted to come here."

"I don't think that particular piece of land was that important to her. She gave it up awful easy."

"Gave it up?"

"Oh, of course you wouldn't know. Not the way you ran off the other day." Mary's curt tone indicated how she'd felt about his trip to Cincinnati. "It turned out her land claim was cross-filed on the old Cooper place. You know how these claims can be. The land officer told her she could hire Wyckford to try to prove her claim, like he's doing for several others."

He sure as hell didn't want to think about April having any dealings, business or otherwise, with Wyckford. "She didn't hire him, did she?"

Mary shook her head. "He isn't back in town yet. And anyway, you know how long those cases can drag on. Look at Lem Sawyer. After three years of trying to prove his claim, he finally gave up and went back to Virginia. April went out to talk to Mr. Cooper. He offered to pay her compensation and she seemed glad to take it. As she pointed out to Scotty, she couldn't very well work the land all by herself. This way she has financial security to start her seamstress business and Mr. Cooper gets clear title to land he's already farming."

"Why didn't she take the money and go back to Philadelphia?"

"If you think she'll go back to Philadelphia, you're mistaken. I've only known her three days, but I can see she loves the land." Mary stood, came around the table to put her hand on his arm. "Loves Kentucky the way you do.

"You could live wild with the Indians, because you were still with the land. Now me, I could live anywhere James and the boys are. The land is not part of my soul, the way Kentucky is yours."

The way Kentucky was part of April's soul, Dan thought. April was staying, and what, if anything, would he do about it?

~ * ~

That night Dan lay on the bed in the storeroom. Sleeping was hopeless. He sat up, resting his folded arms across his bent knees. It wasn't the lumpy bed or the stuffy storeroom keeping him awake. Thoughts of April, in the house, upstairs, in his bed, kept him awake. He wondered what she wore. Nightdress? Chemise? Or was she naked in the hot summer night like he was?

He swore. He grabbed his breechcloth, tying it on but not bothering with his leggings or queue ribbon. Hair loose about his shoulders, his bare feet carried him silently across the yard. Going past the barn, he walked part way in to the meadow where he threw himself down at the base of a magnolia tree.

He sat cross-legged and leaned back against the smooth bark, looking up through the canopy of large, shiny leaves at the moonlit sky. The air hung heavy with the scent of magnolias and the music of frogs and crickets.

The same thoughts had gone round and round in his head for the last three days. What to do about April? He loved her; he admitted that. But what he felt for her wasn't the problem. He'd made love to her, and now what did he intend to do about it? Of course, he'd thought her a widow, a totally different proposition from taking a virgin. Not that it mattered now, what was done was done.

It hadn't been fair of her not to tell him. What really bothered him was the twinge of suspicion she'd misled him on purpose. He remembered that day in Philadelphia when Scotty told him she was an old man's widow. He'd wondered then if she married for the comfort and security. Maybe she hoped to do it again.

He absentmindedly picked up a stick, breaking it into small pieces. The trip out had been hard on her. Maybe she realized she would need a man to protect her. Maybe he should feel pleased she thought him capable, but he felt manipulated, trapped.

He tossed the last piece of the stick away, and stood up. He'd taken her virginity. A man who didn't own up to his responsibilities wasn't much of a man. Duty and honor required he offer her the protection of his name. He walked back toward the house. He'd do his duty. He didn't have to say anything about Blue Licks. She'd backed him into a corner, so she'd have to take him as he was.

Returning to the storeroom pallet, he felt better. No point in putting it off. He'd tell her she didn't have to worry, they would get married. Yes, he thought, he'd tell her tomorrow.

~ * ~

Crrra-ack! The single rifle shot echoed across the meadow. The cloud of dense, white smoke slowly thinned to a pale blue-gray, drifting over the clearing in the heavy, early evening air, searching to join the remnants of the sharp sound.

Dan slowly lowered the rifle and glanced to where April stood. "See," he said, "it's not hard."

She gave him a dubious look. This morning at breakfast, when Dan had offered to teach her to load and shoot, she decided it was a skill an independent frontier woman might have need of.

"Here, you take it." Dan handed the rifle to her. "Be careful. It's heavy," he warned belatedly, as she almost dropped the gun.

Holding the unfamiliar weapon in her hands, she studied the fine craftsmanship. The smooth, muted gray of the metal barrel joined with the glossy, high-grained maple stock, the whole gun highlighted by the warm shine of its brass fittings. The firearm had the same lean, hard, powerful look as its owner.

"I had it made by John Philip Beck." He must have seen the name meant nothing to her, for he explained. "He's a gunsmith in Dauphine County, Pennsylvania. One of the best." Dan ran his hand over the polished maple stock. "I saved my money for two years. Beck fit the stock, the grip, everything, specifically for me."

Dan turned the rifle over in his hands, showing her the brass patch box set into the right side of the stock. "This box is built right into the gun." He pushed a small knob on the butt plate, and the cover to the patch box sprang ajar. He pushed the lid closed, letting his fingers trace the ornamental brass work surrounding the patch box. "See, there's my initials." Dan's lean fingers pointed out an engraved 'M,' a 'K,' with the small 'c' between them, all entwined round and about with thistles.

"Here," he handed the rifle back to her, "let's see if you remember how I loaded it."

April took the rifle, letting the butt rest on the ground, the muzzle almost level with her eyes. "First, we have to load the powder," she said, half to herself.

Dan held out the powder horn, having already removed the wooden plug from the small end.

"How do you know how much to put in?" she asked.

"Mostly practice. The quick way is to hold the rifle ball in your hand and pour the powder over it, until the powder covers the ball."

April nodded. She could consistently measured salt the same way. But she had one hand full of rifle, and the other full of powder horn.

Seeing her predicament, he took hold of the rifle. "Here, I'll hold the gun. You can measure the powder with this." Dan showed her a small hollowed-out piece of elk antler, attached to the powder horn by a rawhide thong. "I use the measure if there's time."

She filled the measure, then poured the fine black grains down the barrel. She took the greased cloth patch and laid it across the muzzle opening. "How can you do this all by yourself?" she said in exasperation. "I need two more hands."

He laughed. "Don't worry, you're doing fine." He had a wonderful laugh, deep and rich. He made it hard to concentrate on the lesson.

"Now, the ball." She said the steps aloud as she took a lead ball from the bullet pouch.

"Make sure the lead's not scratched," he instructed. "The ball has to be round to be accurate."

She placed the ball on the patch, and with her thumb, pushed both into the muzzle. She pulled the ramrod from the brass ramrod pipes beneath the barrel. Concentrating, she used the rod to force the patch and ball down.

"Push hard," he encouraged. "There are twelve grooves that spiral down the inside of the barrel. The grooves make it more difficult to load, but they're what make the ball spin when it's fired. It's the spin that gives you accuracy."

"There," she said with a sigh, "that's as far as it will go." She pulled the ramrod from the muzzle and threaded it back through the pipes under the barrel. Dan nodded his approval. To lose the ramrod was to render the gun useless.

She handed the powder horn and bullet pouch back to him, and picked up the rifle, cradling it under her arm. Pushing the frizzen forward, she carefully poured powder in the pan, then pushed the frizzen closed, its upper face ready for the flint to strike. With her thumb, she pulled back the goose-neck hammer, the flint locked in its jaws.

Setting the stock to her shoulder, she supported the heavy barrel with her left hand. "What do I aim at?" she asked, not at all sure she would be able to hold the heavy rifle steady.

"Here, let me help." Dan stepped up behind her. His arms came around her, his large hands covering hers as he took the weight of the weapon. Her stomach tightened. She was aware of his arms around her, his chest solid against her back, his hips against her buttocks.

"Line up the sights, like I told you." His breath felt soft and warm against her cheek. She leaned the other cheek into the gun stock, trying to think, struggling not to feel his solid warmth against her. Drawing a deep breath, she concentrated on lining up the front and rear sights.

"Aim at the knot on that oak," he said. "When you get the sights lined up, take a deep breath, let a little of it out, then hold it, and pull the trigger."

She took a deep breath, gave a slight exhale. Her finger tightened on the trigger. The goose-neck hammer sprang forward, the flint striking sparks from the frizzen. There was pffft as the powder in the pan burned though the touch hole to the charge in the barrel. Crra-ack! White smoke exploded out of the barrel. The explosion drove her back against him.

"Oh, my," April gasped, as they lowered the gun. Turning toward him, she allowed him to take the weapon from her grasp.

He reached behind him, propping the gun against a convenient stump

Before she realized what he intended, he pulled her against him, and his mouth found hers. Her body melted against his, her mouth welcoming the invasion of his tongue. Her senses began to swirl as his hand roamed over her body. Needing air, she turned her head to break the kiss, but his mouth held her. Putting her hands flat against his chest, she pushed away.

"Wait," she gasped, her mind fighting her body for control. At the rockhouse she had let her love and her body's response to that love, carry her away. Their bodies had spoken to each other of love. Now their minds, their hearts, must have the same chance to speak.

She tried to pull away, twisting her shoulders. "Wait, Dan," she repeated. "We have to talk."

"Later," he murmured against her skin. He nibbled down her neck and his warm lips traveled over her throat.

Her knees began to turn to water, then a prickle of annoyance danced along her spine as she rebuked herself for letting her body govern her mind. The annoyance spread to include Dan. Did he think he had only to kiss her and she would melt in his arms? This time she pushed harder, her voice firm. "No, Dan, we have to talk now."

Dan's head came up. Her tone had startled him and he frowned in puzzlement. What was going on? He had felt her melt against him, knew she wanted him as he wanted her. They would marry, so what difference did it make? He gripped her upper arms, still holding her close. His exasperation showed in his voice, "Come on, April, give over."

Taking her startled silence for acquiescence, he started to kiss the other side of her neck. With surprising strength, she shoved him again.

"Let go!" she said through clenched teeth.

His exasperation burst into full annoyance. Still gripping her upper arms, he gave her a small shake. "What's the matter with you?" he questioned, letting his displeasure show. She was angry and he was getting that way. A thought struck him. Did she think he was without honor? The type of man to sleep with a virgin and then not be willing to do right by her? Hadn't he—No, he realized, he hadn't told her they would marry.

He ran a hand through his hair, then making a helpless gesture he let it fall to his side. He drew a deep breath, striving to control his rising temper. "I know the right thing. Reverend Carroll can marry us tomorrow."

Chapter Seventeen

Marry! April's heart soared at the word, but the next instant it plummeted to her stomach.

"I'll do my duty," Dan continued, "I'll marry you."

The word duty mocked her. She felt sick. He would marry her, not because he loved her, but because of his duty. She wanted to know what the night in the rockhouse had meant to him. Now she did. A mistake to be paid for. And he hadn't bothered to ask her. He was telling her what he, alone, had already decided. His arrogance increased her anger.

Fury made her stomach queasy and she felt the tingle and tightness in the back of her throat, warning her she was about to cry. She began to struggle, her fingers prying ineffectively against his grip on her arm.

"Let me go!" she demanded, still trying to break his grip.

"Stop it," Dan commanded, giving her arm a small shake, his grip tightening. "What's the matter with you?"

"I won't marry you, I won't," she half-shouted, anger and tears in her voice. The ease with which he held her made her furious at her own helplessness, the casual way in which men dominated women. "I had a husband who married me out of obligation, I won't do it again. I won't." She heard the rising hysteria in her voice but no longer cared. "I won't marry you. If I marry again, I'll marry someone who loves me. There are plenty of men in Kentucky. Men who'd want a wife."

Dan's jaw clenched. He felt his body stiffen, and wiped the emotion from his face. The thought of her with another man shot jealousy through him. Anger followed. He'd offered her his name and she threw it back in his face. What the hell did she want from him? Her 'I won't' twisted in his gut like a knife. He held his temper by the slenderest of threads. His voice low and harsh, he gritted,

"You think so? How will you explain to your new husband the fact you're not a virgin?"

Ceasing her struggles, she looked at him with disdain. "I don't have to explain. I'm a widow, remember? You did me a favor by—" But the rest of the words didn't come out as Dan gave her a sharp shake.

"Dammit, April," Dan snapped, his temper escaping his control, "don't be foolish. You may have to marry me." She shook her head no and began to struggle again, her fingers prying and scratching at his hand. "What if you're carrying a baby?" Like a slap, the words halted her fight, her mouth opening in surprise.

"I'm not," the answer came a split second later.

Dan's eyes narrowed at the abruptness of her answer. Her look of astonishment told him it hadn't occurred to her. Quickly he counted back to the night in the rockhouse. "Do you know for sure?" he asked.

Again, April tried to jerk from his grasp. He brought his free hand up to capture her chin, turning her face to look at him.

"Do you know for sure?" he demanded.

Her lips were compressed into thin, angry lines, and she jerked her chin free of his grasp. She looked off in the distance, keeping her chin high. "No, I don't know for sure," she admitted in a cold, controlled voice.

Drawing a deep breath, he released her. She hugged her arm to her waist, her hand going to the spot he'd held. She looked angry and indignant standing there, in spite of the tears streaking her face, her hand rubbing her arm. His own body vibrated with tension and anger. He forced himself to stop grinding his teeth.

A distant roll of thunder echoed across the meadow. Large drops of rain began to fall, leaving damp spots on April's skirt. Dan swore under his breath, and turned to gather up the rifle. He raised his hand toward her elbow, but allowed it to fall away.

"Let's go." His voice revealed no emotion, no feelings. He gestured toward the house. Without a word, she picked up the powder horn and bullet pouch and headed across the meadow, the gusts of wind whipping her skirts.

Behind them, lightning flickered, momentarily illuminating the pathway. A few steps later, a rumble of thunder and another gust of wind hurried them along. Ahead, the house beckoned, the warm rectangle of lamp light spilling across the dog-trot from the open kitchen door. April and Dan reached the shelter of the dog-trot just as a shadow filled the doorway.

"Here they are, Mary," Scotty called over his shoulder, stepping out. "And just in time, too." Another flash of lightning, the peal of thunder on its heels, lit the dog-trot. "I was about ta be sent out ta find ye."

Mary appeared in the doorway. "Just look at you two," she exclaimed. "Come inside and get dry, I'll fix you a cup of tea to keep off the chill." Taking April's arm, she led her into the kitchen.

Scotty grinned. "How about you? Would ye care for some 'tea' to keep off the chill?"

"Sure, why not," Dan answered in a tight voice. Without a backward look he stalked into the storeroom.

A minute later Scotty returned to the storeroom, a jug in one hand and two tin cups in the other. To his surprise, Dan hadn't changed. His wet shirt plastered to his chest, he stuffed his clothes into his saddle bags. Scotty put the jug and cups on the plank table just as Dan scooped up his shaving gear, pushing it in with his clothes. With a sigh, he dropped onto the side of the bed. "Where's that drink?" he asked.

Scotty filled the two cups. "You'll like this," he said, handing Dan a cup. "I bought it last fall while you were with the Legion. A man up in Bourbon County makes it. Claims the stuff's older than Alexander."

The men drank in silence. Scotty glanced around the room. All Dan's belonging were packed. "Ye planning on going somewhere?"

Standing and putting his cup on the table, Dan exhaled sharply. He ran his hand through his hair. "I'm moving out to my place. Tonight."

He picked up his saddle bags and throwing them over his shoulder, he was gone, the steady rain blurring his shape as he walked toward the barn.

~ * ~

The rain had stopped. Lying on Dan's bed, April heard only the rhythmic drip of water from the eaves. Under the cover of the thunder and rain, she'd cried out her anger and pain. Now, she lay, exhausted and miserable, unable to sleep. She had cried so hard her stomach hurt. She rolled onto her side, drew up her knees and hugged her arms around her middle.

In spite of everything, she loved him. She'd tried to hate him for the crude way he'd proposed, for the way he looked on marriage as a duty.

She rolled over trying to find a comfortable position for the ache in her stomach. For one wild moment she had been tempted to accept his proposal. She could marry him, and hope that love and caring would replace duty. But what if it didn't? She would rather love him and not have him, than have him but not have his love.

And what if she were pregnant? Her hands moved to rest on her stomach. The thought of Dan's baby brought tears to her eyes once more. But a baby would mean she would have to marry him, and she would have another duty marriage. She wanted a marriage of love not one of obligation.

She must have slept. The square of gray light from the window showed dawn was not far off. The room was not cold, but she awoke huddled in a ball. This time she recognized the stomach cramps for what they were. They would not be forced to marry. But before she could relax, an unexpected tide of sorrow rushed to join the relief. How could she be glad and sorry at the same time? After a few moments she pushed back the sheet and got out of bed.

April crossed to her trunk and made the necessary preparations before returning to snuggle back in the bed. She must have slept again, since the next thing she knew there was a soft knock on the door.

"Yes?" April answered as she sat up and pushed her hair back from her face.

The door opened to reveal Mary. She hesitated for a moment in the doorway, before coming to sit on the side of the bed. "Are you all right? I thought I'd better check on you, you slept so late."

"I... I'm fine," April stammered, and tried to sit up straighter. Of all things, she blushed.

Mary's look of concern deepened for a moment, and then cleared. "I did hear you moving around early this morning, didn't I?. It's your time of the month, isn't it?" Mary patted April's hand. "Don't you worry. Just stay here in bed as long as you like."

With a swish of her skirts, Mary was gone, and then in a few minutes returned. She carried what looked like a bunch of towels in her hands. She sat the bundle on the floor and removed the tray from the bed, putting it beside the mysterious bundle. "Lay back, now," she instructed April.

"Why?"

Mary picked up the packet of towels. "So you can rest this on your stomach." Mary handed the bundle to April. Surprised, she found the bundle heavy and warm.

"What is it?" she questioned.

"A brick I put in the fireplace, nice and warm from breakfast, wrapped it with a couple of old towels."

April placed the bundle on her stomach. The weight felt good. The warmth which began to seep though felt even better. "This is wonderful," she sighed.

"I thought one of the McKenzies should be nice to you," Mary replied, her voice laden with unasked questions.

"Dan's left, hasn't he." The words were not really a question.

"Yes. He went out to his cabin. James said he'd be back in a week or so."

April made a show of snuggling down in the bed while she thought. She couldn't answer Mary's unasked question by saying Dan left because she refused his marriage proposal. Or that he had asked only out of a sense of duty because they'd made love in the rockhouse. The satisfaction she'd felt at the hurt in his face when she'd refused to marry him wasn't at all comforting this morning. Wanting to be alone with her thoughts, April smoothed her hands over the towels. "Thank you, Mary."

Mary smiled as she moved toward the doorway. "Call me if you need anything. Janie will be here day after tomorrow, and you two have a lot of sewing to do to have the reverend's clothes finished." She stopped in the doorway and looked back, saying, "Men can be such idiots at times, but we love them anyway."

Over the next few days April's moods alternated between anger and misery. Anger whenever she thought of Dan's peremptory offer of marriage. Misery whenever she thought of Dan's hurt at her refusal. Anger at herself that she should feel Dan's pain in addition to her own. Misery when she wondered if her life in Kentucky would be lived without Dan.

Gradually her innate cheerfulness and enthusiasm took over, helped by the distraction of Janie and the making of the reverend's new clothes.

On Wednesday, after breakfast, April and Janie commandeered the Murray kitchen table to lay out the bolts of material. Several men in the community had loaned the reverend clothes. From these the two women took the best fitting shirt, breeches and coat. They carefully picked apart all the seams to use the pieces as a pattern. Janie carefully cut pattern pieces April had arranged on the black broadcloth. April started to stitch.

Watching April take small, quick stitches, Janie sighed. "Guess I never did enough sewing to be a fair hand at it. Ma and Mary took care of it all."

"Mary?"

Janie nodded and waved a hand in the direction of the door leading to the McKenzie and Murray store. "Mary. Everyone around here knows my folks took Mary in after her ma died. Seems their pa didn't want to stay around here with his wife dead. He couldn't drag a young girl around with him, so he left her here and took off with

Dan." Janie paused, then continued in a rush, "And they went to live among the Shawnee."

"Dan told me," April replied, her voice calm as she continued to place the pattern pieces. Janie nodded, and looked relieved. "So you and Mary grew up as sisters?"

"That's right. My parents had given up hope of having any young'ns of their own. Ma always said having Mary was a blessing, for in less than a year I came along. Guess I was a handful, Pa used to take me with him to give Ma and Mary some peace in the house. Tagging after him all day long, I just naturally learned to hunt, shoot and such, better than I learned to sew."

April glanced up, "There's not much else for a young girl to do in Philadelphia. My mother gave me the chore of doing all the sewing when I was ten." Her gaze returned to the seam. "All that practice will hold me in good stead now that I need to earn my living. This coat for Reverend Carroll will be advertisement, but only if we get it finished on time for him to wear it to church."

Janie sighed and picked up the shears. "Maybe if I'd learn to sew instead of shoot, somebody would look at me the way Dan looks at you."

Her heart thumped, thinking of the last look she'd seen on Dan's face. Her needle faltered, but Janie didn't notice.

Cutting through the broadcloth, Janie continued, "All the men around here look at me as if they're wondering if I'm a better shot with a rifle than they are.

"Land sakes, April. You sure can make that needle fly. The reverend's clothes will be finished by Sunday for sure. Everyone in Oak Point will be there to hear the new preacher."

April took two more stitches, tied the thread in a knot, and bit off the end. Would Dan return for the service? She half-hoped, half-feared he would.

Chapter Eighteen

"Hello. Anyone home?" Reverend Carroll called as he reined up in front of Dan's log cabin. Holding a heavy basket in one hand, he dismounted. Not trusting his hired gelding to remain ground tied, he kept hold of the reins, as he walked toward the open front door.

A quick glance inside took in the stone fireplace dominating one end of the cabin. One bench held washing things, while another closer to the fireplace held cooking utensils. In the corner a pile of furs covered by a faded quilt served as a bed. Dan's clothing hung neatly on a row of nearby pegs.

After setting the basket just inside the door, he looked around for a place to tie his horse. Around the north side of the cabin, he found a barn, a corral, and split rail fence that enclosed several acres of meadow shaded on the far side by a grove of trees.

As the reverend tied his mount to the corral fence, he heard the ka-chunk, ka-chunk, of an ax. Following the sound, he soon found its source at the edge of a small copse of trees behind the barn.

Dan looked over his shoulder, seeing the reverend approaching. "Be with you in a minute, Reverend," he called out, never breaking the steady swing of the ax. Two chestnuts trees already lay on the ground. With only a few more strokes, the third began to lean and creak. He stepped back, watching with satisfaction as the trunk cracked, popped, and broke. The whoosh of its branches preceded its solid 'thunk' against the earth. Then he stooped and picked up his hat, shirt, and rifle, and walked toward the reverend.

"What brings you out this way?" A sudden thought struck Dan. "Everything's all right in town, isn't it?"

The reverend's smile immediately reassured him. "Everyone's fine. I just came for a visit."

"Let's go up to the house, Reverend."

"Please, call me David. If I may call you Dan?"

Dan nodded and put on his hat as the two men started back. He debated putting on his shirt, but he wanted to wash first, and in any case he now had the chance to find out if David Carroll was the type to judge a man because he wore a beaded medallion and a tattoo.

"How long have you lived here?" the minister asked.

"Scotty and I built the cabin three years ago, the barn winter before last. Can't say I've really lived here, though."

"Why not?"

"Too busy. When we first started the company, I lived with Sis and Scotty. Wasn't 'til three years ago I had the time and money for a place of my own. But that's when I started working as a scout for General Wayne. I spent all last year with the army in Ohio territory."

He'd neglected the place while scouting for the army, but that hadn't been the only reason behind his efforts of the last week or so. Only by working himself to exhaustion could he keep thoughts of April from haunting him when he lay down to sleep.

Even then he couldn't keep her out of his dreams. But regardless of the dream—whether he saw her standing on the porch of the Twelve Tankards Inn, her green silk dress vivid in the morning sunlight, or her body, pale ivory in the moonlight of the rockhouse—the dreams ended the same way, tears streaming down her face as she refused to marry him.

Unused to examining his emotions, it took Dan a few days to realize he'd used his anger at her rejection as a weapon, to block the hurt of April's refusal. Too late he saw she might have reacted in the same manner, that her anger might have been caused by hurt.

He jerked his mind back to the present, hearing the end of the reverend's sentence. "...you intend to breed horses?"

"That's right," Dan replied, shoving away his previous thoughts. They crossed between the cabin and the barn. "Care to take a chance on my cooking and stay for dinner?"

"No need, your sister sent me out with this." David Carroll picked up the basket as they entered the cabin. "She said this way she was certain we'd get a decent meal."

"She's right about that," Dan agreed as he placed his rifle on the pegs by the door. He crossed to a bench beside the fireplace. Taking a length of toweling from a peg on the wall, he dipped it into a bucket of water on the bench. Once he'd finished washing the sweat and dust from his upper body, he pulled on his shirt. He turned toward the table, and gestured to David to sit. "Let's see what she sent."

The contents of the basket, cold fried chicken, thick slices of salt-rising bread with fresh butter accompanied by a jug of apple cider, made a satisfying meal. The reverend stretched out his legs, while Dan sat relaxed with one arm hooked over the back of his chair.

"This was all a sort of bribe, you know," David said.

"A bribe?"

David nodded. "Your family wants to make sure you'll come to town for the Fourth of July celebration tomorrow."

The thought of returning to town intrigued Dan. Maybe he'd let David persuade him.

David leaned back in his chair. "They half expected to see you on Sunday. As a matter of fact, I thought you'd show up to see if the preacher you rescued was any good at his job."

Dan smiled, as he knew David intended. He decided to take the bait. "Are you? Any good, that is?"

"How good a preacher I am remains to be seen," David replied. "The Lord blessed me with a smooth tongue, fine voice, and an eye for good horseflesh."

"You say you have an eye for horses," Dan stood, "I'm going out to check my horse, come take a look."

Outside, the sun had set, the colors of the day faded as evening came on. The two men walked across the yard to the fence around the meadow.

Dan whistled shrilly between his teeth, looking out across the meadow. "Tell me what you think of this one."

From beneath the shadows of the trees, a bay mare emerged. She trotted up to the fence, putting her muzzle into his outstretched hand. She nickered softly as he stroked her neck. David gave a long, low whistle of appreciation.

David observed the mare's slim head while her large, intelligent eyes turned to study him. He held out his hand, and the mare trustingly nuzzled it, her nose like soft velvet, her breath gustily warm against his palm. "Great topline. Lots of balance. How does she move?"

"As smooth as she looks. Fast, too."

"If she's a product of your breeding program, you already raise the best horses in Kentucky."

"No, I didn't breed High Stakes." Dan gave the mare the bucket of oats he'd brought from the barn. "I won her from George Wyckford last year. But she's in foal to a Sinclair stud."

Still scrutinizing the bay, David nodded. "Sinclair's a noted stud around here?"

"Not here, in Virginia."

"If I didn't know better, I'd say this horse had a lot of Baxter blood." He glanced at Dan. "The Baxter plantation next to ours was noted for their horses. The Baxters were Tories though. The whole family left Charleston and returned to England during the War of Independence." David crossed his arms on the top rail of the fence. "Four or five years ago, in England, I ran across some of the family. They still raised horses. Your mare looks like one of those animals."

"Wyckford could have bought her in England, I guess," Dan said.

"Well?"

Dan knew what the reverend meant. Who'd have thought a minister would turn out to be a friend? Dan would do what Mary wanted, and besides, he needed to see April. He took a deep breath and said, "Would you care to spend the night, ride into Oak Point with me in the morning?"

"I would be delighted, Daniel," the reverend replied.

Dan slapped him on the shoulder. "Good. Let's put High Stakes and your horse in the barn."

~ * ~

The midmorning fourth of July sun warm on his back, Dan and the reverend turned their horses into the corral behind the McKenzie and Murray house, and walked toward the open kitchen door. Dan took off his hat as he entered the building, the reverend behind him.

"Welcome home," Mary said, moving across the kitchen to give Dan a quick hug. "Thank you, Reverend Carroll."

Dan gave Mary a non-committal smile, and looked around the kitchen. "Where is everyone?"

"The boys are off with their friends. I'm surprised you didn't see them on the main street. They're supposed to be back here in time for dinner." She poured each man a cup of coffee. "James and the others are making sure everything is ready for the speeches this afternoon."

Mary pulled out a chair and sat down. "You'll stay for dinner, of course, won't you, Reverend?"

"He'll stay." Dan's voice must have been rougher than he'd intended, as the comment drew puzzled glances from both Mary and David. Having to ask about April aggravated him. "Where's April?"

With a smile that looked smug, Mary rose from the table. "She and Janie are out in the meadow. Janie's teaching her to ride. Why don't you two go visit with them? I can work better without you two cluttering up my kitchen."

Dan and David walked down the path in companionable silence. Near the meadow, the voices of the two young women floated on the warm summer air. The men rounded the corner where the path curved to the left and the meadow came into view.

Dan spotted April and the heat in his belly halted him in his tracks. He watched the scene in front of him.

Unaware of their audience, Janie maneuvered a placid brown gelding to stand next to a large stump where April waited to mount. She sure didn't look like a city woman now, Dan thought. Like Janie's, April's dress was plain, the color, originally midnight blue, now faded to an hour or two before sunrise. April gingerly settled herself on the animal's bare back. She sat at an angle with her two bare feet dangling over the horse's left side.

Even from this distance, he saw April draw a deep breath before kicking Old Jack twice with her heels. At a sedate pace, the animal started across the meadow.

Dan and David moved to join Janie where she stood watching April's progress around the perimeter of the meadow.

"Since when did you ride sidesaddle?" Dan asked Janie, nodding in the direction of the horse and rider. "There's probably not even a sidesaddle in the state."

Janie shrugged. "I told her that, but that's what she wanted. Besides, Jack's such a quiet old thing, I just wanted her to get used to the horse."

The three of them watched the horse amble along the brush at the far side of the meadow.

"Well—" Dan never finished the sentence.

As Old Jack passed a mulberry bush, a covey of quail erupted, wings whirring. They shot across in front of the horse. Dan's heart jumped into his throat, stopping his breath. He swore and started to run, his eyes never leaving the rearing animal and the small figure clinging to its mane.

The horse broke into a ragged run. April slipped toward the ground. "No!" Dan yelled, running harder. She hit the ground, a flurry of skirts and petticoats as she rolled over and over amidst the running hoofs.

Dan swore as he skidded to a halt. She lay face down, one arm flung out to her side. His heart hammering, he dropped to his knees. Carefully he turned her over, relieved to see her breathing was deep and easy. Dirt streaked one side of her face, her eyes were closed.

"April," he said gently, his hand brushing the hair from her forehead. She sighed, and his stomach untightened a notch. Checking for broken bones, he felt her arms. He paid no attention when Janie and the reverend panted up behind him. His hands moved to check her legs. He had one hand on her bare ankle when Janie's cry of "Dan!" broke his concentration.

His head snapped up, and the look of shocked dismay on Janie's face registered. The reverend noisily cleared his throat.

He snatched back his hand. "I... I... Something might be broken." He clenched his hands into fists on his thighs. Regard for April's reputation warred with his need to touch her.

Janie knelt on April's other side, David going to one knee beside her. Janie's steady hands checked April's legs. David looked tactfully away, but Dan couldn't force his gaze anywhere else. Janie settled back on her heels. "Nothing's broken. I'm sure she'll be fine."

Dan let out a sigh of relief and managed to unclench his fists.

April chose that moment to groan, her hand going to her face. "What happened?"

"You fell off," Dan bit out. To hell with what anyone thought. He gathered April into his arms until she half-rested across his lap.

"Are you hurt?"

"I'm fine." This time her voice sounded closer to normal, and her clear hazel eyes studied his face.

Dan gave a sigh of relief. He looked over to David. "Why don't you help Janie catch the horse?"

"Shouldn't I stay here?" Janie said, concern for April in her eyes.

"She's fine. Get Old Jack so we can carry her back to the house," Dan said. Beyond caring what might be proper, he looked with appeal to David. Dan needed a minute alone with April.

David hesitated a second, then gave Dan an almost imperceptible nod. He stood and dusted the knees of his breeches. "If you would accompany me?" he asked, offering his hand to Janie and helping her to her feet.

Once the others were several paces away, Dan turned back to April. Shifting his weight, he settled her more comfortably across his lap.

"You sure you're all right, now?" Dan asked. Why was she still so pale? A heart-stopping thought hit him. "You didn't faint or anything, did you?"

"Faint?" Her eyebrows pulled together in a slight frown, and she brushed back an escaped mahogany tendril from her cheek.

"Faint." He had to ask, had to know. And, God help him, he didn't know what he wanted the answer to be. He cleared his throat. "When Mary was expecting Alexander, she fainted a couple of times."

Comprehension replaced puzzlement on her face. Color rose in her cheeks and she turned her face from his.

When she spoke, her voice was low, but steady. "No, I didn't faint. I have no reason to faint."

His clenched jaw eased at her words, then the meaning sank in. His gut dropped away in a surge of sadness so unexpected it shook him. This woman fascinated him, frightened him with what she could make him feel. Damn if he didn't love her.

Unable to resist, Dan pulled April to him and kissed her quick and hard. "I'm glad you're not hurt." He wondered if her confused expression meant she was considering smacking him for his effrontery. Not giving her time to decide, he said, "I hear David and Janie coming. Can you get up?" Without waiting for an answer, he helped her to her feet.

The reverend and Janie walked up, the reverend leading Old Jack. "He didn't go far," David remarked, apology in his voice.

"Let's get her back to the house," Dan said. He made sure April could stand on her own, then took the reins from David. He grabbed Old Jack's mane and swung up on the horse. "Hand her up," he instructed.

David lifted her up, and Dan took her across his lap, settling her to lean back against him, one arm around her shoulder. With April securely in front of him, Dan gently gigged the horse. "We'll meet you two back at the house," he said to Janie and David.

Other than being dusty and grass-stained, she appeared to be fine. He'd been glad for the chance to hold her in front of him as they rode toward the house. But the way she'd straightened and held herself away from him told him she hadn't forgotten the angry words that had passed between them. A hug and a quick kiss weren't going to make her change her mind about marrying him.

He reined Old Jack to a halt by the dog-trot and lowered April to the ground as Janie and David came up. Mary appeared, and hearing Janie's explanation of the fall, hustled the two young women inside to get cleaned up. Dan watched April disappear. After the weeks alone, and then holding her in his arms, he knew he couldn't live without her any longer.

Now all he had to do was convince her. He grinned. She might be a stubborn woman, but he'd been called stubborn a time or two himself.

~ * ~

April lay on the bed, a cool cloth over her eyes, under Mary's orders to rest a bit while Janie helped with the final preparations for the noon meal. While lying down eased her slight headache, the inactivity gave April entirely too much time to think. She'd felt so warm and secure in Dan's embrace. The temptation to stay there had been difficult to resist. Her life would be easier if the physical attraction between them had diminished while they were apart.

She sighed with the realization that the attraction was as strong as ever. She could no more ignore him than she could ignore the sun or the wind or the rain. He was just as forceful, just as elemental

She shifted position, turning her mind to the perplexity of Dan's reaction when she told him she wasn't expecting a child. She'd been so unsettled from the fall, she wasn't sure she'd gauged his reaction correctly.

"Dinner's ready." Mary's call echoed up the stairs.

April sat up. She felt fine. Only a few minor aches remained. In any case, she thought as she made her way downstairs, she'd told Dan there was no tie between them. He could walk away with a clear conscience. She had her business; he had his farm. Both of them were free to do whatever they wanted.

So why, then, did she feel delighted at the thought of spending the rest of the day in Dan's company? She hurried downstairs.

~ * ~

The afternoon sun shone brightly and the streets were filled with people. Store fronts draped with red, white, and blue bunting provided a colorful background for the people thronging the streets. In and around the more sedate adult groups, flocks of small children circled, laughing and shouting.

Within minutes the two older Murray boys had joined several of their friends. Scotty and Mary, Alexander holding her hand, were walking in front of the group. April walked next to Janie. Although April chatted with Janie, her attention wanted to focus on Dan and David who walked behind them.

"Look who's coming," Scotty called over his shoulder. A group of people, centered on a well-dressed blond man, strolled toward them. April recognized the man as the lawyer, Wyckford, remembering him from the dance in Pittsburgh. She also recognized the catty Mrs. Miller and her daughter.

The two groups came together. Scotty introduced Reverend David Carroll to Wyckford.

"Glad to have you with us, Reverend." George Wyckford shook the reverend's hand.

"It's thanks to Mr. McKenzie and Mrs. Williamson I'm here at all." David gestured toward Dan and April.

"Ah, yes. I've met Mrs. Williamson." Wyckford turned toward April. "My dear," he said with great solicitation and took her hand. "I've heard all about your terrible journey."

As graciously as she could, she withdrew her hand from Wyckford's. "Really, Mr. Wyckford, the trip wasn't all that difficult. After all, here I am, safe and sound."

"But your flatboats were attacked by Indians. That must have been horrifying," Wyckford continued.

"It was disgraceful, that's what it was," supplied Mrs. Miller. She looked toward the lawyer, then back toward April. "Really, dear girl, perhaps you should have waited and traveled with Mr.

Wyckford." She cast another admiring glance in the lawyer's direction. "It surely would have been safer."

"Why would it have been safer?" Dan's question caused a chill of apprehension to crawl up April's back. His voice sounded neutral, but April heard the effort Dan took to sound that way.

"Well... ah..." Mrs. Miller stammered.

"But, Mama," her daughter answered, "didn't you say 'how safe can you be from Indians when you're traveling with an Indian?'"

April gasped. Beside her, Dan stiffened at the verbal slap. Wyckford smoothly broke the tension. "I've heard you studied in England, Reverend Carroll. Where did you study?"

Not bothering to listen to the polite exchange, April studied Dan out of the corner of her eye. He stood tall and straight, as though the insult had never happened. She clasped her hands together, battling the urge to snatch Mrs. Miller and her odious daughter bald-headed.

After a few more polite exchanges, the groups went their separate ways, much to April's relief. Without seeming to, she listened to Dan and the reverend as they walked behind her.

"He's very smooth," David said, "Wyckford, I mean."

"Smooth?" Dan growled.

"Like glass. I was watching him, and he almost laughed out loud when the Millers insulted you. And he jumped in with a question to me before anyone had a chance to refute what she said."

The rest of the conversation drifted out of April's hearing. As if in response to some unseen signal, the crowd began to converge near the platform erected for the speeches. While the mayor appropriated Reverend Carroll for a seat of honor on the platform, Mary spotted the twins and called them over.

"But, Ma," Matt protested. "We don't want to listen to any speeches."

"Yeah," Mark chimed in. "The mayor will say the same thing he says every time he makes a speech. 'We, here, in Oak Point, are bringing civilization to the wilderness.'" Mark's adolescent tenor parodied the mayor's heavy bass and bombastic style.

"Be that as it may—" Mary started, but Dan interrupted her.

"Why don't I have the boys go back to the house and get my rifle. They can meet us out in the north meadow in an hour or so, once the speech is over."

April watched the boys turn pleading eyes to their mother. With a sigh and a smile, Mary gave in. "Oh, all right, but—" she got no further.

The boys whooped "Thanks, Ma," and tossed a "Thanks, Uncle Dan" over their shoulders as they darted through the crowd, heading toward the McKenzie and Murray store.

What seemed like a long time later, the mayor's oration drew to a close. A hearty round of applause welcomed its end. The crowd once again broke into milling groups and drifted toward the meadow north of town for the annual shooting match. Dan and Scotty walked on ahead, taking Alexander with them. Janie excused herself to visit with old Grandma Anderson, so Mary and April walked on alone.

Mary hurried April to a quicker pace. "I know a good place to stand." A few minutes later, they stood on a small rise in the shade of an oak tree. About fifty yards from the edge of the meadow stood the targets. April studied the line of four-foot sections of upright logs, each bearing a paper target tacked to its side. The rectangular targets bore a deep triangular notch from the two top corners to the middle of target. Mary explained the goal was to shoot as close to the apex of the 'v' in the paper as possible.

Dan joined them just as the twins raced up carrying his rifle, powder horn and bullet pouch. "Thanks, boys," he said, as he swung the straps of the powder horn and bullet pouch over his shoulder. He tucked the rifle under his arm and went to join the men on the shooting line.

Chapter Nineteen

Ten men stood on the shooting line in the harsh afternoon sun, but April only had eyes for one. Dan stood relaxed, yet ready, his lean hips at an angle, his weight on one leg. The rifle butt rested on the ground in front of him. As the judge called out the rules, Dan lifted his broad-brimmed hat from his head and wiped his forehead with his sleeve.

"Three shots," called the judge. "Fire."

In a ragged sequence, the men raised their rifles to their shoulders, aimed and fired. April jumped at the rolling thunder of the volley. Before the echo died away, Dan had the next charge of powder down the barrel. With growing excitement, she watched him reload. His smooth, steady movements belied their speed as he rammed the ball down, removed and threaded the ramrod home. The breeze had barely dissipated the smoke of the first volley before Dan shouldered the rifle again.

This time the crack of individual shots stood out above the noise of the crowd as they shouted encouragements. The acrid stink of gun smoke hung heavy in the air. Dan reloaded once more, his movements ones of controlled power. The rifle spoke again, succeeded by other shots, now well-spaced.

The echoes died away. The sluggish breeze rolled the smoke from the meadow, the sharp smell of gunsmoke stronger now. The crowd quieted as the judge walked out toward the targets. He stopped by the first, "Jackson," he called out, "one cut paper in the notch, two in the wood!" The crowd cheered.

He walked to the next target and examined it. "Jenkins, all in the wood!" Catcalls mixed with the cheers as Jenkins looked chagrined.

The next target was Dan's. April held her breath as the judge examined his target. "McKenzie, two cut paper in the notch, one in the wood!" She cheered with the rest of the crowd.

Two of the remaining marksmen scored the same as Dan.

"Second round!" the judge called. Two other men moved out into the meadow, removing old targets and tacking new paper to the upright logs. The buzz of the crowd increased as the new targets were set.

Dan and the two others leisurely repositioned themselves to stand before the center three targets.

"Three shots, fire when ready!"

The three reports rang out simultaneously. The crowd cheered louder than before. "Come on, Jack!" someone yelled. "Give 'em hell, Dan!" someone else roared in reply.

The second volley was almost as close together as the first. Once again, she watched Dan, his muscles clearly delineated as his shirt clung to his body. Dark, damp patches showed between his shoulder blades and at the small of his back. The third and last shots cracked across the meadow.

The echoes and the cheering died away together. The judge strolled toward to the targets, and April clutched her hands together. "Rogers, two cut paper, one in the wood!" The crowd murmured.

"Arneal, two cut paper, one in the wood!"

The crowd shifted, and the murmurs increased as the judge walked to the last target. He bent to examine the target. When he straightened, it seemed to April he was smiling. Beside her, Mary held her breath. "McKenzie, two cut paper, the third's smack-dab in the middle, cut paper on both sides of the notch!"

Scotty gave out a whoop, followed by the rest of the crowd. Mary let out her breath and shook her head. April gulped air into her starved lungs.

Well-wishers crowded around Dan, slapping him on the back, shaking his hand. As the milling crowd began drifting toward town, April, with a sense of wariness, watched Dan and Reverend Carroll, come toward Mary and her. Although Dan had treated her in a circumspect manner since this morning, she sensed an underlying sense of purpose in him. A chill of excitement scampered up her back.

"That was excellent shooting. I'm impressed," the reverend said to Dan as they approached.

"Thanks." Dan smiled and accepted a congratulatory hug from Mary. Muttering something about finding Scotty, Mary left. Dan turned toward April. The gunpowder smudging the right side of his face served to accent the tiny lines at the corner of his eye and made his smile a white flash against his dusty-bronze skin. He wiped his sleeve across his face once more leaving a streak on his cheek.

"Congratulations, Dan," Janie said as she joined the group.

"We're just lucky they don't let you compete, Janie."

She shook her head. "I'm not good enough to cut paper three out of three times."

"You shoot, Miss Ferguson?" David asked, looking puzzled.

A blush crept up Janie's face.

"Sure does," Dan answered. "She's good, too."

Janie didn't answer, but looked down at her hands, clasping them together in obvious embarrassment.

Wishing to come to her friend's rescue, April said, "I wasn't much help when the flat boats were attacked, I couldn't even help reload."

"Yes," David said slowly. "I see frontier women must possess a variety of skills." David's gaze rested on Janie's tousled brown curls, while she continued to look at her hands. April resisted the urge to give her a nudge, to make her look at the reverend.

"Perhaps," the reverend continued, "I should consider taking shooting lessons."

Hesitantly Janie raised her head. "Maybe you could get Dan to teach you," she suggested.

David turned to Dan. "You give lessons?"

Dan gave a quick glance toward April. Now it was her turn to blush.

"I gave lessons once," Dan answered, his blue-gray eyes flicking back to April.

David glanced from Dan, to her, and back to Dan. To her consternation, David said, "I see," as if he really might. "And how did they turn out?"

Dan shrugged. "Don't know. Got interrupted."

"Interrupted?" Janie asked, her nose crinkling as she tried to make sense of the men's remarks.

"Never mind," April said. To her relief, she saw Mary heading their way. Right behind her was the mayor, coming to claim the reverend. A minute later, just as the rest of the groups started walking back toward town, the twins came rushing up. Matt held his hat upside down in both hands.

"Here ya are, Uncle Dan." Matt shoved the hat at Dan.

Mark grinned at her puzzled expression and explained. "It's Uncle Dan's prize. The winner gets to keep the lead from all the shots fired. We—" he gestured to his brother and himself, "dug 'em out of the targets for him."

"Congratulations again," she said.

"We think you're the best shot anywhere," the twins added over their shoulders as they raced off toward town, leaving her and Dan suddenly alone.

Dan continued to look at her, his blue-gray eyes seeming to look past her words for more meaning. Her heart beat faster. When he spoke again, she wondered if he'd really meant to speak aloud. "What do you think of me, I wonder."

For a long moment she did nothing. Then carefully, she reached up and gently brushed at the smudge on his face. "I think you have dirt on your cheek." His skin felt warm and alive under her fingertips and a tight knot in her chest made it hard to breathe. She withdrew her hand, turned, and hurried to catch up with the twins.

~ * ~

A gentle breeze moved the warm night air. Music combined with conversation and laughter. The scents of smoky pine torches, the occasional sharp bouquet of whiskey overpowered the mellower one of cider that drifted on the heavy night air. Lighter, and more distant, came the sweet Kentucky-green scent of the surrounding meadows and woods.

Like most of the men, Dan had removed his jacket and hat in deference to the warm evening. Dressed now in his linen shirt, buckskin breeches, and top boots, he lounged back against the side of the tinsmith's shop. One knee drawn up, his booted foot rested against the building. Before him in the large open area, created by the converging streets, a number of people danced. People milled about at the fringes of the dance area. Others sat on chairs brought from home. Dressed in their best bib and tucker, the people of Oak Point celebrated Independence Day.

His eyes followed April while she danced with Alexander in a set that included Scotty and Mary. He'd partnered her twice tonight. Both times when he'd asked, she'd agreed, though he'd be happier if she'd been a little more enthusiastic in her acceptance.

He sighed because he was going to ask her to dance again in a minute or so. Oak Point's frontier heritage was such that when he did, everybody would know he was 'courting.' A man only danced twice with a woman, unless he wanted to publicly declare himself interested in her. And a woman only accepted the third dance if she was willing to be thought of as his girl.

With another sigh, he peeled himself from the wall, and started toward her.

~ * ~

The music ended and April took Alexander's small, warm hand in hers and followed Mary and Scotty to the edge of the dance area.

As Scotty and Alexander left to get refreshments, a lady on the next bench leaned over to speak to Mary. Glad for a moment alone, April scanned the crowd. Her glance moved back out over the crowd. In spite of the flickering torchlight and beginning shadows, her gaze found the tall, trim figure of Dan McKenzie with ease. Headed in her direction, he was intercepted by a worried-looking, heavyset, middle-aged man holding a piece of paper in his hand.

She watched as the man gestured and spoke to Dan. A frown appeared on Dan's face. One hand raked through his inky hair as he shook his head. The heavyset man looked familiar. Where had she seen him? A few seconds reflection brought back the memory. He'd been sitting on the platform while the mayor made his speech.

She turned to ask Mary who the heavyset man was, but she was deep in conversation. April glanced back to see Dan trying to soothe the agitated man. With a few more words, the man heaved a deep sigh and nodded. He and Dan parted company. The heavyset man hurried off to show the paper to the group of men around the whiskey barrel, while Dan continued slowly in her direction.

Mary turned back as Scotty and Alexander arrived with the cider an instant before a worried-looking Dan.

"What did Harris want with ye?" Scotty questioned as he handed the cider to Mary.

"The militia commander?" Mary asked. "I didn't know he was here at the dance."

A shiver of apprehension slithered down April's back. Dan's eyes swept over her, but she could sense his mind was still with whatever Harris had said.

"This afternoon Harris got a letter from General Wayne reprimanding him. Seems orders went out from Army Headquarters in Philadelphia weeks ago. Orders for the Kentucky militia to reinforce Wayne when he moves on the Indians this summer. Harris was supposed to have sent an acknowledgment to Wayne, but he never received the orders."

Scotty muttered a curse under his breath.

"Yeah," Dan agreed. "In any case, now Harris has only a little over a week to get word to everyone. The militia is supposed to join up with General Wayne no later than the twentieth of this month." Dan glanced toward the whiskey barrel. The group of men had broken up, and now the news was spreading through the crowd. "General Scott, the head of the Kentucky militia, will be here soon to take charge. We'll be under his command when we move north into Ohio."

We. Dan had said 'we move north.' April's heart withered, shrank, and then sank into her stomach. She clutched her hands together in her lap.

"Do ye think ye'll be ready in time?"

"Harris is sending riders tonight to spread the word to the southern and eastern counties."

"Will you be one of them?" Mary asked, concern in her voice.

"No."

April's heart started beating again.

Dan explained, "I'm a civilian scout, serving directly for Wayne. But I'll accompany the militia, if I don't receive specific instructions otherwise. When General Scott comes, he may have orders for me."

"If Wayne has called up the militia," Scotty said, thinking aloud, "then he's verra sure there will be a major battle." He looked sharply at Dan. "Just as ye predicted, eh, Dan?"

Dan nodded absentmindedly as he looked over the crowd. The mayor stood in front of the musicians and made shushing motions with his hands. The crowd quieted.

"Guess you all heard the word by now," the mayor said. "The militia has been called up. But we got a whole week, so let's go ahead and finish celebrating the Fourth. Let's dance, everyone!" At the mayor's signal, the musicians struck up a tune. The mayor grabbed his wife, earning a cheer from the crowd.

As the dancing started again, April tried to read the expression on Dan's face. Knowing he would be leaving took the joy out of the evening. His expression serious, he looked at her for several long moments. She tried to smile, but it wasn't a successful effort.

"Will you walk with me?" he asked abruptly.

Instantly, the memory of his body pressing hers against the Quartermaster hut swept through her. She hesitated, not knowing whether to say no because of what might happen, or to say yes for the same reason.

"Please," he said. "I need to talk to you." He held out his hand. She found herself placing her hand in his and rising to her feet. Dan led her away from the dancing, past the livery stable and out toward a small adjacent meadow.

In silence, they walked along the split rail fence that zigzagged along the edge of the pasture land. Here the music was faint, but the warm, green scent of Kentucky summer strong. In the meadow, the winking lights of fireflies danced.

By unspoken mutual accord they stopped and turned toward each other. Swallowing to clear her throat, she asked, "What did you want to talk about?"

Dan drew a deep breath and with seeming deliberance, took a step closer, so that his boots brushed against her skirts. Her own sharp intake of breath brought his musky, masculine scent. She took a half-step back, her shoulders coming up against the top rail of the fence. He followed, moving even closer, his body only inches from hers. He placed his hands on the fence rail, his arms on either side of her shoulders, creating a prison from which she had no wish to escape.

"You didn't answer my question this afternoon." His voice was low and soft, his breath whispery against her cheek.

All her senses overloaded. The scent of him, the warmth emanating from him. Her body shivered deep within and she clutched her hands together to keep from reaching for him.

"What do you think of me?" his low voice rasped. Before she could form a coherent thought, he lowered his head and his lips found hers. His kiss was hot and soft as he moved his mouth gently over hers, igniting a fire within her. Only his lips touched her, but sweet, hot, flames circled through her breasts, her stomach, her thighs.

He broke the kiss and she gasped for breath. He began to plant tiny kisses over her face. At her temple, her eyelids, her cheek. She couldn't breathe, could hardly stand upright against his tender onslaught.

"Tell me," his dark voice entreated between kisses. The kisses trailed along her jawline and down her neck. Her breath became rapid.

"Tell me." His voice sounded ragged with desire. His kisses traveled across her collar bone, then down to the beginning swell of her breast.

"Tell me you love me," he murmured, his voice a velvet entreaty. "I want to marry you, April," he whispered. "You said you would only marry for love, so tell me you love me. Marry me."

Her eyes flew open. He'd said *want*. Her hands slid up his chest and wrapped around his neck, leaning her body into his.

"I love you," she said against his lips.

He groaned as his arms swept around her. This kiss was hungry, passionate. She eagerly accepted the invasion of his tongue. She heard a small moan of pleasure, startled to realize it came from her.

When they finally broke the kiss, he continued to hold her close. She rested her forehead against his cheek while his hand lightly ran up and down her back. Finally, after a gusty sigh, his hands moved to her shoulders. She kept her arms locked around his waist, but leaned back so she could look at him.

The light of the rising moon illuminated the lopsided grin on his face. "I take it that was a yes?" He sounded both happy and smug.

"Couldn't you tell?" Her feet definitely not on the ground, she felt so light-hearted she could fly.

"Just wanted to make sure."

"You want me to kiss you like that again?" She tried to look innocent while she wiggled her hips against his.

"God, yes," he groaned, but his hands stilled her hips. "But not until after we're married." Holding her at arm's length, his smile faded. "I'm sorry, April, honey, but I want to get married right away. Now, tonight. I was going to court you, do it proper, but I can't wait, I have to report back—"

She put her hand to his lips, stopping his explanation. "It's all right." She lifted her fingers, and he started to speak again. "No," she said, putting her fingers back to his lips. This time he brought his hand up and covered hers, pressing a kiss into her palm.

"Let's go find the reverend, then," he said.

~ * ~

Half an hour later all the participants streamed into the Murray kitchen. Moments before, everyone had talked and laughed as they made their way home from the dance—Scotty teasing Dan, Mary, and Janie conferring with her about household furnishing. But when they entered the darkened kitchen, conversation dwindled away. Mary hurried to light several candles, and the room took on a warm, yellow glow.

"Are we ready?" David Carroll asked.

April suddenly felt too shy to speak, so she only nodded. Surely everyone could hear her heart thudding.

"We're ready," Dan said.

The reverend positioned himself in front of the corner fireplace. Dan slipped on his coat before he took her by the elbow to lead her the few paces to stand before the reverend. She heard the shuffle of footsteps, and knew Janie, Mary, Scotty, and the boys grouped around behind them. She felt grateful for their presence. They had treated her like family, and now she was about to become a part of the McKenzie-Murray clan.

All further reflection fled as the reverend said, "Please join hands." When Dan took her hand in his, the whole world narrowed down to the two of them. His hand was warm, sturdy, and solid, like the man. As if through a heavy mist, she heard the words Reverend Carroll spoke; heard her own low, steady answer, at odds with the quivery way she felt; heard the confidence and conviction in Dan's voice. She was acutely aware of her hand in his. Their linked hands formed a physical symbol of the mystical bond that now irrevocably linked her—her life, her body and her soul with Dan McKenzie.

The ceremony ended. She looked up at the man standing beside her. Her husband.

"Ye two can spend the rest of the night standing around looking at each other," Scotty interrupted as he stepped forward to shake Dan's hand, "if ye canna think of anything else to do."

"James!" Mary admonished. She came forward to embrace first April and then Dan. The babble of voices filled the room as everyone hugged and laughed.

Mary and Janie escorted April upstairs to help her pack. Scotty brought out the whiskey and the three men toasted the marriage.

"Well," David said, putting his cup on the table. "I'll escort the boys back to the dance. Maybe no one will notice we were gone. I take it you want to keep this somewhat of a secret?" He looked at Dan.

Dan gave a lopsided grin. "You're right. I'll take April out to my place tonight. You could say I'm right anxious to avoid a chivaree."

As David herded the boys back toward the dance, Scotty poured another drink for Dan and himself. After a sip, Scotty cleared his throat. "I know it's none of my business, but have ye told the lassie about Blue Licks?"

Dan's contentment wavered. "No." He knew he should have, but he pushed aside the thought. "I'll tell her one day," he rationalized, "but now's not the time. Not when I have to leave so soon." He shrugged and continued, "I'll tell her someday. When there's more time."

A burst of giggles caused Dan to look toward the stairs.

"How long can it take to pack one bag?" he grumbled.

"Ye sure ye want to ride out to your place tonight? Ye could stay here, ye know."

Dan shook his head, smiling. "No, thanks. All she needs to take is a change of clothes." He took a sip of the whiskey in his cup. "You can hitch up the wagon and bring enough of her things for the next few days, like we said."

"Aye. I'll be there bright and early."

"Right. Bright and early, about noon."

Scotty's smiled broadened. "Bright and early, about noon," he agreed.

~ * ~

April gave a sigh of relief as Old Jack plodded to a halt in front of Dan's cabin. The rush of excitement which had buoyed her since Dan's proposal had drained away about half an hour ago. Her body reminded her that it was unaccustomed to horseback riding for any length of time. And the myriad of small aches and pains reminded her she had fallen off this very horse only this morning.

Dan dismounted from High Stakes, and came around. In spite of her intentions, a small sigh, more like a groan, escaped as he lifted her down.

"You all right?" he asked, his hands lingering on her waist.

"Yes, just a little stiff. Guess I haven't had enough riding lessons yet."

Dan swore under his breath. "I'm sorry, April. Maybe we should have stayed in town."

"No, I'm fine, really." But she gave herself away the next instant with a wince of pain as she started to walk toward the house.

He swept her up in his arms, ignoring her gasp of surprise. Her arms went around his neck, and cradling her against his chest, carried her to the cabin. At the door, he said, "Hang on." Without putting her down, he pulled the latch string, then used his booted foot to push the door open. With his bride in his arms, he entered the darkened cabin.

Chapter Twenty

Dan's first thought was to put April down on the quilt-covered pile of furs in the corner, but it seemed too presumptuous. A few steps took him to the pine table, and stopping there, he lowered her feet to the floor, the rustle of her skirt and petticoats loud in the silent house. Just having her in his arms made his hands itch for what was under that dress and all those petticoats. Patience, he thought, as he lit the candle on the table.

"I'll go get your bag and then take care of the horses."

He retrieved her bag from Old Jack's back. When he reentered the cabin, April still stood by the table where he'd left her. "Make yourself at home," he said, feeling like an idiot. He escaped again to put up the horses.

When he returned, the warm candlelight glowed through the open door—a welcome signal someone waited for him. Not just someone, but his wife. He walked a little faster. Stepping through the door, he placed his rifle on its pegs, along with the powder horn and bullet pouch. His hat followed, his movements habit. When he turned from his task, there she stood, the light of the single candle making her look small and fragile. Behind her, he noticed she'd hung her other dress and some underthings on the pegs next to his shirts and leggings. The sight pleased him.

Without thinking, he held out his arms, and she came to him. For a long minute, they simply stood, embracing each other. He marveled at how the angles and planes of their bodies fit together, pieces of an age-old puzzle.

What started as a kiss of tenderness quickly became one of passion. He pulled her hips and belly against his own and held her there.

April's arms went around his neck. She rocked her hips against his, drawing a groan of pleasure and need from him. Dan's hands moved to the back of her dress to fumble with the buttons. She gave a low moan of anticipation, her breasts aching to be free of confinement. After a few seconds, however, he broke the kiss, and with a mumbled curse, spun her around to attack the buttons. His warm, gusty breath caressed the back of her neck as he unfastened her dress.

Finally, he finished. "There," he said.

She took a step forward and turned to face him. In the soft light, his eyes were dark with passion and his chest rose and fell with his ragged breathing. Her heart trembling at her boldness, she let the bodice of the dress fall forward, afraid to watch him as she pulled the bodice down and drew her arms free of the sleeves. Loosening the skirt, she pushed the dress down to the floor and stepped out. Swallowing her nervousness, she glanced up. The look of hunger on his face made an adequate reward for her boldness.

Without a word, he pulled his shirt tail from his waistband and, in one smooth motion, stripped the shirt off over his head and tossed it away.

Returning the compliment his gaze had paid her, she allowed herself to study him. The warm candlelight alternately flowed and flickered over the muscles and sinews of his chest and shoulders. The beaded medallion hung in the center of his chest. The tattoo and the scar on his left side were merely shadows in the candlelight.

She reached to the back of her waist to undo the tapes of her petticoats. At his sharp intake of breath she glanced down. Her actions had pulled her chemise tight across her bosom, her peaked nipples clearly visible. Enjoying the anticipation, she loosened one petticoat, pushed it down, and stepped out. She did the same with the second. She found herself smiling as she added the petticoats to the shirt and the dress.

Wood scraped on wood as Dan pulled out a chair, sat down and pulled off one boot. As the boot clumped to the floor, she stooped and untied the laces of her slippers. His other boot followed as she peeled off her stockings.

Straightening, she stood clad only in her chemise. The warm night air gently moved over her bare arms and legs. She looked at him, and as if he'd been waiting until she watched, he slowly stood upright. The buckskin breeches clung to him like a second skin. He might as well have been naked.

Her heart pounded at the visible effect she had on him. Swept up in the recklessness, she reached for the ribbon at the neck of her chemise, but he shook his head.

"Your hair," he rasped, "take it down."

Obeying his command, she raised her hands to her head, aware of his hot gaze on her legs as the hem of her chemise rode up to mid-thigh. She slowly removed all the pins, allowing her braids to fall free. He took a step forward and held out his hand. She gave him the pins and, without taking his gaze from her, he put them on the table. She undid the braids, the ribbons braided in them falling to the floor. She ran her fingers though her hair, shaking her head. He groaned her name and pulled her into his arms.

Her aching breasts flattened against his chest. She arched against him wanting to feel all of him. His back felt warm and damp under her hands. He tangled his hand in her hair and tugging gently, he pulled her head back. His hot kisses traveled down the exposed line of her throat to her breast. He took her nipple in his mouth, sucking it through the material of the chemise. At the exquisite sensation she moaned and writhed against him. His hot mouth moved to the other nipple, giving it the same attention. His calloused hand moved over her buttocks, pulling her to him. He was hard, hard against her belly as his hips moved rhythmically against hers.

The tingles shooting through her body grew warmer and warmer. Her knees buckled, and she would have collapsed had he not held her. Her hands clutched his upper arms, her fingers digging into his muscles, as he continued to suck and nip at her breasts. "Please, Dan," she sobbed.

In response to her plea, Dan's body shuddered. He pulled her away from him and stripped her chemise from her. An instant later he peeled out of his breeches before carrying her down to the quilt-covered pile of firs.

He made her feel on fire, and she wanted him, too, to feel the flames. She put her arms around his neck and when he thrust his tongue into her mouth, she sucked rhythmically. With an agonized groan, he rolled over her. His wonderful weight pressed her into the bedding as he entered her. Then, staking his hands beside her shoulders, he thrust within her, each movement hard and deep.

She drowned in the raw passion. Each thrust pushed her closer and closer to the edge. With a keening cry, she wrapped her arms and legs around him, as his driving body took her over the edge and into the abyss. Through the roaring which filled her ears, she heard him cry out. His body shuddered, and collapsed upon her.

After a moment, he slid off to one side, and pulled her against him. Beneath her cheek, she felt his breathing slow as did hers. Exhausted and utterly content, she drifted into sweet sleep.

~ * ~

Breakfast was over and Dan lingered over a third cup of coffee, watching her do the dishes, when she heard a wagon coming up the road.

"Hello, the house!" Scotty called out, even though he saw them standing in the doorway.

"Hello, yourself," Dan replied. Scotty pulled the wagon into the yard. Seated next to him was Mary, with the three boys amid several baskets and boxes of supplies in the back.

Smiling at the assemblage, April asked, "Who's minding the store?"

Scotty laughed. "Janie. Her dad's still 'resting up' from the Fourth of July in the back storeroom." Scotty climbed down from the wagon, and Mary slid across the seat. He turned to help her down as the boys tumbled out the back.

"Just a few things to tide you over for the next day or so." Mary hugged April as the boys carried in the boxes.

The 'few things' included a ham, half a cheese, a basket of eggs nestled in straw, a peck basket of potatoes, carrots and onions, some fresh string beans and early ears of corn from the garden, as well as salt, sugar, cornmeal, and flour. The last box contained three loaves of bread, a small crock of butter and an apple pie.

April's throat ached in happiness, the sight of the ladened table a statement of Mary's welcome of April into the family.

After a noon meal of stew, also supplied by Mary, Scotty rounded up the boys, and the Murrays started back to town. April traded one last wave with Alexander as the wagon disappeared around the bend in the road. "That was nice of them."

Standing beside her, Dan put his arm around her waist, snuggling her against him. She gave a sigh of contentment. "It was nice of them to go, too," he said, bending down and kissing her cheek. Her heart began to beat faster. "Come on." He suddenly released her waist and grabbed her hand. "Let me show you around."

He showed her the barn, corral, the spring. "This fall, Scotty and I can dig it out, build a spring house over it," Dan said.

"Come on," he said taking her hand. He led them northwest. The path went uphill, following the ridge. He continued to hold her hand as they passed though stands of ash, beech, oak, and hickory, the shade cool and green. The path narrowed and April fell back to walk behind Dan. By the time she reached the top of the ridge, she was breathing hard.

Dan led her out of the sheltering woods and on to the top of a huge boulder that sat flush into the brow of the ridge. Standing directly behind her, he drew her into the circle of his arms, snuggling her back against him. "What do you think," he asked softly, gesturing to the view.

Kentucky, green in the full splendor of summer, lay spread before them. Hundreds of shades of green—leaves, grasses, bushes. To the right, ridge after dark-green ridge marched toward the horizon. Somewhere beyond the line of ridges lay the Ohio river. Off to the left, the same march of ridges lay washed with gold by the late afternoon sun.

"It's beautiful," she whispered, leaning back against his solid chest, "just beautiful." The beginnings of an evening breeze stirred her skirts.

"Look there," he gestured, "you can see our place." Our place. His words made her heart warm. Down through the trees, she saw the dusty brown ribbon of road, the cabin and the barn, the meadow enclosed by the split rail fence.

She took a deep breath and let it out, letting the moment imprint itself in her memory—the land at her feet, her husband's arms and love surrounding her. Kentucky land that belonged to them. And they would belong to the land, she thought. Here, she and Dan would live, see their hopes and dreams fulfilled, raise a family. A deep, abiding contentment filled her soul. Dan must have felt the same, for he held her, unmoving, for several minutes. Finally, he gave a gusty sigh, and let her go.

"Let's go home." He took her hand once more, and started down the trail.

~ * ~

George Wyckford cast a hurried glance around his office. Everything appeared neat and tidy, reassuring, for his departure. Since the fourth of July when Wayne's messenger arrived, he had experienced a growing uneasiness.

For the past several days, he'd gathered information. He commiserated with the local militia leader about the difficulty of getting everyone called up in so short a time. He bought drinks for the militia men themselves and gained a good idea how many men would be reinforcing the Legion.

He clenched his fist in anger and frustration. In spite of the late notice, the Kentucky militia would number over one thousand men. He'd leave now to warn Captain Campbell at Fort Miamis.

Wyckford strode toward the stable. His chestnut gelding stood saddled and ready, the reins held by a skinny, unshaven man. Dipping his fingers in his vest pocket, he withdrew a coin and flipped it toward the man. Wyckford smiled. Anything for money, that's all scum like this was good for, he thought. Their greed and no inclination to ask questions were their only virtues.

~ * ~

Reverend David Carroll rounded the corner of the inn just as Wyckford spurred away from the stable. Watching the skinny fellow slink back into the stable, he shook his head in amazement. Why an elegant gentlemen like Wyckford employed rather disreputable men was a topic of discussion in Oak Point.

Still looking at the stable doorway where Wyckford's man had disappeared, David rubbed the back of his head. Why did Wyckford employ such men? He chided himself for the uncharitable suspicion that it was not out of the goodness of Wyckford's heart. Perhaps his suspicions stemmed from the resemblance Wyckford's men bore to the brigands who had attacked him. Once more he found himself rubbing the back of his head where the blow had landed.

He turned to look down the street, but Wyckford and the chestnut gelding were already a blur. David thought about his fine-looking horse. The animal reminded him of Dan's bay mare. Not too surprising, though, as Wyckford had owned both of them. The animals definitely reminded him of Baxter horses, as he'd told Dan. Now that he thought of it, Wyckford himself had the blond, well-bred look with the aquiline nose and aristocratic profile of a Baxter.

But that was absurd. Surely all the Charleston Baxters had returned to England years before. David rubbed the back of his head again, deep in thought. Perhaps the next time he wrote to his sister in Charleston, he would ask about the Baxters.

~ * ~

April sat beside Dan as he drove the team back to town. Scotty had brought the wagon out yesterday evening with the information that the militia would leave this morning.

Occasional bird calls or chatter of squirrels punctuated the clop of the horses' hooves and the creak and rattle of the wagon. The new day already warm, April ran her hand over her forehead and gave a sideways glance at Dan. His features, in the shade of his broad brimmed hat, looked calm.

She supposed she looked calm, too. But in her stomach, the small gnawing feeling grew. The closer they got to Oak Point, the closer they were to Dan's leaving.

The last few days had been better than anything she'd ever imagined with just the two of them together. Dan gave her more riding lessons on Old Jack, more shooting lessons with the rifle. They laughed, talked, made love.

"Trouble is," Dan had said, "I don't know how long I'll be gone." He lay on his back in the middle of the quilt, a sheet pulled across his hips. With one hand behind his head, he wrapped the other around her shoulder as she snuggled against his side.

"Will you be back by Christmas?" she asked. Her head rested on his shoulder, while her fingers idly traced the thong and beaded medallion. She liked the unexpected intimacy of conversation with a naked man.

Dan sighed. "We'll just plan on spending this winter with Scotty and Mary. They have room, and Mary will be glad for the company. You can continue your sewing that way, too." He removed his hand from behind his head, and placed it over her hand where it lay on his bare chest. "Maybe we can move back out here next spring. That will give me enough time to get this place fixed up."

"Fixed up?" She frowned. "What's wrong with it?"

He shifted, as if uncomfortable. "There's the spring house to build, a well to dig so you won't have to carry water. I want to add on to the cabin as well as to the barn." He shifted, half-rolling toward her. "Are you sure you want to live out here? It's civilized in Oak Point. We could live there."

Live in Oak Point? How could he raise horses if they lived in town? Then suddenly, she understood. He loved her, had married her, but he still wasn't sure she could survive out here. In time she would show him she could survive and even thrive on life in Kentucky. But for now she would take comfort in his concern.

"Everything here is fine, Dan," she said, and pushed him so he once more lay flat on the bed.

"But—" he started, but she interrupted him, coming up on one elbow so she looked down at him.

"Someday I expect to have a spring house, and all the other things you mentioned. For now, I have the one thing I can't live without. I have you."

She leaned over and kissed him, her hair falling around them. He'd opened his lips to deepen the kiss, and she'd thrust her tongue into his mouth. She'd felt his jolt of surprise, and then his groan of delight as his hand had come up to hold the back of her head.

The screeching of a jay as they passed under his tree jerked April from the delicious memory. She felt the heat in her cheeks and glanced over to see Dan grinning at her.

"It's good just remembering, too, isn't it," he asked with a teasing laugh. She felt her flush deepen and he laughed again. "Tell me." He dropped his voice to a conspiratorial whisper, "which time were you remembering?"

"Dan!" she gasped, shocked but somehow pleased. "You just shush," she admonished. Ahead, the outskirts of Oak Point appeared. "We're practically in town. It's bad enough everyone will know what we've been doing without you making me blush."

He laughed again. "April-honey, with the militia leaving, every married couple in Oak Point did the same last night."

"We shouldn't be talking about this," she said, her voice faint, hoping he would drop the subject.

He grinned and shrugged, "Don't see why it's all right to do it, but not to talk about it. Seems foolish somehow."

"Foolish or not, we will not discuss it anymore right now," April replied, trying to sound stern. She sat up straighter on the wagon seat, as they rolled into Oak Point.

At the Murrays', April let herself be swept up in the excitement and commotion of the large household. Anything to keep thoughts of the impending separation at bay while every passing second brought Dan's leaving closer.

Chapter Twenty-One

Behind the Murrays, April and Dan walked toward the center of town as the entire population of Oak Point gathered in the main square.

Each step she took increased the tightness in her chest. How would she live through the next hour? She clenched her jaw tighter to keep silent the plea her heart made. In time with each step, her soul cried, please don't leave me, please don't leave. But she wouldn't say the words.

As if they were something outside her body, outside her control, she watched her shoes as they walked beside Dan's moccasins. Walking together, carrying them apart. She remembered the way he had held her, had touched her last night. How he told her without words he loved her and didn't want to leave. The knowledge was all she had to cling to.

As they neared the center of town, the crowd thickened. A woman, clinging to her husband, bumped against her. To steady her, Dan took her hand. The calm composure of his expression camouflaged tight muscles in his hand and arm.

Dan and April came to a stop, part of the general crowd of people milling about in the square. Several women cried into their handkerchiefs. One clutched her husband, sobbing. She and Dan exchanged looks, and he gave her a small nod, as if thanking her for not making a spectacle.

She gave him a smile that belied the lump in her throat she simply couldn't swallow. The itchy, tingle behind her eyes warned of tears not far away. She longed to throw her arms around him and beg him to stay. She clenched her jaws so hard, the muscles ached.

Just at that moment, Harris, the local militia leader rode up, accompanied by Major General Scott. "Well, men," Harris shouted, "are we ready?"

The crowd raised a ragged cheer.

The major general surveyed the men. "Mount up!" came the order. Matt and Mark led up High Stakes and handed the reins to Dan.

"Thanks, boys," Dan said, shaking hands with each of them.

"Bye, Uncle Dan," they said, obviously proud to be treated like adults.

Dan turned and gave Mary a brief hug.

"Have care," she said.

"Always do." He reached down to ruffle Alexander's curly hair where he stood beside Mary. Dan and Scotty shook hands. The Murrays discreetly drifted away and Dan turned toward her.

She could read the love in those pale blue-gray eyes. Dan swallowed and opened his mouth as if to speak, but instead gave a deep sigh and a half shrug, as if words were beyond him, too. He nodded to her once more, and turned to mount.

She bit her bottom lip to hide the trembling.

Before he put his foot in the stirrup, Dan turned back. Without a word, he reached inside his shirt and withdrew the beaded medallion. He took off his hat, and pulled the thong off over his head. Holding the medallion in his long brown fingers, he gave it one last caress, before he placed the thong around her neck.

The medallion with its purple thistle hung low on her abdomen and she brought one hand up to encircle it, her heart thudding. She blinked rapidly to clear her vision.

Reaching out, he lightly ran the back of his knuckles over her cheek. "Remember me," he whispered. In the next second, he turned, mounted, and was gone.

The rest of the day seemed a week long. The lump in her throat wouldn't go away. The loneliness sat, already rock-like in the pit of her stomach. That night, in the Murrays' upstairs room, alone in Dan's bed, she surrendered to tears.

She clutched his medallion to her breast, gripping the memento so tight the beads made impressions in her palm. He'd said 'remember me,' in case he never came back. Please, God, she prayed, please take care of him. I love him. Please keep him safe.

During the days, she kept busy with her sewing, as well as sharing the household chores with Mary. She had helped before, but now sharing the work reinforced the sense of belonging, of being part of the McKenzie-Murray family. Even though Dan was gone, she was at home. She was grateful for the noise and energy of the Murray household as they helped to fill the days.

The month of August arrived. "You know," April said to Mary one morning as they did the breakfast dishes, "it doesn't seem fair. Even if he didn't want to go, Dan is off doing something exciting— taking his thoughts, his time and energy. He's someplace else, doing things that I've never been a part of." She struggled to make her thoughts clear.

Mary nodded. "Go on."

"He's missing from my life, but I'm not missing from his. Here I am, where he was a part of everything, and now he's missing from the table when we eat, missing from the store, from everything." Missing from my bed, she thought.

Mary gave a sigh, her hands still in the dish water. "I know what you mean. I miss James every year when he goes to Philadelphia." She turned to look at April. "But don't worry, once he's home, you look back and say to yourself that wasn't so bad. And feel proud you could handle him being gone."

"I guess you're right. I suppose I'm just selfish enough to hope he's as miserable without me as I am without him." While she spoke, April's hand absent-mindedly stroked her midriff, caressing the beaded medallion where it rested under her bodice, next to her skin.

"I'll be glad when this hot weather breaks," Mary said, drying her hands.

"I know what you mean. The heat's made me so tired. It's all I can do to stay awake in the afternoons. Too bad I'm too old to take a nap," she joked.

The dishes put away, April followed Mary out the kitchen door. The two women wandered to the north end of the dog-trot, enjoying the suggestion of a breeze.

"Look," Mary said, indicating the clouds building in the distance. "I bet we'll have a storm this afternoon or this evening. Then maybe the weather will break."

The women looked north, toward the Ohio territory, where the storm clouds gathered.

~ * ~

Late on an August afternoon, Dan lay silently in the dense undergrowth, the sweat running down his face while he watched and listened. The Indians had chosen the field of battle well—the blow-down of a tornado. The massive maze of fallen trees would be a wicked spot for a fight. Doubling the Indian advantage, the British fort on the Maumee river overlooked the meadow beyond the blow-down. British guns could bear on the open area, giving the Indians cover should the Americans force them to withdraw from the helter-skelter of the fallen timbers.

Having seen enough, Dan carefully slithered backward through the rank overgrowth. An hour later, he reported what he'd seen to Lieutenant William Henry Harrison, General Wayne's aide.

"I saw warriors from at least six different nations. Between fifteen hundred and two thousand men, almost double the number they've been able to assemble before. And it looks like Little Turtle's no longer the main war chief. Blue Jacket is in charge now."

The lieutenant gave Dan a hard look. "Blue Jacket? He's a Shawnee."

"That's right," Dan agreed, keeping his voice flat.

"You know him?"

"Know of him. Never met him."

"Stay close by, Mr. McKenzie, the general may wish to speak with you."

Dan watched the lieutenant walk toward Wayne's tent, its position marked by the general's personal flag. He wondered what Harrison had heard of Blue Jacket. What did the lieutenant think about the fact that the combined tribes had chosen as their war chief a man who had less Shawnee blood than Dan himself. When it came to a fight, the Indians always selected the best leader, regardless of his tribe or blood. Few people realized the tribes hated and distrusted each other as much as they did the whites. Only the threat of the white man's expansion held them together.

Harrison would report to Wayne how Dan had watched the warriors chanting and praying, purifying themselves by fasting before the battle. Wayne knew the Indians well, Dan thought. The longer Wayne stalled the attack, the better his chances.

For the next three days, Wayne made as if to attack. Three days during which the warriors waited in the dense timber, fasting and praying, preparing themselves to face their mortal enemy.

~ * ~

As the long, hot August days rolled over Oak Point, April felt willing to be uncharacteristically idle. The mornings she spent sewing and the afternoons helping Mary. April wondered about her sleepiness until one morning in the middle of August.

She had placed the knives and forks on the table for breakfast, when Mary slid a platter of hot cakes in front of her. The aroma assaulted her like a blow. Queasiness flooded up from her roiling stomach. The suddenness of the nausea was as unnerving as its severity. Covering her mouth with her hand, she stumbled out of the kitchen door, only vaguely hearing the questions following her. She made it to the edge of the dog-trot. But her empty stomach had nothing to give up.

In a few moments Mary was there. "Here, rinse your mouth out with this," she said as she handed April a cup of water. April took a tentative drink, unsure of her stomach, letting the water roll around her mouth. "Now spit," Mary instructed.

"I'm sorry," April apologized, embarrassed. She'd expected Mary to look concerned over the sudden illness, but a smile hovered about her sister-in-law's face. "I don't know what came over me."

"Don't you?" Mary half-laughed.

April felt her mouth fall open. Of course. She laid her hands over her stomach as she mentally counted back. Her hands flew to her face, covering the huge smile on her lips. "Oh, Mary. What will I tell Dan?"

"Well, we've always bragged about what a good shot he is." Mary smiled at April's blush and gave her a hug.

~ * ~

Dan stumbled to a halt, amazed. We made it. We're still alive. They had fought the Indians all the way through the fallen timbers. Breathing in labored gasps, he leaned on his rifle. Around him, other soldiers staggered to a stop, their breathing a chorus with his own. A sudden quiet seemed to surround the small knot of men. The sounds of battle continued in the near distance as the Indians began retreating across the meadow, calling for the fort to open fire.

Dan's breathing beginning to ease; he wiped the sweat from his face with his sleeve. Once he came out of the timbers and into the meadow before the British fort, the late morning sun shone hot and bright. He squinted as he looked around at the men who'd made it through the battle. Bent over his rifle, a veteran sergeant still gasped for breath, his gray-streaked hair was matted to his forehead. "Damn," he gasped, "we did it."

Next to the sergeant, a young private swayed and clutched his belly. "Oh my God," he groaned. He twisted around and fell to his knees, heaving up the contents of his stomach. The rest of the men ignored him.

That's the way they all felt, Dan thought, swallowing his own nausea. During the battle, the fear-excitement, terror-thrill kept everything at a distance. Afterwards came the sickness, the shakes, the remembered close calls. In his mind's eye he saw the swinging tomahawk. He'd ducked just in time, catching the blow on the flat of his shoulder, the stone ax leaving a throbbing ache instead of taking off his head.

The private finished retching. Cheer up, Dan thought, watching the boy struggle to his feet. The first time was always the worst. He knew when the private lay awake tonight, he'd see again all the men he'd faced in battle. But, unlike Dan, the private wouldn't have a nagging ache in his gut, dreading he'd recognize one of the faces.

A howl rising from hundreds of throats jerked Dan back to the present. On the far side of the meadow, warriors massed before the gates of the British fort. Even from his position at the edge of the timbers, he could see British officers watching from high on the walls of the fort. The howl became one of anguish, frustration, and anger. Not only were the British refusing to fire on the American army, they were refusing to open the gates.

Witnessing the betrayal, Dan cursed under his breath. He'd always said the British would never support the tribes when push came to shove. He prayed this defeat would be the one to convince the Indians to agree to a peace treaty. Let this be the end of the killing. One final war whoop swelled as the Indians broke apart, fleeing around the sides of Fort Miamis and escaping into the surrounding woods.

General Wayne and Lieutenant Harrison rode from the cover of the fallen timbers. They stopped and began to re-order the American army, now strung out all across the meadow. Intending to join the general, Dan tucked his rifle in the crook of his left arm, but his arm and shoulder refused to bear the weight. He bit back a groan-turned-curse. He gripped the weapon in his right hand and began to trot across the meadow, angling to meet Wayne before the gates of the fort.

~ * ~

From high on the palisade of Fort Miamis a man in civilian clothes tried to swallow the bitter taste in his mouth. He'd most likely watched the end of the British attempt to maintain the Ohio territory. His gaze caught on the tall frontiersman who joined the American general and his aide. A sudden jolt of recognition swept over Wyckford. His eyes narrowed. "McKenzie." He hissed the name like a curse. Somehow, someway, he vowed, he'd make the half-breed pay for his part in the British defeat.

~ * ~

"What?" Wayne's eyes never lifted from the massive amounts of paperwork before him.

Dan shifted his feet, both irritated and understanding about having to repeat himself. "I said, I'm going back to Kentucky for a few weeks."

"The hell you are." Wayne replied without heat, his eyes on his report. "I need you here."

Dan kept his voice calm. "The battle was more than a week ago. Nothing's happened since then, except you and that British Captain Campbell sending insulting notes back and forth. Neither the British nor the Indians have made a move. There's no scouting for me to do."

Wayne put down his pen and rested his folded hands on the campaign table. "Be that as it may, I still need you. You know and understand the Indians. I need you to talk for me."

"You have other men who can interpret. It'll be months before they finally decide to parley. Probably not until after the first good snowfall. They'll wait to see if the British will promise them any help. Then they'll wait to see if the British keep their promises, before they come to you."

Wayne grunted his acknowledgment. "That still doesn't explain why you're so all-fired impatient to go back to Kentucky."

"Remember that letter you wrote to Colonel Barker in Philadelphia? The one ordering me to escort a widow named Williamson?"

For a moment Wayne looked puzzled. "Oh yes, Williamson. But what's that got to do with anything?" A speculative look came into the general's eye, and he leaned back in his chair. "Was she some crotchety old crone who gave you a lot of trouble on the trip?"

"Oh, she was a lot of trouble. But she wasn't old and crotchety. In fact, she was young and good-looking. I married her on the fourth of July."

"The hell you say!" Wayne shouted, leaping from his chair.

Dan smiled. "Now you know why I'm going back to Kentucky. I'll give you one more week and then I'm leaving."

After a supper of tasteless beef stew and hard biscuits, Dan went to check High Stakes. She playfully bumped her head against his chest. "Be patient, girl. We'll be on our way home soon."

One day down, and only six to go, Dan thought as he lay on his bedroll looking at the stars. He reached into his makeshift pillow to remove the cross stitch sampler.

He'd been surprised when he'd found April's sampler the first night he'd unrolled his pack. Then, clearly as if he were living the day over again, he was in the Sinclair kitchen in Pittsburgh, her soft voice saying, "...slept with this sampler under my pillow... like a good luck charm to take me back to Kentucky."

His fingers traced over the stitches. He missed her. He was beginning to understand why the married men always talked about going home. Like most single men, he'd thought only in terms of sex. Oh, he'd missed that. He had only to think of her and his body was ready. But he found he missed other things as well.

He missed the sounds her skirts made as she moved around the cabin. Missed her bringing him a cup of coffee. The way she lightly touched his shoulder as she walked past his chair. How she brought him a drink of cool water in the middle of the afternoon while he split rails for more fencing.

He rolled over and carefully tucked the sampler into the bedroll. Six more days, then he could be on his way home. Home to April.

~ * ~

Late at night, the doors to Fort Miamis opened. Wyckford, mounted on his chestnut gelding, paused beside Captain Campbell. "You're sure now, you can make it to Oak Point, finish up your business there, and get back in two weeks?" the captain questioned sharply.

"Of course," Wyckford replied, his voice just missing condescension.

"I still don't understand why you think it necessary to return to Kentucky before you return to England," Campbell grumped.

"No, you wouldn't," Wyckford replied. Jabbing his spurs into the chestnut, he rode through the gate, his horse headed south toward Kentucky.

Chapter Twenty-Two

"Only Fess Raymond would be lucky enough to break his arm the day before the battle," Janie said as she, April and Mary walked down main street.

April didn't share Janie's concern. "He can have all the glory he wants. We're lucky he did break his arm. This way we know none of the Oak Point men were hurt." The knowledge of Dan's safety made the day brighter.

"I guess you're right." Janie shrugged off Fess Raymond. "Are you feeling better this week?" she asked.

"A little," April lied.

"You'll feel better soon," Mary reassured her.

"Knowing Dan will be home soon makes me feel better."

Almost as if he was intercepting them, April saw George Wyckford cross the street, heading in their direction. He hadn't been in town since the fourth of July. The man looked as handsome and well-dressed as usual. Though others thought him charming, she didn't like the man since he seemed to go out of his way to bait Dan. "What do you suppose he wants?" she whispered to Janie.

"Afternoon, Mr. Wyckford," Mary said as he approached. "How was your trip to Cincinnati?"

The blond lawyer removed his hat. "I think the trip proved profitable." He looked speculatively at Mary. "I suppose any day now the militia will return. Do you expect McKenzie to return, now that word is out?"

A glimmer of apprehension tightened her chest, April frowned. "What word?" she heard Mary ask as she stepped to her sister-in-law's side.

"You haven't heard?" Wyckford asked, raising an eyebrow. "My sincere condolences." April's heart began to thump. "It seems the Indians recognized McKenzie during the battle. They wonder why a man who fought with them at Blue Licks was now fighting on the other side."

Surprise and shock rippled through April. "Blue Licks?" she said, unaware she spoke.

Wyckford looked in her direction. "Yes, ma'am. McKenzie's always been a traitor. He fought alongside the Indians at Blue Licks."

Wyckford's words cut like broken glass in her stomach. The image of her father's body draped over the back of his horse filled her mind. "No," she whispered, "Dan couldn't have." Her chest hurt, and she fought to get her breath. Wyckford lied. Why would he lie like this?

"You must be mistaken," Mary countered Wyckford, her voice cold.

"It's the truth," Wyckford declared. He raised his voice, and other people began to pay attention to their conversation. "McKenzie fought under British orders when the Indians massacred the settlers at Blue Licks."

April exchanged looks with Mary and Janie. Mary's pale face and wide eyes reflected the foreboding April felt. Desperate, she searched Wyckford's face for a sign that he lied. A small crowd of people now clustered around. "Dan would never do anything like that," she said, her voice rough with held-back tears. "Come on, Mary, Janie. Let's go home."

As they walked away they heard Wyckford say, "I assure you all, McKenzie was one of those massacring savages."

The women quickly returned to the Murray kitchen. Mary started to fuss with making tea. April sat at the table, her skin cold in the hot afternoon. "Why would Wyckford lie like that about Dan? What does he have to gain?" Infuriated, she looked to Mary for an answer, waiting for her to deny Wyckford's words.

"Why would Wyckford make up a story like that?" Janie asked.

April drew a harsh breath. "Mary, did Dan or Scotty tell you we met Wyckford in Pittsburgh? He accused Dan of being a traitor then, too."

Mary shook her head.

April swallowed, the suppressed tears clogging her throat as she tried to think. Her sense of foreboding took the shape of memory. Dan telling of his Indian heritage that night in Pittsburgh. His voice saying, "I lived as a Shawnee Brave. I did things I don't want to think about. Things you don't want to know about." Uncertainty gnawed at her stomach. "Was Dan living with the Indians then?" she asked her sister-in-law.

Mary shuddered as if shaking off a thought "This is nonsense. Janie, go tell James we need him. You can mind the store."

Janie disappeared through the door to the store without a word.

Mary said, "Maybe Scotty knows something about all this."

Silently, April and Mary waited.

Scotty came through the door, a smile on his face. "Aye?"

Mary launched into an account of their meeting with Wyckford. Scotty's smile slowly died and April's hope died with it. His expression went from stunned to dismayed. "He thought no one would find out," Scotty blurted out.

Voices seemed distant, garbled, and senseless to April. The hard lump of misery expanded to encompass her heart. She turned and ran. One hand pressed to her mouth, the other clutching at her skirts, her vision blurred from the hot tears streaming down her face, she fled to the sanctuary of the hay loft.

She lay huddled in a ball, arms wrapped around her, trying to hold the hurt. How could he, how could he? Tears of hurt, shame, humiliation, burned her eyes. Dan knew, knew from the first day he met her that her father had died at Blue Licks. How could he not tell her? The betrayal made her sick.

And how could she still love him, knowing how he'd deceived her? Her love for Dan became like the jaws of a trap. What else had been a lie? Did he really love her? How could he love her, she thought wildly. How could he have made love to her? Her trembling hands moved to her stomach. Her baby. His baby.

She writhed in the hay, unable to evade the piercing thought any longer—could the father of her child have killed her own father? She heaved a long shuddering sigh, one hand resting on her stomach, seeking and giving comfort to the child-to-be.

Then, her forehead wrinkled and suddenly she sat upright. "How could George Wyckford know Dan was at Blue Licks?" she asked the loft.

~ * ~

April stood at the rear of the Blue Bear Inn, looking up the stairs running up the outside. At the top was a small landing and the door to George Wyckford's office.

Gathering her skirts, she climbed the stairs. A burst of male laughter erupted from within the inn. Wyckford's office must be directly above the common room.

She reached the landing, knocking on the door as she came to a halt, afraid if she stopped to think about what she was doing, she wouldn't do it.

As she knocked, another burst of raucous laughter came from the common room. "Mr. Wyckford?" she called. Impulsively, she put her hand to the latch, opening the door. The first thing she noticed was the partially open door leading into the inn's interior hallway.

Clothes were flung across the bed, but the orderly fashion looked more like packing than unpacking, even though the lawyer had just returned from Cincinnati. A fire was laid in the fireplace, when the weather didn't call for it. On a desk next to the fireplace, papers and a book had been sorted into two stacks. She entered the room slowly, still not certain what was wrong. She'd reached the desk when a voice cut across the room.

"What are you doing in here?"

She flinched, and her hand knocked a stack of papers and the book from the table. She glanced up to see Wyckford standing in the inner doorway, one hand on the latch, the other holding a tinderbox.

Flustered and embarrassed, she stammered "I-I..." and then stooped to gather up the things she'd knocked from the table. The book lay open on top of the pile of papers. She heard Wyckford say something as he started across the room, but the words on the flyleaf of the book jumped out at her, blocking out everything else.

Written in a fine copperplate hand were the words, "To my beloved nephew David Carroll, upon the occasion of his ordination." She closed the cover of the book to read the legend, Holy Bible. "David's Bible," she breathed. Directly under the Bible lay a thick sheaf of papers. Lifting the Bible she scanned the official-looking page "...you are hereby and forthwith directed to raise... ordered to join and reinforce General Wayne..."

She saw Wyckford's boots next to the papers the instant before he jerked her to her feet. "What are you doing here?" he demanded, shaking her so hard she dropped the book.

"I came to ask you how you knew about Dan," she said, surprised to hear her voice steady. Wyckford frowned, his cold grip on her arms tightening. "Dan never told Mary or me about being at Blue Licks. I came to ask how you knew. The only people who could have told you—" As if someone else were speaking, she heard her voice slow, her thought translating themselves directly into words. "—were the Indians, or... the British."

She looked down at the Bible and the papers at her feet, and then back into Wyckford's face, seeing the cold calculation there. "It can't be," she whispered. "You work for the British."

Wyckford gave her an icy smile in answer, his hands tightened on her arms. His glance swept over her. Before she realized his intentions, he yanked her against him. As he forced her body against his, she shivered in horror. Struggling, she pushed against his chest. He held her tight within his arms, moving his body against hers. Anger and fright mixed as she twisted and turned, trying to escape.

He chuckled. "You're a nosy little thing, aren't you? What's McKenzie to you, anyway?"

"He... he's my husband," she gasped, still struggling.

Instantly Wyckford's body stilled. He shoved her away from him so hard her head snapped. Holding her at arm's length, his eyes narrowed as he hissed, "Your what?"

She struggled to control her rolling emotions. "Dan McKenzie is my husband. We've been married since the fourth of July."

Disdain and disgust swept over Wyckford's face. He slowly released her arms, then wiped his palms on his pant legs. Wyckford stood between her and the door, looking inward. She drew a deep breath, readying herself to run. Suddenly Wyckford's gaze sharpened on her, the disgust on his face replaced by cold calculation.

"Sit down," he said, shoving her into a chair. "Stay there." With determined movements, Wyckford picked up the tinderbox and moved to light the fire in the fireplace.

As soon as he turned his back, April sprang from the chair, and ran on wobbly legs toward the door.

With an oath, he was after her. She made it halfway across the room before he grabbed her arm, swinging her around to face him. Preparing to scream, she gasped, filling her lungs with air. Wyckford's blow caught her across the face.

The blow stunned her. Dazed, she couldn't resist as he snatched a lace-trimmed cravat from the clothing on the bed and used it to tie her wrists together. He pulled a handkerchief from his pocket, and forced it into her mouth before spinning her around to knot it behind her head. He pushed her, bound and gagged, back into the chair.

Immobilized by shock, she watched Wyckford feed the papers and Bible into the fire. Hot flames crackled and leapt, the increased light illuminating the lawyer's cold face. He straightened and turned to look at her.

Wyckford reached down, and grabbed her tied wrist, dragging her to her feet. She saw the blow coming, but she couldn't avoid it. Once again pain exploded in her head and the world went dark.

~ * ~

Hearing came back first. She was outside, in the forest. Horses nickered nearby. The remains of a campfire glowed a few feet from her. On the other side of the fire sat George Wyckford. He stood and walked around the fire toward her. "Did you tell anyone you were coming to see me?"

Still dazed, April shook her head. When he gave a sigh she realized her mistake.

"You're lucky," he informed her, "if you'd told anyone, I'd have to kill you." His voice was as calm and charming as if they were in a drawing room. "We still have to travel fast. Don't cause me any trouble. I don't want to leave you, but I will if you make it necessary." The contrast between his tone and his words made her shiver. "Do you understand me?"

April nodded. After a long moment, Wyckford's hard expression relaxed. Then he smiled. "Wish I could be there when that Indian bastard returns. Not only will everyone know he's a traitor, but they'll all think his new wife ran away rather than stay with him."

~ * ~

April didn't know how long they rode or how far they traveled. The first few days passed in a haze of despair and physical illness. Every morning her rolling stomach refused breakfast, and with a shrug Wyckford simply packed the food away. They stopped only briefly during the day to rest the horses. With no food, exhausted by ceaseless riding, she could barely eat her share of supper before she fell into a fatigued sleep. The next morning the cycle would start all over.

She lived in a world of her own. Wyckford rarely spoke and only touched her when necessary, to lift her on and off the horse. She rode Old Jack. She assumed Wyckford must have stolen him to make it look as though she had run away. She wondered if Scotty and Mary would believe what Wyckford wanted them to.

And Dan, what would Dan think? Would he think she'd run away? Would he come after her? She prayed for her rescue. But even this thought was fraught with despair since Wyckford bragged he'd kill Dan if he followed them into British territory. How could she live if he used her as bait to get Dan killed? The two-edged sword of worry cut across her spirit and soul as she alternately prayed for rescue and for Dan's continued safety.

Slowly she drew on her inner reserve of strength, telling herself she must remain strong for the baby. She mentally put the worries of Dan and Blue Licks away, concentrating instead on survival. She had no doubt Dan would come for her. Her job was to guard the baby and stay healthy and alert. She would wait and be ready.

Late one morning Wyckford led them out of a stand of trees. Across a river lay a meadow, the blackened remains of a building and the burnt stubble of crops, blotched its beauty. At the far side of the meadow sat a fort. From a corner blockhouse a British flag ruffled in the light afternoon breeze. She swallowed her panic. She straightened her back, sitting tall on Old Jack.

~ * ~

Dusk settled over Oak Point, the heat of the day fading with the light as Dan rode into the yard between the McKenzie and Murray store and the barn. The kitchen door cast an oblong shaft of lamplight into the dog-trot. Home had never looked so good. He was tired and hungry, but he felt good.

Reining in High Stakes, he called out, "Hey, April. Hey everyone! I'm home!" He swung down from the saddle.

Mary came to greet him, and he saw tears streaking her face as she hurried toward him. Scotty followed close behind her. A cold chill settled in Dan's gut. He swallowed convulsively, but the cold tendrils radiated outward from his belly and into his limbs. Numb, he put his arm around his sister as she sobbed against his shoulder.

Dan looked over her shoulder at Scotty, his brother-in-law's tired face full of compassion. Again he swallowed. But the lump stayed in his throat. With an effort of will, he managed to get the words out. "Where's April?"

Chapter Twenty-Three

"The lass is gone," Scotty said.

"Gone? Gone where?" Dan's mind skittered in a dozen different directions. "Did she go back to Philadelphia?" The question came without thought.

"Nay, lad. She found out about ye being at Blue Licks."

Pain, blunt and heavy, hit Dan. Blue Licks! He could hardly make his voice work. "How?"

Scotty sighed. "Wyckford."

Mary explained. "He'd just come from Cincinnati, or at least that's what we thought." Scotty put his arm around her. "He met us on the street three days ago, Dan. Asked if you were planning on coming back now that everyone knew you were a traitor. He said Indians at Fallen Timbers recognized you. Said you fought on the side of the Indians at Blue Licks."

He flinched under Mary's reproachful gaze.

"You should have told us, Dan," Mary said. "You certainly should have told April."

Dan eyes flicked to Scotty who shrugged.

"At first, Mary and April thought Wyckford was lying, but when they told me what he said..." Scotty looked down and shifted his feet before looking up at Dan again. "I'm sorry, lad, I'm afraid my reaction gave everything away."

The dull pain crawled over Dan as he asked, "Then what?"

Mary put her hand on his arm. "April wanted to be alone for a while, so we didn't go out to the barn to look for her until she didn't come in for supper."

He thought of April, tears streaming down her face because she was married to him, a half-breed who'd been at Blue Licks. A chill settled in his gut and he began to shiver.

Scotty cleared his throat. "That was when I noticed Old Jack was gone."

"We thought she'd ridden out to Janie's or your cabin. We sent Matt to Janie's and Mark out to your cabin, but she wasn't at either place."

"I'd been about the town," Scotty said, "telling anyone who asked ye're side of the story. Ye best be warned, some people aren't asking for your side."

Dan made a dismissive gesture, "Tell me about April."

"'Twasn't 'til the twins got back that I went to Wyckford's. Figured by then I was calm enough to talk to him without being tempted to take a poke at him. His room was empty, his horse gone from the stable." Scotty exchanged a glance with Mary. "Ye'll not believe this, but in the fireplace in his room you could see where he'd tried to burn some papers and a book, so he must have left in an all-fired hurry. One of the papers was the militia's call up orders that never arrived, the book was David Carroll's Bible, taken when he was ambushed. The only thing we can figure out is Wyckford was spying for the British. He must have arranged for the robbery of anyone traveling alone this summer to get the militia's orders."

"A spy," Dan breathed, trying to take it in. Somehow it seemed to make sense. He swallowed, fighting to get out the next question. "He has April?"

Scotty nodded, and Dan's insides went stone-cold dead.

"David and I rode out yesterday morning. Neither of us is the tracker you are, but even we found traces of a camp. Looked like two people and two horses. One of the horses was Old Jack. Anyone can recognize that crooked print of his."

Anger flared at the thought of April with Wyckford. But the anger couldn't overcome the chill that had displaced all other sensations in his body. He drew a steadying breath, judgment beginning to win control over his surging emotions.

Rage and fury wouldn't help him find Wyckford, or get April back. He forced himself to be calm, to think. Even if Scotty showed him the place now, he couldn't follow a trail at night. Think. He couldn't take High Stakes. She had just made the trip from Ohio and was in foal. He'd need a horse he could push to the limit, since Wyckford had three days head start.

Dan looked at Mary. "Can you pack me some supplies? I'll leave first thing in the morning."

The sun was barely up when Dan ate breakfast. The food tasted like sawdust, sticking in his throat. He doggedly swallowed bite after bite, knowing his body would need the nourishment. Just as he finished, he heard the sound of a horse entering the yard.

"That'll be David," Scotty said. The two men left the kitchen, going out through the dog-trot.

Reverend Carroll tied a big, dirty-brown colored gelding to the corral fence. "Dan!" the reverend cried, delight momentarily lighting his face. Just as quickly, the delight washed.

"Aye, I've told him."

"It's not your fault she's gone," David told him.

"It is my fault. I'm the one who brought her here. I'm the one who was at Blue Licks. Wyckford's always hated me, now she's in danger because of me. All she ever did was..." He stopped before his voice broke. All she ever did was love him. The cold, shivery feeling which had settled over him last night was still there. Vaguely he wondered if he would ever be warm again.

"Let me lend you my horse," David insisted. He gestured to his mount. He was tall, long legged, with a powerful chest and hindquarters, his dirty-brown color broken only by a white blaze.

"Thanks. I'll do my best to bring him back." Dan looked at David, and saw the reverend understood what he'd left unsaid. Dan would take the gelding, but there was no guarantee either the gelding or Dan would return.

A few moments later Dan finished tying his supplies and bedroll to the saddle, then patted the gelding on the neck. "What do you call him?" he asked over his shoulder.

"Sir Walter Raleigh, because he looks like he fell in a mud puddle," David said with a small smile.

Dan mounted the horse. "Raleigh," he crooned, stroking the animal's neck. "You ready?" The horse tossed his head, bridle jingling, as if eager to get started.

Dan looked down at the two concerned men standing in the yard. "I'll find her." He swung Raleigh around, facing north. Looking straight ahead, he said, "I'll bring her back." He paused and his voice dropped, "If she's willing to come back."

Would a woman be willing to come back to a one-room log cabin on the uncivilized frontier and live with a half-breed who'd been present at the battle that claimed her father's life?

As he rode north he prayed she would. No matter how long or how hard he had to search, he'd get her back or, by God, die in the attempt.

~ * ~

Dan followed Wyckford and April's trail north, crossing the Ohio river. Followed them long enough to feel certain they were heading for the British Fort Miamis. The only other choice for the spy was to head straight for Detroit. But since he had April, Dan gambled Wyckford'd stop at Miamis first. Dan needed help to get inside the British forts, so he cut west to find his cousin, Standing Bear.

Fortunately, the Shawnee village was still in the same place it had been two summers ago, the last time Dan had been there. Hoping he would be remembered and recognized as a friend, Dan galloped Raleigh straight into the center of the cluster of wigwams, scattering women and children as he shouted his cousin's name. To his relief, Standing Bear appeared from one of the wigwams.

Stopping short of the stamping animal Dan held under tight control, the warrior paused a moment, then spoke. "What brings the Man With Eyes Like Gun Smoke in such as hurry to see his cousin?"

"I need your help."

~ * ~

Dan and Standing Bear crawled forward, halting at the top of a small hill overlooking the British fort on the Miamis river. Dan wiped his sleeve across his forehead. The fort sat quiet, calm, the Union Jack on the block house hanging limp in the hot summer air. He turned to Standing Bear. "What do you think?" he asked in Shawnee.

The warrior shrugged. "Looks the same as always. Do you think she's here?"

Dan stared back at the fort, using not just his eyes, but his whole body, trying to see inside the log-walls. He drew a deep breath and let it out slowly. "She's there... I can feel it."

Standing Bear grunted, accepting that a man could know things through some mystic sense. "Now, what?"

"You keep watch." Dan slithered backward, down the hill.

Once off the crest, he stood and walked back into the woods where he and Standing Bear had tied their horses. The gelding's ribs were clearly visible. "Sorry, fella," Dan patted the gelding's neck.

Dan untied his pack from Raleigh, and made his way to a small stream. He prayed his intuition was correct; that he had, indeed, intercepted April. He took off his hat, stripped off his shirt, and then pulled soap and a razor from the pack.

A few minutes later, he ran a hand over his jaw, then over his breastbone. Satisfied, he rinsed the razor, dried it on his pant leg before folding it and putting it away. He untied his queue ribbon and shook out his hair. From the pack, he pulled a roach of red deer skin and feather and fastened it, like a crest, to his head. Standing, he stripped off his leggings. Dressed in only a breech cloth, knife at his waist, moccasins, and feathers, he looked as much an Indian as he could. He tied the pack back on Raleigh, and crept back up the hill to join Standing Bear.

His cousin looked him up and down and grunted his approval. "You could be one of my braves." Then with a small smile he added, "Except for those eyes."

Dan managed a smile in return. His heart pounded, and he knew it was more than the heat causing him to sweat. Fear he'd fail to rescue her tightened his gut. He stood. "Let's go."

They began to walk leisurely toward the fort. Dan's stomach clenched. To calm himself, he mentally went over what Standing Bear had told him about the layout of the fort. As a leader of his village, Standing Bear had been to Fort Miamis for parleys with the British on several occasions. According to him, the British allowed Indians in the store inside the fort.

As they strode across the open area in front of the main gate, Dan's stomach tightened with each step. She had to be here. He forced himself to breathe slowly. His skin felt two sizes too small. The guard on the parapet watched them in a desultory fashion, only calling over his shoulder, "Couple of heathens comin' in."

Unchallenged, Dan and Standing Bear walked through the open gate. The hot noon sun burned down on the packed dirt of the parade ground. After the noon meal, the fort dozed. Three soldiers lethargically loaded a wagon. A few others lounged in the shade. Just as Dan started to breathe a little easier, a burly sergeant stepped in their path.

"An' where might you two be headed?"

Before Dan could do anything, Standing Bear answered. "We go store," he said in bad English, pointing across the compound.

The sergeant answered with a non-committal grunt, but stood his ground. Dan's tongue felt like flannel, stuck to the roof of his mouth. He repeated Standing Bear's words, "Go store."

The sergeant's beady eyes looked him up and down before coming back to linger on his face. "A bloody 'breed,'" the sergeant muttered. He looked back at Standing Bear for a moment as he rubbed his chin. "Oh, what the hell," he muttered as he stepped aside, waving them on their way.

Beside the store, Dan spied a stable, its open doorway a rectangle of shade hiding the interior. "I'll check the stable," Dan mumbled. "Watch my back."

With an imperceptible nod, Standing Bear slowed his steps. The two passed the hitching rail serving the store, Standing Bear stopped on the porch while Dan melted through the open doorway into the stable.

The warm scent of horse, hay, leather, and dust lay heavy in his nostrils. He stood quietly, his back against the wall for a moment. As his eyes adjusted to the shadowed light, he recognized the chestnut gelding in the third stall. A tingle of exhilaration shot through him. He'd reached the stall when the quiet stable echoed with the sound of a pistol being cocked.

"Hold it right there."

Dan froze.

"Don't move."

His heart thumped at Wyckford's familiar voice. Quiet footsteps rustled behind him, keeping well to the other side of the wide center aisle. His mouth went dry as his opponent came into his line of sight.

Wyckford moved past him toward the rear of the stable, but the cocked pistol in his right hand held steady on Dan's chest. The Englishman stopped several paces in front of him, eyes narrowed as he inspected his target through the gloom. A slow smile crossed Wyckford's face. "No, not a savage... a spy."

Dan had only one thought. "Where is she?"

As if in answer, a rustling came from the gloom behind the Englishman. The shape moved forward, as if responding to Dan's will, coming out of the shadows to stop one pace behind Wyckford. April. Inexplicable relief swamped him. Then he made out her pale face, her hair scraggling down in pigtails, the exhausted slump of her body, the sight of her bound wrists signifying her prisoner status. The relief and joy surged into fury.

His gaze flicked back to Wyckford, whose smile broadened at the hatred directed toward him. "Keep coming, McKenzie," he ordered.

At his name April gasped. "Dan?"

The exhausted breathlessness of her voice stabbed at him. He started forward, but Wyckford's silky voice stopped him. "That's far enough."

Dan trembled with the effort of containing the rage that consumed him. After the one glance at April, he riveted his gaze on his opponent. The pistol held steady, as did Wyckford's eyes above the dark muzzle.

"Let her go," Dan demanded.

"I think not."

"Let her go," Dan repeated with quiet intensity, "or you're a dead man."

Wyckford laughed. "No, my dear fellow, I'm afraid you're going to be the dead man. In a few minutes you'll be just another savage, shot trying to steal a horse." He glanced to where April stood, then back to Dan. "Killing you will give me great pleasure, McKenzie. You've been a thorn in my side this whole mission."

"No!" April gasped.

Dan heard, but kept his concentration on Wyckford. His whole body tensed as he watched Wyckford raise the pistol. The muzzle became a dark hole pointed at his head. He drew a deep breath as Wyckford spoke again.

"You can wonder what happened to her while you rot in hell, McKenzie." The Englishman's finger turned white on the trigger.

"No!" April cried again. Her bound hands made a grab toward the spy's arm the same instant Dan sprang. Before Dan could reach him, Wyckford gave April a wicked shove. The Englishman's thrust sent her against one of the stall partitions. Her head hit with a solid thunk. Without a sound she collapsed into the straw.

Dan slammed into Wyckford. The Englishman shuddered but didn't go down. With his left hand, Dan grabbed the pistol. He jammed the soft flesh between his thumb and forefinger under the flint. His right hand went for his knife. Wyckford caught his wrist, keeping his hand from the haft. In a deadly embrace, the men strained against each other.

"Damn," Wyckford hissed. They struggled for possession of the gun. The spy pulled the trigger. Both men jerked. Wyckford in anticipation of the blast which didn't come. Dan when the flint bit deep into his hand. Still locked together, upper bodies straining, their scuffling feet made a cloud of dust rise from the stable floor.

In a desperate move, Wyckford let go of Dan's wrist to use both hands to regain the pistol. Dan's freed hand sought his knife, even as he felt the pistol being pried from his grasp. Wyckford drew in a deep breath, preparing to yell for help. Dan's knife found its target. The heavy blade sank deeply between the spy's ribs. His own belly clenching and rolling, Dan stared into Wyckford's eyes. Wyckford's intended shout became a soundless expulsion of air.

For a long second, Wyckford stood motionless. A warm wetness trickled down Dan's hand, the hot, sweet scent filled his nostrils. The Englishman's eyes flickered. "Damn," he breathed, as his body became dead weight. Dan let go. Wyckford folded onto the ground, a dark, wet stain across his shirt.

Without sparing Wyckford a second glance, Dan knelt beside April. His left hand trembled as he stroked the hair back from her face, more scared now than he'd been seconds before. "April," he called softly. He found a large lump on her forehead, and she moaned at his touch. His heart knotted in his chest.

At a sound behind him, Dan whirled, the stained knife ready. Standing Bear stood in the doorway, his own knife in his hand. Dan let his breath out and turned once more to April. Her eyes opened and closed and she moaned.

"April, honey, wake up," he urged. He gave her a shake, "We have to get out of here."

"Dan?" Her voice sounded far away. She tried feebly to sit up.

"Yes, sweetheart, I'm here," He helped her into a sitting position. She looked dazed. One bound hand dragged the other up to touch the lump on her forehead. "We're going to get out of here, but you have to be able to ride. Can you?" She nodded hesitantly.

Motioning to Standing Bear, Dan turned toward Wyckford's body. "Help me get his coat, breeches and boots off." Tugging at one boot, Dan continued, "I'll dress in his clothes. She and I will ride out on Wyckford's horses." Breathing rapidly, Dan pulled off his moccasins, and pulled on the breeches and boots, while Standing Bear rolled the body over to strip off the coat. "Can you cause a diversion while we leave, then follow us?"

A confident smile was Standing Bear's only answer.

Shrugging into the coat, Dan led Wyckford's chestnut gelding out of the stall. The chestnut was saddled with a pack tied on. Handing the reins to Standing Bear, he did the same with Old Jack.

He knelt beside April. Her eyes were open, but unfocused. "Can you ride Old Jack?" he asked, helping her to her feet. Please let her be able to ride, just for a little bit, he prayed. He lifted her on to Old Jack. Her hands curled into the horse's mane to hang on. The sight of her bound wrists made him want to kill Wyckford all over again. Instead he stripped the roach from his head, cutting off one of the ties to use as a queue ribbon. He picked up Wyckford's hat swung onto the gelding. Standing Bear put Old Jack's reins in his hand.

"Two minutes," the Shawnee said. He slipped from the barn.

Dan took a deep breath, trying to calm his thudding heart. He turned to look at April. She sat slumped on Old Jack, her eyes closed. She looked so tired and bedraggled his heart ached. Everything she'd suffered had been because of him. He buttoned the coat across his blood-smeared chest. He heard a rising chorus of voices and laughter from the parade ground.

"Hang on a little longer, honey," he called to April. He gently tapped his heels against the gelding. Holding his breath, he led them out of the barn and toward the gate. Dan guided the horses across the parade ground unnoticed, unhindered. Everyone was too entranced with the 'drunken' Indian making a spectacle of himself in front of the commanding officer's quarters. Dan kept the horses at a walk as they passed through the gate and headed toward the woods. A burst of male laughter rolled out the gate after them.

The horses crested the hill, and as soon as Dan knew they were out of sight of the fort, he vaulted from the saddle and hurried to

April. He put his hands on her waist to help her down. With relief, he saw her gaze seemed to be focused. For an instant she stared into his eyes. She gave a small smile, sighing "Oh, Dan." Then all the color drained from her face and her eyes fluttered. Her body went limp and she fainted into his arms. He still sat on the ground holding her unconscious body in his lap a few minutes later as Standing Bear came over the hill.

Chapter Twenty-Four

April lay quietly with her eyes closed. The scent of smoke, food, and the warm, closed smell told her she was indoors. She felt so good, so safe, she didn't want to open her eyes and find it was a dream. She gave a deep sigh. The sound of steady breathing she had thought her own abruptly ceased. She wasn't alone. Curiously unafraid, she opened her eyes.

Overhead, an arched framework of sapling covered with woven mats met in a star pattern opening in the center. Sunlight poured in through the smoke hole. She turned her head. She lay on a bench that ran all around the inside wall a few feet off the floor. More bright light came from the arch on the far side of the wigwam, silhouetting the man rising to his knees from the floor beside her.

Her eyes locked with his pale blue-gray ones, and her heart flipped. The safe comfortable feeling hadn't been a dream, Dan had come for her. She whispered his name as he gathered her into his arms.

His chest was bare, and his hair hung loose about his shoulders, just as in the hazy, half-remembered images. Only now his warm, male scent surrounded her, his chest was smooth against her cheek, not splattered with blood.

"It's all right. You're safe," he comforted.

Her crying tore at his heart, but they were necessary for her. The tears would leach away her fear and terror, so the memory could fade.

"I was so tired," she mumbled against his chest. "So afraid. He... caught me in his room, and then I saw David's Bible."

"Go ahead, cry it all out," he urged.

"He... he hit me, and then he..."

Dan's body stiffened and he cursed himself for his involuntary reaction. He'd sworn he wouldn't ask if Wyckford had... he couldn't even think the word.

Her face hidden against his neck, she shook her head. "No, he didn't touch me. He hated you so much he didn't touch me knowing I had been with you."

He thanked God Wyckford had despised him. All the hatred, scorn, and prejudice he'd ever faced—was worth it, twice over, for her safety. "I'm so sorry, April. I never wanted anything bad to happen to you." Even to him, his voice sounded raw.

She shuddered against him and his heart wrenched. "It was so horrible," she sniffed. "We met him on the street. He said you were a traitor." As soon as she said the words, her body tensed in his arms. He knew what else Wyckford had said that day and he let his embrace loosen.

She pushed against his chest and he released her, letting his arms fall to his sides, still on his knees beside the bench where she sat. The light from behind him glistened on the tears in her eyes, on her cheeks. "It's true, isn't it?" she whispered.

He couldn't run anymore. He'd been running since Blue Licks, though he hadn't known it until he'd met April. Now, if she couldn't accept him as he was, he would lose her. If he lost her, he would die inside. "Yes, I was there." Struggling to keep his voice calm, his hands at his sides, he began to explain.

"I should have told you, but I was afraid of what you would think. I was afraid that day, too. I was a scared fifteen-year-old boy the Indians forced to join them. I didn't realize what was happening until it was too late and they'd dragged me into the battle. I swear to you, April, I only fought to defend myself."

Her expression never changed. She sat motionless, her hand resting on her stomach. The chill in his own belly began to spread again. He waited. Still she said nothing.

"You're safe now." He made his voice neutral. "After you rest for a few days, I'll take you..." he paused, swallowing. "I'll take you anywhere you want to go." He wanted to put his arms around her, beg her to come home with him. But where he took her had to be her decision. His mouth was dry. With a conscious effort, he unstuck his tongue. "I'll do whatever you want."

April looked at him for a long time, collecting her thoughts. She looked down to where her hand rested on her stomach. "I wanted to hate you," she said softly. "But I couldn't. Even when I wondered if you could have killed my father, I still loved you. I went to see Wyckford to see if he knew why you were at Blue Licks.

"All the time I was with Wyckford, I remembered the times we'd been together, all the things we wanted to do together. Being kidnapped, thinking I'd never see you again, made me realize what happened in the past is past. The only truly important things are the people you love. What matters is I love you, Dan."

She barely got the words out before she was in his arms again. "Take me home," she said against his chest. "Take me home to Kentucky."

His grip around her tightened, and he pulled her off the bench and into his lap. His mouth covered hers and with a moan, she melted into his arms. His kiss consumed, demanded, and she reveled in its possessiveness. She lost herself in the touch, taste, and feel of him.

Gradually the fierceness of the embrace passed, and the need for air broke the kiss. Not knowing what else to say, she whispered "Take me home. Home to Kentucky."

"Home to Kentucky," he echoed, then surprised her with a shaky laugh. "Home to Kentucky. That's what you said to me the first time we met." He pulled her back into his embrace. "And this time, see that you stay put, woman," he whispered fiercely in her ear.

She snuggled against him, her face nestled into the juncture of his neck and shoulder. "You've already made certain I'll have to stay home. The baby we're going to have this spring will keep me busy."

He went completely still, then after a long moment, put his hands on her shoulders, holding her away from him while he stared at her. Her heart thudded with joy, watching the expressions follow one another so plainly across his usually unemotional face. First he looked puzzled, his forehead wrinkling, as if the word "baby" was foreign. Then the wrinkles cleared, and for another long moment he looked stunned. That expression was quickly replaced by the beginnings of a smile, as his mouth turned up at the corners. And how, with that smile, did he manage to give off a glint of masculine smugness that made her want to giggle, or hit him, or both. But before she could, concern replaced the smile.

He looked so solemn as he held her as if she were suddenly made of fine porcelain. "Are you all right?"

She laid her hand against the angle of his jaw. "I'm perfectly all right, just tired." His expression didn't alter. "Really, Dan, I'll be fine," she reassured him. "All I need is a little rest and to know you're here with me."

Dan sat dazed for a moment. She loved him. He'd known, but not really understood until now. She truly loved him. He hadn't taken—you can't take what was freely given. That was the way she loved him, unreservedly, holding nothing back. And it was the way he loved her. He swallowed, and when he spoke his voice was rough with emotion. "I love you. More than I ever thought possible. I need you. Without you, I... I don't know." He paused, "Let's go home."

He covered her mouth with his, and for the next few minutes, they were the only two people in the whole world.

~ * ~

Dan and April stayed at the village with Standing Bear for three days, which was a shorter time than Dan felt necessary for April to rest, and longer than he wanted to wait. They said goodbye to Standing Bear and headed south for Kentucky. Dan once again wore his beaded medallion under his shirt. April's sampler traveled secure in her bedroll.

They traveled home through the glorious fall. The crisp autumn nights had turned the countryside into a mosaic of colors. They rode at a steady pace, Dan finding a suitable place to rest early each evening. They made love, sometimes in the twilight, by firelight, or by starlight. One afternoon they stopped to rest in a fern-lined grotto at an unnamed spring.

The sun had dipped below the western hills when Dan and April rode into the side yard of McKenzie and Murray. As Dan reined in, someone lit a lamp in the kitchen, casting an oblong of light into the dog-trot.

He dismounted and walked back to help April down. "We made it," he grinned up at her, savoring one last small moment he would have alone with her for the next few hours.

She smiled back at him. "Thanks to you."

"We did it together," Dan replied, putting his hands to her waist and then setting her on the ground.

At that moment Scotty, coming out of the kitchen, caught sight of them. "Dan! April!" he shouted. "They're back!" he yelled over his shoulder, then hurried across the yard. Within seconds everyone poured out of the kitchen. Scotty, Mary, the boys, even the reverend and Janie. Pandemonium took over as the yard surged with people exchanging hugs, kisses, questions and answers, all at the same time.

"Enough of this," Mary said, finally taking charge. "Boys, take care of the horses. Come on Janie, we'll get the bath ready, and after April and Dan clean up, we'll eat dinner." Dan watched April disappear in a flurry of skirts as his sister shooed the women toward the house. The three men stood in the suddenly quiet yard until Scotty grasped Dan's hand. "Glad to have ye back."

"Glad to be back."

"So Wyckford was a spy?" David asked.

Dan nodded. "I ended up with the papers he had in the chestnut gelding's saddlebags. He was sent here to spy and cause trouble. He was even behind the attack on the flatboats." The irony of Wyckford causing the attack wasn't lost on Dan. As a result of the attack, he ended up alone with April in the rockhouse.

"I'll be glad to show those papers about the town," Scotty said. He looked toward the house where the women had disappeared. Then he turned to Dan. "Did the bastard hurt her?"

His blunt question drew a smothered gasp from David.

Scotty looked at David. "Everyone will wonder. Dan might as well tell us, and we can tell everyone else whatever Dan wants them to know, discreetly, of course. If there's nae mystery, the gossip will die down."

"Scotty's right," Dan acknowledged, though Wyckford and April wasn't something he wanted to talk about. "April wasn't hurt. Wyckford didn't, didn't... she said when she told him she was my wife, he looked at her like something that crawled out from under a rock." He straightened his shoulders. "Reckon he thought any woman who'd been with a 'breed was too contaminated for him."

"That sounds about right," David commented.

Dan frowned. "What do you mean?"

"Remember when I came out to visit you the first time? And I said High Stakes reminded me of our neighbor's horses? When I saw Wyckford, he looked like a Baxter, too, all handsome, blond and aristocratic. So I wrote to my sister in Charleston, to see if she knew what happened when the Baxters went back to England.

"I received her letter just after you left. Clarissa said the Baxters had gone to live with Mr. Baxter's brother on his estate in England. The name of the estate was Wyckford and they were still noted for their horses. Nothing was more important to them than the purity of bloodlines, for either their horses or themselves."

At the sound of the boys' voices coming from the barn, Scotty asked quietly, "Wyckford himself?"

Dan kept silent for a long moment. "He won't bother anyone ever again."

The men looked at each other.

Several shrieks came from the kitchen. Dan started to bolt forward, then realized the shrieks were followed by feminine laughter. His curiosity deepened as Scotty elbowed David.

"Tell him, lad," Scotty said to the reverend.

David shrugged his shoulders. "Janie and I are getting married. We were just waiting for you and April to come home. We want you to stand up for us."

"What if we hadn't come back?" He gave David a crooked smile. Being home, among friends and family made an ache of good feelings in his chest.

"Oh, I had great faith in your ability," David replied with a straight face. "Besides, I had to convince Mr. Ferguson that I was suitable son-in-law material. That took some effort."

"Congratulations," Dan said. Then before he could say anything else, the boys burst out of the barn, and Mary yelled from the kitchen for him to hurry and get cleaned up.

~ * ~

A few hours later, April sat in the middle of Dan's bed in the upstairs room. A single candle gave the room a soft glow as she brushed her hair. She heard steps on the stairs. The door opened and Dan entered.

Dan smiled as he closed the door. His shirt went over the back of the chair. He sat on the bed to take off his boots. She placed the hair brush on the chair as Dan blew out the candle. Snuggling into the mattress, April listened to the soft sounds as Dan shed the rest of his clothes. The bed dipped as he climbed in. Stretching out, he heaved a contented sounding sigh.

"Are you tired?" he asked as his arm went around her.

"A little."

He ran his hand over the sleeve of her nightdress. "What is this thing?"

Trying not to giggle, she answered, "A nightdress."

"Why does it cover so much of you?" he asked as he pulled her to his side.

"Because," she answered, running her hand up his bare arm, across his bare chest and then down to his bare hip and thigh, delighting in the way his breath caught before she ran her hand back up to rest over the beaded medallion. "What you wear to bed covers so little of you."

With a laugh, he pulled her on top of him. "Can we get rid of this nightdress thing?"

She lay limp, not helping as his hands started to pull at the hem. "Why?" she teased.

"Because I want to make love to my wife," he growled.

She sat up and gave a dramatic sigh. "I don't know. Do you think it will work here?"

He paused, his hand full of her nightdress which he had up around her waist. "What do you mean?"

"We've been on the ground in the rockhouse, on a pile of furs, in a wigwam or on the ground again these last few days. Do you think we can do it in a bed?"

He stripped the nightdress over her head and tossed it aside. "Only one way to find out," he muttered before he rolled her under him.

Author's Notes

For most people the words "frontier" and "the west" conjure up visions of the Great Plains west of the Mississippi. But for the early settlers, the western frontier was the uncharted wilderness beyond the eastern tidewater, the land first glimpsed by frontiersmen such as John Finley and Daniel Boone. The colonial American desire to expand into these lands, and the British restrictions against such expansion, added to the desire for American independence.

With the start of the American Revolution in 1776, early settlers west of the Appalachians were attacked by British-backed bands of Indians. One such battle was at Blue Licks, which Dan recounts to Scotty. In the decade that followed the signing of the Treaty of Paris 1783, the official end of the Revolutionary War, citizens of the new United States swarmed into the newly acquired Northwest Territories.

The various Indian tribes did not take kindly to what they viewed as an invasion. Forming a loose confederation, they turned to their traditional allies, the British, who in violation of the Treaty of Paris, still occupied forts in the Ohio Territory.

To make the Ohio Valley of Indians safe for settlers, President Washington sent expeditions in 1790 under Hammer, and in 1791 under St. Clair. Both armies were defeated. Washington then gave the task to Anthony Wayne, a revolutionary war hero. Taking time to discipline and organize the army, Wayne moved his Legion, toward the British forts. Wayne did indeed rely on civilian scouts. The most famous of these was William Wells, a white man raised by the Indians.

As in the case of the words "frontier" and "the West," the words "Indian Wars" also bring to most people's minds the US Calvary versus the Sioux and Cheyenne on the Great Plains. But the confrontation between the Americans and the Ohio Valley tribes—Miamis, Shawnee, Ottawas, Sauk, and Fox—was by far the more fiercely contested. At the Battle of Fallen Timbers (August 20, 1794) Wayne commanded 3,000 men against an Indian force of around 2,000. Compare this to General George Custer, who 80 years later at the Battle of Little Big Horn commanded 265 men.

Also, as Dan predicts, after the defeat of Fallen Timbers, Wayne was able to negotiate the Treaty of Greenville (August 1795) in which the Indians ceded most of Ohio and large sections of Indiana, Illinois, and Michigan.

Historical people in this book are General Wayne and his aide, William Henry Harrison, who would be elected President in 1840. To avoid geographical confusion, I have used the archaic spelling of Miamis (instead of Miami) for the British Fort. Those familiar with the history and the area will recognize the fictional community of Oak Point is based on Lexington.

Author Bio

Terry Irene Blain was lucky enough to grow up in a large Midwestern family with a rich oral tradition. As a child she heard stories of ancestors' adventures with Indians, wildlife, weather and frontier life in general, so she naturally gravitated to the study of history and completed a BA and MA then taught the subject at the college level. Married to a sailor, now retired, she's had the chance to live in various parts of the country as well as travel to foreign places such as Hong Kong, Australia, England and Scotland.

INTO THE WILD

Daniel McKenzie was an army scout—quiet, capable, handsome...and utterly unwilling to be the trail guide April Williamson needed to reach Kentucky. The Indian attack at Blue Licks was but one bitter taste of the American frontier, a massacre that had taken her father just as cholera had taken her mother. But April would not give up on her dream. At journey's end was independence, and nothing would stand in her way.

The young widow was beautiful and determined, but the months of travel involved in her plan would be too hard. Without the general's order Dan would have told any woman no, but April especially. His secret would destroy her—or she might destroy him. April's kiss was like the country itself. Restless and sweet, it promised a love that denied every boundary and looked only to freedom and the future.

 Boroughs
Publishing Group

Did you enjoy this book? Drop us a line and say so! We love to hear from readers, and so do our authors. To connect, visit www.boroughspublishinggroup.com online, send comments directly to info@boroughspublishinggroup.com, or friend us on Facebook and Twitter. And be sure to check back regularly for contests and new releases in your favorite subgenres of romance!

Are you an aspiring writer? Check out www.boroughspublishinggroup.com/submit and see if we can help you make your dreams come true.

www.ingramcontent.com/pod-product-compliance
Lightning Source LLC
Chambersburg PA
CBHW051455170626
46811CB00002B/488